Book 1: The Urban Samurai Series
by N.S. Kelly

COPYRIGHT

DEDICATIONS

Thank you to Deidre Knight who mentioned something about wanting to read a story about female samurai during a RWA conference one time. From her comment, Shia and her sisters were born. Of course, they took a totally different turn than I intended!

To our son, who gets that some nights are just writing nights.

To the Write by the Rails members, thank you for the love and support in this crazy career.

To my writing partner and partner in everything, thank you for wanting to run with this idea.

To my Sparkling Hearts crew, JT, Elizabeth & Cat - you guys keep me sane and in awe of your skills.

PROLOGUE

3600 M Street NW, Washington, D.C.
2:37 AM

"Get out of the car, Abigail." The voice demanded.

"Please. You don't have to do this." She pleaded.

He reached over, grabbed her hair, and slammed her head against the passenger side door.

Abigail screamed, half in pain, half in shock. He'd promised her so many things, love, money, happiness-and hell to pay if she didn't listen.

Abigail scrambled for the door handle. It was dead weight in her hands. She was breathless, scared. He'd always made good on his promises in the past.

She pulled the handle upward and stumbled forward as the door opened. She struck the pavement, barely able to get her hands in front of her face on the wet asphalt. She whimpered when the asphalt shredded her palms. She knew she had to get up and run. Run. Run.

She pushed herself up to one knee. The downpour of rain matted her hair to her face and washed the blood from her hands. She stood and fell backward against the side of the car as a wave of dizziness tugged at her stomach and her head. She tried to steady her breathing, blindly reaching a hand before her. She couldn't determine direction, but she knew she couldn't stay where she was. He'd catch her if she stayed there.

She took an unsteady step forward then a second. She bit her lower lip and shook her head. For a moment, her mind cleared. A flicker of confidence lit its way within her.

"You can't run from me." He voice wrapped around her.

Pain spread like fire along her back. She dropped to her knees, the scream frozen in her throat. Her hands failed her. Her head bounced off of the wet asphalt, more blood mixed with the rain.

Someone lifted her, hands wrapped around her waist, and she was adrift, floating. Pain and water washed over her in exchanging tides. His voice was distant, but his words still terrified her.

"Do you remember, Abigail?" He asked. She shivered as his tone raced over her.

Her head lolled, eyelids fluttered. Her limbs numb.

"Do you remember what I told you I would do?" He asked.

She recognized her surroundings. She'd been there before. There was anguish and pain...so much pain.

"If you ever let him touch you again?" He continued.

Abigail tried to scream. Her voice failed her. Fear constricted her throat and seized her breath.

She fell for so long that she thought she'd fall forever.

Until she struck the stairs.

CHAPTER ONE

Crunch. Crack. Bones split.

She knew the sound of bones snapping under the pressure of a predator's jaws. She froze. Her nightly run forgotten. She stopped in the shadows of the building next to her, tilted her head, and listened.

She paused as silence descended.

Her stomach tightened.

Human, animal, or other?

She remained still, hiding, listening, as she'd always done and been trained to do.

Her breathing steadied. She fought the sounds, willing them to not be what she'd thought she'd heard. This was not her battle.

She'd wanted to get in her nightly run without a demon sighting. The long days at the morgue shredded her stamina. A medical examiner's daily routine fatigued her enough without adding in this. She'd been working days on end and welcomed the brief respite. She'd started her run to get rid of the stress, not add more.

No, thank you, Universe, for whatever planetary alignment that was causing such upheaval.

She wrinkled her nose. The rusty, metallic smell of blood reached her as she passed by an alleyway. She sniffed, shaking her head, adjusting to the scent. She suppressed the involuntary urge to sneeze by pressing the tips of her index fingers and thumbs together. The minute gesture gave her something to focus on. She took in a deep breath and exhaled. She'd deal. She'd been made for this. It was her calling.

Technically, she wasn't on duty. Shellie was on tap for this. North America was her domain, her responsibility.

Crack.

Growl.

Wet lips smacked together in satisfaction and repulsion rolled through her entire body. She bit back a physical response and focused on her breathing.

This was work, nothing more.

Her stomach tightened. She listened and then crept forward toward the sounds. She stopped and stilled in the shadows of the building, and her hearing expanded. Her hands curled to her sides. Her spine tightened. A plastic bottle clattered down the alleyway, blown by the wind. Tires splashed through puddles several blocks over. The endless rhythm of go-go music playing in Adams Morgan a mile away pulsed in her ears. The city never rested.

Crunch.

Lick.

Slurp.

Purr.

Growl.

She hesitated, every cell in her demanding a response. Pinpricks raced over her skin. She forced her heart rate to slow as she began to take stock. The local samurai wasn't responding. Shellie was late.

Shellie was never late.

Every bit of her being tuned into the sounds. Shellie

either was either ignoring her mission or she'd been called elsewhere. She hoped it was the latter. She heard it all, bad sign.

And then, the scent hit her.

She sniffed again, and odd combination of smells — ashes, bones and baby powder—whiffed across her nose. Demon. Rissu, recently born at that.

She shuddered. She wished no one a run in with a mature Rissu. Baby killers. She'd slain several before. A newborn meant an adult had to be nearby.

Who was calling demons into the Nation's Capital? Did they have a vendetta against the current administration?

Stupid, stupid, stupid.

She would never understand those she'd been sent to protect. They did the dumbest things in the name of power, and calling a demon into being was very, very dumb. Although, D.C. provided a daily dose of all levels of stupidity. She'd chronicled them through the years. Someday, she'd post them up to some website. Or, maybe she'd send an anonymous article. Her sister Samurai wouldn't kill her then.

Focus, Shia, focus.

The sound of another crack reached her ears, and her body began to hum. She couldn't ignore a demon. As tired as she was, duty called...demanded. Shia cast aside the desire to turn the other cheek and move on because this wasn't her domain. The tenets of the Samurai prevailed. Their code was simple: Loyalty, honor, obedience, duty, filial piety, and, when necessary, self-sacrifice.

Cold energy rippled over her, pulsed in her veins, growing with each heartbeat. Her eyelids fluttered. The static from within caressed her skin, escaping through every pore and every hair on her head. The familiar satisfaction of upcoming battle crept into her psyche. The feeling of perfect harmony with her body granted a heightened consciousness only true Samurai achieved. Her swords hummed against her back. Her hands reached back without a second thought. The sound of metal against leather whispered as she pulled the hidden blades from their sheaths.

What other woman ran the streets at night with swords strapped to her back? Thankfully, she'd never had to explain it.

Swords in hand, she rounded the corner, and the alleyway opened up before her. Bricks, trash, shadows. Nothing ever changed in the alleyways, unless you counted the probable appearance of hungry homeless, hungrier rats, or a prostitute turning a quick trick, darkness and night.

She moved forward, inch-by-inch. She should have taken up needlepoint or some other mindless, home based activity. There were thousands of things to occupy her body and mind, yet somehow, she still had to be out moving and engaging.

Demon junkie.

That had to be it. All her years spent tracking, teaching, it was a drug in her system. She was taking a vacation once this latest infestation died down or when she found Shellie.

She moved further into the alley and saw him. Male, not that she'd ever seen a female Rissu outside a portal shimmer. The spines always showed on the males, deep, dark, spiky, through the clothes, if they happened to wear any. No matter how hard they tried to pass off as human, Rissu never quite managed to keep the spines from protruding from their backs.

"No sir, we don't eat the resident beings on the planet we were just called to." She tsk'd him as she stepped out of the darkness.

The creature before her stopped, hunched over in the shadows of the alley. His head turned at the sound of her voice. Shia couldn't make out the demon's victim from this angle, but she was certain it was dead. The Rissu's claws stilled. Chunks of flesh stuck between its fangs. Blood dripped from its long razor like nails and covered the brick wall before him, sprayed forward like the work of an avant garde artist.

Messy kill.

She wrinkled her nose as the scent of wet dog overwhelmed her.

Oh, thank the stars, he'd started with the four-legged beings rather than the humans. She sent a silent prayer for the lost canine soul and focused on the Rissu before her. He was large for a newborn. Her best guess put him over 6'4", though his weight was impossible to estimate, given the anatomy of his race, top-heavy, a brawler, well muscled and powerful. His claws easily tore through the carcass of his prey, a Rottweiler. His teeth had severed its neck and bones. The thing was famished, and she had interrupted its first meal.

Shia weighed her odds. She'd hunted Rissu before. This one outsized her by at least a couple hundred pounds and over a foot in height. She'd bet he wasn't going to like her much after this.

Oh well, the bigger they are, the harder they fall. Right?

When he turned his massive head to look at her, she struck. Her katana whispered through the night air, intent on taking his head from his shoulders. She cursed under her breath as he moved, the tip of the blade grazing his shoulder rather than severing his head from his neck.

"No sir, be a good demon. This is not your realm." She shook her head at him and sing-songed as she followed his movements. She twirled the longer blade in her right hand, her wrist rotating the long metal blade as an extension of herself. Her motions were almost musical as she stepped closer, separating the beast from his snack.

The Rissu remained hunched over like a cat, back bowed, teeth bared, eyes lit up, studying her every move from the center of the alley.

He growled.

She smirked. "Bring it, fledgling."

She stepped to the side, preparing for his attack. They never learned. When he launched into her, she switched the grip on her sword. He drove against her, and Shia fell backward under the force. She jabbed into his upper ribs; the hilt of her katana in one hand, a hardened strike with the wakizashi in the other. Each blow found the soft space between ribs, and she allowed herself a brief feeling of success. The Rissu's momentum carried them both deeper into the alley. His weight shifted again, and she shoved hard. He slammed into the wall behind them.

The demon howled in pain as the spines on his back struck cold stone. Shia grinned and rolled out of his grasp. Her foot lashed out, kicking his jaw sideways.

His claws slashed out, nails elongated, sharp and spiky, reaching to her. She bit back a cry of pain as his hand knifed down, catching her across her abdomen.

She clamped a hand over her mid-section. Blood rushed to her center. She frowned as she rolled, coming to her feet in a crouch. She chided herself for the premature assumption of victory.

Rookie Rissu, 1, centuries old Samurai, 0.

"Oh no, demon boy, it's not gonna be that easy."

Ohh, come closer demon...ashes to ashes and dust to dust.

She'd send him back into the alternate dimensions,

multiple realities, in pain, and definitely in several pieces. Shia satisfied herself with the memory of sending an enemy into a dimension portal once without his limbs. She wondered if she'd have time for such a ritual before the pre-dawn traffic interrupted her.

She blocked out the pain and switched hands with her katana, watching as the blood red eyes tracked her movements. Back and forth. Back and forth, she played.

She waited.

In the pause between shifting of hands, he leapt.

She darted aside, grasping his neck. She pushed down into the pavement as he tried to overtake her. Her body shifted and flowed, one sword swept out and around in the other, intent on taking his head and ending this fight. He darted to the side and slid past her blade. Her sword tip hit the ground, metal ringing on asphalt. She almost bit her tongue in frustration. Her hand let go, claws retracted as the demon tumbled over and away from her. She didn't need him taking her with him. She watched as the Rissu rolled to his feet.

She crouched, ready, waiting as he stared down at her. When he dashed towards her, her arm lifted in a block to his shoulder, pushing him past her, she ducked, taking her swords with her as his tail sailed over her, ducking under the deadly spikes. They both rolled, standing off.

The Rissu threw a haymaker at her.

She blocked, arm on arm, the impact resonating through her as the wakizashi blade barely touched him. Her other arm and katana arced out and over. She sliced down, severing his shoulder from his body and then lifted the blade, turning to slash across his neck.

Slice.

A lock of her hair drifted in the air.

She missed.

The blade swirled around her in a defensive posture on instinct. Losing sight of such a beast for a second could be fatal. She drew the katana back, her eyes shifting through the shadows to catch the Rissu before its next strike. After several breaths, she stood upright, cursing her luck and her performance. The Rissu had executed the only move with worse consequences than blindsiding her.

The demon turned tail and ran.

Shia groaned under her breath. She'd get her run in yet. Rissu weren't the fastest demons in the realms, but they left a good trail. She slid both swords back into place on her back and palmed several throwing stars while forcibly ignoring the pain in her abdomen as her body began to stitch itself back together. The metal stars offered comfort and familiarity as they slipped into her hands. Metal vibrated against her skin.

Her vision shifted and red lights danced across the ground in the darkness.

Demon trail.

He'd darted out of the alleyway. He had made an escape attempt, but she could still catch him. Shia sprinted down the alley, nearing full speed in a few steps. She raced forward, intent on the unholy light along the street.

Her focus split between human reality and the otherworld. She reached the end of the passage and turned the corner. She collided with something solid. The air left her lungs. Stars danced in her vision, and she struggled to draw in a breath. This wasn't Rissu, far too physical and of this realm.

She forced her need to fight deep down, focusing on the night.

The figure staggered backward, spinning before stabilizing against a parked truck. A beam of light darted over the ground, over the car, into the sky and then stopped. A flashlight.

A demon wouldn't have a flashlight.

Human.

She struggled to right herself and dropped the throwing stars down her sleeve.

Breathe, Shia, breathe.

She didn't attack humans without cause. She shifted, and she took another deep breath, stabilizing.

The man stood upright, leveling the flashlight at her face. Standing, yet still craving air in her lungs, Shia lifted her hands in self-defense. She blinked, willing her eyes to adjust to the sudden glare in the dark.

"You okay, lady? Someone chasing you?" He asked.

It was bright.

"No, no one chasing me." She answered.

It took seconds for her vision to right itself. When it did, she could make out his silhouette against the grey night air, but nothing more. She frowned. As if hearing her thoughts, the man moved the light from her to his own form. He focused the light on a piece of paper in his hand. Centered on the paper was a black and white picture of a Rottweiler.

He turned the light beneath his face, illuminating him in campfire ghost story fashion.

"Have you seen this dog?" He asked.

She bit her tongue. Hard. If she hadn't already locked her knees, they might have buckled in embarrassment. Oh, gods. Ryan. She took a deep breath, forcing her heart rate to decelerate, demanding her body come back into her control.

"Good evening, Detective Calder." She watched as his eyes widened.

He switched the light from himself back to her, studying her as she winced from the pain of the sudden brightness.

"Dr. Ronin, out for an evening run?" He asked.

Shia dropped her gaze, taking in her black sweats. Not something she wanted to be seen in, but there you had it. Thank the Universe the dark fabric hid the cuts it suffered and any blood loss she'd suffered.

"Yes."

She darted a glance over his shoulder, the red lights still hovered over the street. Had the demon sprinted right past him? Her gaze swept over him, making sure he held no hint of red light. She shifted her shoulders, settling her swords in lower. Protected by the same magic protecting her, he shouldn't be able to see them, but she didn't need to take the chance with the eagle eyed homicide detective. As odd as he seemed sometimes, he appeared very aware in the human realm. She wouldn't put it beyond him to notice the otherworldly going-ons.

Ryan tilted his head and followed her gaze for a moment over his shoulder before focusing on her again. "Well, I figured you weren't grocery shopping. Looks like you worked up a good sweat." He flashed the light at her feet and along the entrance to the alleyway. "You drop anything?" The light crisscrossed over the demon trail, which glowed like fire in Shia's eyes.

She wished he'd kill the light, but knew he wouldn't. The glare amplified in her head a hundred times over. She squinted. "Thought I heard something in the alley, but no one's there. Decided I better make up my time." She shifted, torn between letting her eyes drink in his dark form and chasing after the Rissu.

Wait a minute.

Rottweiler?

A shiver raced through her. "You're out looking for a Rottie?"

Please tell her this wasn't his dog she'd failed to rescue.

Ryan nodded, "Yeah, Mrs. Bradbury in Apartment 4-G is missing her dog. She's pretty broken up about it. I figured it was the least I could do to help. Especially because Mrs. Bradbury listens to Joe Cocker when she's upset...and her hearing aide isn't always up to par." He moved the light from one side of the street to the other, checking for any uninvited guests. "Nothing inspires a man to community service like Joe Cocker at a hundred and twenty decibels."

Despite her duty, her lips twitched. Decorated homicide detective way laid by an elderly neighbor and 70's soul-singing icon. Priceless. She sobered. She didn't want either of them finding out how the dog died. The crack of bone in teeth still echoed through her head. She wished she'd found the Rissu minutes before. The four-legged little beast should have lived.

"You live nearby? Rottie's stay pretty close to home. I can keep an eye out for him while I run." Over Ryan's shoulder the trail began to dim.

"That would be great. You can't miss him. He's got a collar with rhinestones...something about his resemblance to Elvis. I don't know." Ryan handed her the flier. "Two blocks south of here. Trust me. You'll hear 'I Get by with a Little Help from my Friends' before you ever get in the door. My number's on the flier if you find anything, but I think you have it from the Felder case."

Shia nodded. She knew more about Ryan than she cared to admit even before their cold case, the Felder homicide. She bit her lip as the Rissu's trail dimmed and faded. She shouldn't have let him side track her. She was faster than him. He never would have realized it was her if she'd kept moving. Her entire body warmed.

"What's his name?" She'd replace the dog. She

11

couldn't in good conscience let an old lady mourn the loss of her beloved family member because a demon decided to make him dinner.

This job sucked.

Ryan shrugged. "What else? Joe." He gave her a quick once-over. "You mind me asking something personal?"

"You can ask. I may or may not answer." She'd already delayed too long. She rocked from foot to foot, ready to be on the move again.

"The nation's capitol isn't always the friendliest place, especially in the dead of night, for a good looking girl. You have some pepper spray or something handy?" He half-grinned. "Professional courtesy and all..."

Shia smiled. "Don't you know, Detective, I am a weapon. I run the nights. It's the best time. No one out to stop me."

She wasn't about to reveal the swords, throwing stars, or baton hidden on her body. He didn't need the influence. The worst she encountered was a stray homeless or a demon. The demons, well, they were hers to handle anyway. The homeless wandered on their way, thinking she was an illusion. She preferred it that way.

"I'd like to share your confidence, Dr. Ronin. I'd feel better hearing you had some tools to help you stay safe." He unbuckled a small container of pepper spray from his belt. "This is compact. It shouldn't affect your running stride, but it could help in case you bump into the wrong night creature."

Her hand lifted. He didn't know about the other creatures of the night. The pepper spray dropped into her palm. The one detective who she thought would do well in her realm had never questioned her findings. Sometimes, she'd had to reach to explain a death. He worked the cases, focused on the facts. She wondered what he'd do if she presented him with a demon, the Rissu?

She sighed. He'd never even see it. Few did.

"Thank you, Detective. I'll be sure to return this to you tomorrow, if you stop by the morgue."

He nodded. "Thanks. I have the Huang results to pick up. I'll adjust my schedule. Enjoy your run, Dr. Ronin."

Shia shifted, unsure. Ryan never spoke more than a few words, directed at work to her. He was quiet, but he was out looking for a Rottie who belonged to a neighbor. The Rissu was long gone. She'd have to hunt it down tomorrow. And Ryan? He wasn't of her realm, but one of those to protect who now had a demon in his neighborhood. She'd be sure to keep her running route close by. She didn't want some Rissu munching on him or his elderly neighbor.

"Good luck with your fliers and finding the Rot. I hope she eventually turns the music down, for your sanity," she murmured.

She pulled her hood up over her hair and took a step forward.

She stopped and turned, casting a glance back at him. "Detective Calder?"

"Yes, Dr. Ronin?"

"Be careful of the shadows."

It was the only warning she could give him. She wished she could have given him more. She turned and set out at a sprint on her regular path. She didn't need him asking for clarification. He was one to do so. She sprinted away from him faster than she should have.

CHAPTER TWO

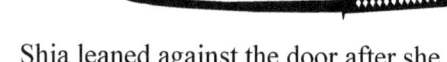

Shia leaned against the door after she closed and double bolted the massive weight behind her. Her eyes drifted shut. The back of her head rested on the cool metal. Her palms flattened as she let the coolness seep into her bones. The calmness of the condo swept over her. The bite of the swords still strapped to her back didn't faze her, and she took a deep breath.

What had that been about?

She'd been sidetracked by a human. In all her centuries, she'd never deviated from her course. She was a samurai, yet Ryan slowed her down with his stories about the dog and the neighbor. Albeit, the sexiest detective she'd ever met and totally uninterested in talking to her outside a case. She'd let him stop her and running headlong into his hard body blew her concentration. Her entire being itched, resonating on a different frequency now.

He'd been looking for a dog.

Her chin dropped to her chest. Her hair fell over her face, tickling her skin.

She'd found the dog—the canine gave his life, rhinestone collar and all, to a newly born Rissu demon. Better him than what the Rissu routinely hunted, but it still horrified her.

She sighed. She didn't need new connections or attention. A rhinestone collar on a Rottie? She would replace the four-legged. She couldn't leave an elderly lady, no matter how much she annoyed Detective Calder with her choice in music, without her protector. Honor required it. And, he was going to have to be...

"Lady Ronin, I've started your shower." Her AI's voice intruded.

She jumped. Her head banged into the door as her eyes flew open. "Thank you, Jace."

She had to be out of it to let Jace startle her. Her sisters would have a field day with that one, not that she'd be sharing. She loved the technological advances and the conveniences they offered, but sometimes they intruded. She pushed herself forward.

Lamenting accomplished nothing.

She dropped her weapons in their resting place near her desk in the living room before striding across the hardwood floors of the barren condo and entering the bedroom. She should buy some furniture. It wasn't like people randomly stopped by, and her sisters didn't count. She'd bought the place as a safe house, but she rarely used it until a few months ago. She preferred her warehouse home to this one. Then the work hours doubled after the retirement of another M.E. so she'd moved closer to compensate for a while.

She shed her clothes, dropping them to the floor. She'd pick them up later if Jace didn't have one of those creepy little bots sweep up behind her. The shiny bug like creatures still made her shiver in repulsion. She'd skewered the first few, but he'd rebuilt them. You install an AI. You get all the gadgets. She wasn't willing to part with Jace, as much as he annoyed her some days.

She strode into the shower. "Jace, boot up my laptop. I need to check in and figure out where Shellie was tonight. Research any Rissu sightings."

"Yes, m'lady."

She checked her stomach where the Rissu had slashed her. The skin already knitted together and pink. Good, limited damage. When the warm water hit her body, she smiled. Her head tilted back, letting the liquid warmth pelt her skin. She loved running the streets after sunset, but she might love her late night showers more. Add in the fact she had a state of the art computer system at her beck and call, being a samurai demon hunter had never been better. After all the years of sleeping in the dirt, she refused to take her surroundings for granted. She couldn't predict when she'd be back to living on the move.

Of course, no one trained her to watch out for killer energy radiating from one lead homicide detective. Demons, human assassins, drug traffickers, she knew how to deal with so many facets of evil and death. But one living, breathing, on-the-right-side-of-the-law male enters, and she looses all train of thought and reasoning. Shia reached out to grab the soap, sliding the sandalwood scented bar over her body.

What was she supposed to do with one detective who caused every one of her cells to go on red alert? He shouldn't have that power.

"Lady Ronin, your report is ready."

She shut off the water. Jace was more efficient than anyone she'd ever employed, more so than any human apprentice. Too bad he was electronic.

Then again, maybe that served her better. She wouldn't have to mourn his death. Eventually all humans had to die. But not her. Samurais lived forever. Or until a demon killed them.

"Report." She stepped out of the shower and grabbed the teal colored towel off the wall. She shivered at the change in temperature. She clenched her jaw. She needed to do something about this sensitivity before she set out to track the Rissu down. This kind of physical distraction would get her hurt, or worse, killed, again.

"Sightings of Rissu newborns are being reporting across the continental United States. Three occurred last night. One here, one in Dallas, and one in Los Angeles. I'm compiling any unusual occurrences for this evening as the West Coast is still in the early hours."

"And where is Shellie?"

She tucked the towel into place around her, letting her wet hair trail down her back. She ran her hands through the strands, attempting to pull it back.

She needed a haircut.

"Last report, she was in Las Vegas. That Rissu took off with a child. No reports have been filed since."

Shellie would be focused on the hunt for that one and rightly so.

Barefoot, she padded back into the bedroom. "Estimate creation time on three Rissu."

She pulled a pair of soft jersey knit black pants from her dresser and shimmied into them. A long sleeved silky coal colored t-shirt followed suit. Bless her addiction to online shopping and her monochromatic color preference. Old Navy supplied her with the most comfortable clothing. Too bad she kept ripping them. She should look into some more serviceable clothing fetish.

She settled into her office chair, and she set in to work. She tucked one leg under her, the other hanging down. She propped her head atop her hands and scanned the reports Jace pulled up on her monitor. Words passed before her ... attack, night, pre-dawn. It all read the same.

When her cell phone shrieked next to her, she didn't even flinch.

She hit answer on the screen. "Yes?"

"You reading this?" The feminine voice demanded.

"I'm living it. A Rissu has been here tonight too. Shellie's nowhere to be seen." She kept reading.

"Shia, this is unacceptable. What the hell is going on?"

She passed a hand over her eyes, resetting her vision as the words threatened to blur. "I don't know. This is sudden. And for them to be so wide spread..."

The sigh echoed over the line. "You're going to have to stay on top of it."

"I'm not active." She straightened up. Stay on top of it? Manage her day job and active status? Four sisters worked to provide funding while seven remained on active duty. She'd created the protocol. They'd existed too many years on the fringes, barely surviving while battling unseen battles.

"Celeste went active three days ago. Raisa's about ready to do the same. I'm trying to keep myself as the central information hub and track everyone. I need you to shift and balance. You can maintain both responsibilities. Our house cannot survive otherwise."

Shia bit back a groan. She signed up for this. She built everything. If two of the four of them shifted already, she could do no less. "Fine, I'm on it." She shouldn't fuss, in reality she should have been the one running things, but Ilsa, the tall Scandinavian, made a better manager. She'd handed central leadership over without an issue when her protégé showed far more business sense than she did.

She tapped the End Call button on her iPhone and dropped it on her desk, harder than she'd intended. Sure, sit back and run things from Sweden. Ilsa hadn't moved in centuries while she was far from home. When had things gotten so out of control?

She bit the inside of her cheek. Track human killers by day and night...track demon killers by night and day. She snapped the laptop shut and strode to her bedroom. She'd sleep now, taking some respite while she could get it since it might be a long time before she'd rest again. Tomorrow, she'd track her demons, the Rottweiler, and one all out sexy male.

"Jace, find me a Rottweiler breeder and trainer. I want a good guard dog for an elderly lady. He needs to be willing to wear a rhinestone collar. And make sure he's named Joe. Wake me in four."

"Yes, Lady Ronin."

"Eight ... Nine ... Ten."

Ryan racked the barbell, balanced between relief and frustration. He'd compromised on the number of repetitions or the amount of weight during his last few workouts. As he sat up from the bench press and buried his face in his towel, he tried to figure it all out. He looked at the digital readout next to the bench.

Ten reps at 325 pounds.

He cursed and scrubbed the sweat from his scalp. He had been stuck at 325 for a month, but had broken through the plateau a few weeks ago. Suddenly, he was back, unable to push past the hurdle and add weight. He closed his eyes and rested his forehead against the steel barbell.

"... and to recap our top story, Rachel Grimes, personal assistant to Alexander Spyros, head of Spyros International, committed suicide earlier tonight. Our investigation has confirmed that Grimes had a history of bipolar disorder, and that she had a prescription for Vilanzolin. At this time, neither Miss Grimes' personal physician nor Mr. Spyros were available for comment. From the Pentagon, this is Chris Weitzel, reporting on behalf of..."

The huge sound of a Hammond organ and electric guitars replaced the reporter's nasal delivery in the speakers. Styx's rock anthem, "Blue Collar Man" tore through the room. Ryan rubbed his eyes, and the first image that came to mind was the snap shot of Joe, the Rottweiler. Christ, he'd seen that dog so often, he might as well have given birth to the darn creature. Mrs. Bradbury displayed fanatical devotion to the dog's namesake, going through "Mad Dogs and Englishmen" all the way up to "Organic." The woman was a devotee that was certain. Joe was still missing, despite her wailings and 24-7 playback of Cocker's tunes.

Sleep deprivation didn't help. Hitting a plateau in the gym was one thing. What else was he limiting thanks to his neighbor's pooch? Homicide investigation had a timeline that determined success. Waiting meant giving the murderer a longer window to cover his tracks or flee the country. Ryan cursed at the thought of missing a collar because his head was full of the chorus to "You Can Leave Your Hat On."

He ran a hand over his face before reaching for his Rev3 energy drink. He took a swig and set the can back down on the floor.

Ryan replayed the weekend's events in his mind's eye. He had been called out to a murder-suicide on Friday. Those were usually easy to close. The father in this case had locked his four and six year old daughters in the trunk of his car while he killed their mother and then himself.

Bastard.

Interviewing children always reminded Ryan of his own childhood, and he'd seen his sister's innocence in the little girls' eyes.

"Enough," he snapped out loud.

Ryan had promised himself to shut his thoughts off until he hit his desk tomorrow morning with a hot cup of coffee. One more example of losing focus. If there was any living being happier to see Joe returned home, he couldn't think of it...Mrs. Bradbury included. His silver lining? His chance meeting with Shia, the incredible Chief Medical Examiner.

He put aside all thoughts of old ladies and missing puppies at the thought of Shia Ronin. Christ with a sawed-off shotgun, she was one beautiful woman. He'd seen her plenty of times in a lab coat. Her outfit tonight was a refreshing change of pace. The workout gear she donned did more to compliment her lithe form. He could put up with late night doggie rescue if she was part of the deal.

He smirked at his own infatuation. Something about her drew his curiosity. He tossed the towel to the floor and tapped the digital display by the bench. In a moment, the gym filled with shrieking guitars and pounding drums. Ryan dropped back onto the bench. His head swam with the snapshot of Shia, caught off guard, staring up at him, her blue-black eyes wide, in the darkness with a look that wiped aside all other thoughts.

"Eight … Nine ... Ten." He panted.

"Repetition Complete."

"Computer," Ryan said. "Up the weight to 350."

The system complied, adding the appropriate plates. Ryan gripped the bar and pushed it upward from its cradle.

"One … Two ... Three ..."

CHAPTER THREE

Shia glanced over the corpse lying on the main table in the morgue. "Computer, record."

"Recording."

"Twenty-four year old, female. Asian-American." She focused on the woman's body in front of her. "Date of death, August 15, 2015. Approximate time between 1 a.m. and 3 a.m. Bruising on the skin around the throat region. Check for indentation pattern." She glanced at the x-rays posted up on the wall. "Fractured left tibia, a recent break perhaps occurred no more than three weeks ago. Another fracture, left radius. The angle and the ..."

A steady knocking on the door interrupted her.

Shia glanced up and frowned. "Enter."

Her head turned as Detective Ryan started to open the door. He wrinkled his nose as the inevitable first face wave of acrid morgue odor greeted him. Shia smiled. Formaldehyde had to be scratching the top of his pallet and the back of his throat. The smell hit everyone that way.

She heard him exhale as if trying to get the sour taste out of his sinus cavity.

"Dr. Ronin, are you decent?"

Her eyebrow twitched. "Dead body. Of course I'm decent, Detective Calder. What do I owe the pleasure?"

As if she hadn't seen enough of him in her dreams last night. Now he invaded her working space. He had every right to do so. The body in front of her was the victim in his newest investigation. She'd arrived during the night.

He pushed the door open with his elbow, revealing a tray of white Styrofoam cups in his free hand. "I come bearing gifts." Three identical cups occupied the tray. He half-smiled as he entered, casting a glance around and drinking in the sight of specimens lining the steel tables.

She sniffed. The hint of black tea wafted past. "You brought me tea?"

No one came into the morgue baring gifts, much less her beloved tea. Her hand snaked out before she could stop it, snatching the cup. She lifted it up, eyes closed as she inhaled the aroma. She'd evolved from Green Tea to the Black centuries ago, loving the little extra kick the black had on her energy levels.

Ryan shrugged. "You're the only M.E. I've ever seen who doesn't drown in loud music, cigarettes, coffee or some combination of the three. Since you were out running the other night, I figured you must be one of those fit freaks dedicated to purity in the body. I grabbed black tea on a whim."

She studied him over the rim of her cup as he moved to the sink and dumped out one of the other cups, emptying black coffee down the stainless steel drain. He grabbed the final cup and tossed the tray into the plastic trash bin. She bit back another smile as he scowled, the heat of the coffee hitting him when he swallowed more of the heavier drink.

She sipped, eyes closed in a brief moment of pure pleasure. She'd missed brewing her own blend in the pre-dawn hours, running too late and on too little sleep. She needed to program Jace to start the brew as her body began to awake. Then again, even the AI had a hard time with how fast she woke up. She could go from asleep to fighting stance in a matter of seconds.

"Loud music helps sometimes, cigarettes are overpowering--they can kill a body and coffee..." She mentally shook herself and put the tea down, refocusing on the female before her. "Well, the coffee bean has no known predator."

"Other than the overtired homicide detective," Ryan answered as he lifted his cup in a mock toast. "How did the pepper spray work out for you?"

Startled, she stared at him. "Pepper spray?"

Oh, she'd slid the small canister into her pocket and forgotten about it. "I appreciated the offer, Detective, but completely unnecessary. I'll return it. It's sitting on my desk at home."

She'd have to rifle through her clothes to find the thing. Pepper spray never deterred a demon, only irritated them. She'd forgotten the container the moment he'd handed it to her. Throwing stars proved more efficient.

"If it means anything, I'm glad you accepted." He leaned forward with each word. "Not using it means you had a safe run." He laughed into his coffee. "Besides, by the time I left you, I might have turned the pepper spray on Mrs. Bradbury."

She couldn't refrain from smiling. "Was she still playing Joe Cocker music when you went home?" She didn't envy him the music. Yet, while she'd slept, Jace found three breeders for Rotties. She had him looking into training and trying to match the brief picture Ryan flashed at her. She should have asked him for a flier.

Ryan erupted in song, the voice that left his body wasn't his, but lower, raspier. "Sometimes I got to change have a change of scene cause every night I have the strangest dreams." He shifted from side to side in a spastic rhythm, never spilling his coffee. "Imprisoned by the way it used to be, left here on my own or so it seems." He spun in a 360, leveling his gaze on her intently. "I got to leave before I start to scream. But, someone's locked the door and thrown away the key." He paused, looking up at the ceiling in silent contemplation for several seconds. When he exhaled and faced her, his body spun in a circle as he sang, "Feelin' Alright...oh oh, I'm not feelin' too good myself."

He stopped suddenly, as if an exorcism had rid him of demonic possession.

Shia sidestepped him when he started spinning around the room, ready to draw the sword hidden beneath her lab coat. Her heart rate accelerated as fight mode threatened to sweep over her. Had he been bitten by the Rissu? She hadn't seen any bite marks on him. Her head tilted, and she squared off, ready to drop her recorder. Hmm, Detective Calder might be a little on the loony side.

He halted and took a long pull off of his coffee. "Take your scalpel and stab me in the eye if I ever quote another Cocker song to you." He shook his head as if trying to rid his brain from the lyrics he'd sung.

Tension left her. Maybe the late nights and noise had gotten to him. She almost breathed a sigh of relief when her heart rate returned to normal. He certainly kept her on her toes.

"I hope the dog comes home, and you don't have to listen to anymore Cocker songs." She wished him a sound sleep, but she'd also make sure a Rottie so similar showed up even the old lady couldn't tell the difference. She turned her attention back to the corpse in front of her unable to deal with Ryan's flight into the musical realm. "Details. Explain what isn't in the report."

Ryan's stare weighed heavy on her for several seconds. When he replied, any hint of humor or impersonation escaped his tone. "Victim is a 24-year-old female, Abigail Huang, married to Charles Huang, no children. Apparent cause of death is asphyxiation as a result of a broken neck. Our latest cemetery occupant took a header with plenty of stops on the way down." Ryan turned to his right and dumped his cup of coffee into the stainless steel sink. He dropped the cup in the trash and turned back to her. "Did you find anything to dispute these findings?"

She breathed in deeply. He seemed fine, seemed being the operative word. She couldn't strip search him and check every square inch of him for marks. Her body warmed with the thought. Ryan, naked, was ... distracting. She forced herself to turn away from him and pushed the image of him from her mind.

Poor woman. He was dead on, and off, in his findings. Pure human killer.

"Very astute. My study concludes the victim died from a broken neck, and several other fractures and abrasions are consistent with the reported "accidental" fall down the famed stairs in Georgetown. However, x-rays reveal many of these wounds were not suffered on the same occasion. Some of her wounds, including a fractured left tibia and radius, along with a few minor injuries like the phalanges and Calcaneus, occurred more than a week, perhaps up to three weeks, before the fatal injuries."

"Whoa...whoa," he stammered. "Multiple previous fractures?" Ryan stared at the body. "Shia...I mean, Dr. Ronin, are you telling me the victim suffered fractures on different occasions?"

"Yes." She gazed at him. "Minor breaks, severe, but

non-impacting head trauma. She's been beaten before, nothing to raise concerns, if you weren't looking for the connections." She turned towards the light boxes on the wall. Various images of bones silhouetted against the lamps.

"I always look for signs of abuse." She pointed out the faint, additional lines of fractures and damage. "Only a female in a damaging relationship or job suffers these kind of blows."

"I missed it," Ryan said. He stopped and stared back at the corpse on the steel table. "I missed it." He shook his head, before running a hand through his hair. He looked up at her, and then gazed past her. "I've got to find him."

"You didn't miss it. The abuse had been subtle up to this point. Whoever did this, reached a limit."

Ryan's response was distant, vacant. "I need your report ASAP. I'll be in touch."

"This …" She pointed to the woman's neck. "… wasn't planned."

"Detective Calder," She snapped when he tried to turn away from her. "I wasn't done." Her teeth clenched. How dare he ignore her after he'd invaded her domain? "You want your answers, you will listen to my findings."

She watched Ryan closed his eyes and draw in several breaths as if to suppress the adrenaline pumping in his veins. His jaw hardened as he glanced over his shoulder at her. "I'm listening."

"Good. Come here. Learn what you're looking for." She stepped back to the victim. "This faint bruising on her arms is not from this incident. The other breaks are a few weeks old. She suffered extensive trauma to the left side of her body. Injuries to her right side finished her off, but we can trace an underlying history of damage."

She lifted the woman's hand and flipped her palm

27

over. "She has salon nails, underneath, they're shredded."

"Dr. Ronin, my responsibility is to uphold the law. Abigail Huang died of natural causes, or she was murdered. If someone killed her, as we are both beginning to believe, I'd appreciate a precise lead on who her killer was."

Even angry with her, he radiated heat. She swayed closer to him when he stepped up next to her. Every cell went on red alert. She bit her lower lip. She'd run an extended patrol tonight. She suspected she was going to need to work off some energy if he stayed much longer.

"With these kinds of past injuries, this death was not an accident, look for someone who knows her. Someone in constant contact with her. From what I'm seeing so far, I'd recommend starting with her husband." And honestly, who took a header down the Georgetown stairs on their own? The Toxicology report wasn't done yet, but she knew the woman didn't have any alcohol or drugs in her system.

Ryan cursed. "Sorry I doubted you, Miss Ronin. I'll get to the bottom of our vic's injuries ASAP."

"Ryan?" She slanted him a look. "I'm not a miss." She hadn't been a miss in centuries. "It's Shia, professional or personal." She'd been called a lot of things in her life, but she'd never been called Miss. "Get me DNA from the husband. I can most likely link her death to him. In the meantime, I'll work on a precise timeline of her injuries."

He lifted his gaze. Shia's breath caught in her throat as his eyes locked on hers. Her heart threatened to leap out of her chest, a slow sensual heat wound through her body. This man might be more dangerous to her than the Rissu demon.

"And his fingerprints. Clear ones." She'd match them to the full thumbprint on the woman's neck.

She'd already checked, but they weren't on file.

Shia swallowed as he remained focused on her. She might wish he'd pay attention to her for herself, rather than because of a case. Where was her common sense?

"Right. Establish a timeline for me on the injuries that will prove a pattern of abuse. I may have the right pieces in place to confirm this, but it's going to take me some footwork. We've got the exact cause of death and injuries suffered, so I can recreate how our vic wound up in the morgue. If I have the facts, I'll get a confession. Let's confirm what lead to her death and what didn't." He pointed at Abigail's corpse. "I'm coming back to pick your brain on anything leading up to this."

She nodded, anticipating every word.

Ryan turned, striding to the door. He paused before he left, glancing back at her. "Thank you, Shia."

She watched his silhouette disappear through the frosted glass. She blew at a stray strand of hair as it drifted into her eyes. Her heart rate returned to normal.

Well, hell.

CHAPTER FOUR

Ryan sat in his black, unmarked Chevy Impala. His Ray-Ban shades kept the light out of his eyes, if not the exhaustion. Who needed sleep? It seemed over rated, but maybe that was because he wasn't getting any.

The police scanner cut intermittent messages through the car, a jumbled mix of numbers and codes, breaking up the sounds of David Bowie's "Space Oddity." Ryan ground his teeth, tasting the salt and spice of the peppered beef jerky. Major Tom was making his final transmission to Ground Control. No one should interrupt that, much less some petty larceny further up northwest.

Two hours into his stakeout, he resorted to spicy food and an ice-cold energy drink to keep his interest. Perky co-eds out for an afternoon jog were too few and far between, and Ryan's other entertainment option was a neighbor tilling the garden around her perennials. She ripped weeds out with a hypnotic focus. He didn't usually like sharing time with a partner, but he was getting close to talking to himself, or the cartoon icon smiling from the beef jerky package.

He'd parked in the same spot where the private investigator had snapped the pictures sent to the precinct. Ryan had them memorized at this point. Charles and Abigail Huang lived in a two-level, brick house without a garage. In this part of town, the place probably cost them over a half-million bucks. The neighbor to the left was the heavy set, older woman working in the garden. She was a renter, only in the neighborhood since the past winter. The neighbor on the right, Hector Gonzalez, was much more intriguing. Ryan's investigation had turned up a series of calls to local authorities, almost always reporting disturbances at the Huang residence.

Ryan would settle for Hector's return home, but he hoped Charles would make an appearance. By the time Bowie changed gears and launched into "John, I'm Only Dancing", a pale blue Honda Accord pulled up in the Gonzalez driveway. Ryan swallowed the remainder of the jerky, took a long slug of his drink, and shut off the radio, silencing the bizarre marriage of Bowie and Dispatch. Hector Gonzalez was two steps out of his Honda, white plastic grocery bags in hand, when Ryan exited the Impala and armed the deadly anti-personnel alarm.

"Mr. Gonzalez," Ryan stated as he approached. The older man stole a quick glance up and turned back to his bags. "Excuse me." He was at the foot of the driveway, addressing Hector, who simply closed his car door and began the walk to his front door. "Perdoname, Señor."

Hector looked at him and shook his head. "No dinero. No hablo Ingles!"

Ryan rolled his eyes. He was being mistaken for a door-to-door salesman. Priceless. He would love an explanation of what the hell Hector Gonzalez thought he might be selling, but let it go. He lifted his badge, presenting it to the older man and whistled. "Soy policia. Got a minute?"

Hector erupted into light-speed Spanish, and Ryan made out some garbage about immigration and political asylum. He shook his head and waved his hands in the air, badge still planted in his left hand. "Hablas Ingles?"

Hector stared back at him. "No. No hablo Ingles."

"My ass, you don't speak English." Ryan thought, having read multiple police reports quoting Hector's complaints. He smiled and shrugged. "Hablo solamente un poquito de Espanol." He latched his badge back on his belt and then ran a hand through his hair. "Comprende?"

"Si." Hector nodded, a little bit of Spanish.

Ryan nodded with him and smiled. Rules of Police Communication 101, follow their body language. He looked around, as if searching for a way to communicate. "Umm...tengo preguntas de...del..." He pointed at the house next door. "de los Huangs."

Something washed over Hector Gonzalez's face. "Abigail?"

"So, you understand?" Ryan countered.

"Si...yes, yes, I understand." Hector replied, shame and hope mingling in his gaze. "I'm sorry. I did not mean to deceive you."

Ryan's shoulders relaxed, and he allowed himself to grin. "It's okay, happens all the time." He stepped closer, and Hector made no move against him. "Abigail Huang. You two were close?"

Hector looked at his shoes, taking a deep breath, shifting the grocery bags in his hands. "Not exactly. She was muy bonita, a beautiful girl. Her presence made this neighborhood happier, better."

"She was a beautiful girl, Mr. Gonzalez?"

"You know she is dead, or you wouldn't be questioning me." Hector's tone suddenly grew teeth as he stared up at him. His body straightened, attempting to regain the posture of a once taller, stronger man, but age kept a permanent rounding to his shoulders as if the world weighed down on him.

Ryan nodded. "Yes, she is dead. I was just checking on your English comprehension." The mutual dislike was established, but it served neither side of the conversation. Ryan softened his tone. "I need you to tell me about the last time you saw Abigail Huang...alive."

"I told the other officers everything."

"I didn't say the last time you called the cops, Mr. Gonzalez. I said the last time you saw Abigail alive." Ryan gazed down at the older man.

Hector stared at him for a long time. When he spoke again, he was far more reserved, and his eyes moved from Ryan to the brick house next door. "She moved slow...the slowest I've ever seen her. Normally, Abigail is so vibrant, so full of life. This day, it was a Thursday. The sun was supposed to shine all day, but there were clouds, and it was not as bright as it should have been."

"Abigail came out of the home, walking slowly, leaning against el barandilla...the railing, and then the mailbox. She was limping badly. I called to her, and she hardly responded, raising her hand slightly. No tiene la sonrisa bonita. Abigail has such a beautiful smile. This day, she didn't smile. She was hardly...how you say...alive."

Tears filled at the corners of the older man's eyes. "That was the last day I ever saw her, Officer."

Something tightened in his chest before he moved on. He knew a liar when he met one, and Hector Gonzalez didn't have it in him to be anything more than the petty liar he had been minutes before. He'd been willing to feign ignorance to the police, but gave it all up once Abigail's name came into the conversation. He wasn't a liar. He worshiped her from beyond the hedge.

"Walk me through it," Ryan said. "She leaned on the railing and on the mailbox."

Hector pointed, drawing a path; the final steps he'd ever seen Abigail take. She exited her front door, resting against the wall. She took the two steps down from the porch to the sidewalk, leaning heavily on the rail. She made her way down the driveway, resting against the car parked in the driveway. She took the final few steps to the mailbox and then held onto it. She limped each of those few steps she had without something to steady her. Walking back, she switched to the far side of the driveway so she could use the car, the railing and the wall as support.

Support for her left side.

Ryan nodded. "Gracias, Señor Gonzalez. I'll be in touch if I have any further questions."

He turned and strode back to the Impala, leaving the older man in his driveway. There were a few Thursdays between Gonzalez's last call to the cops and the discovery of Abigail's corpse. The x-rays were right. Shia, Dr. Ronin, was right about the injuries to Abigail Huang. Ryan cursed. They weren't the only injuries. He needed proof of when Abigail Huang suffered the laundry list of broken bones, if Dr. Ronin had proof. He needed it solid.

Bulletproof.

Forgoing her nightly run made her cranky. Shia's muscles still carried the weight of tension from the morgue. She couldn't get the muscles in her neck to release. She rolled her head around, the resulting cracks and resettling made her sigh in pleasure.

Finally.

She closed her eyes for a moment before refocusing on the road below her. The lack of run hurt, but not as much as the lack of sleep, still, she'd rather be out running the streets than curled up watching over them. She called on every technique and trick she knew to keep her eyes and senses opened and focused.

She should have set out wireless infrared cameras along her route. She could have been monitoring from the comfort of her own home, letting the AI do his job and keep vigilance while she slept. Instead, she'd stationed herself atop Ryan's building, figuring the Rissu hunted here once, he'd come back for easy prey. She'd been afraid to sleep, that she'd be too late. Her body vibrated with unease all day, and she wasn't willing to lose another soul, four-legged or two.

The newborns had no finesse, at least, not this breed. She wanted to be on hand when he showed up again. This time, he'd lose more than an arm. She'd send him back to the nine dimensions of hell. She wasn't going to let an elderly woman be next on his meal plan. He would have marked her scent from the dog. He could have keyed on Ryan's scent too if he'd been in contact with his neighbor or her dog recently.

Connections. It was always all about the connections.

She tapped a finger against the bud in her ear. "Jace, details."

"All quiet in the paranormal realm so far. But, the Metro Police have had their hands full with drunk and disorderly, plus a mugging in South East. And something about having to catch a noisy rooster."

"Rooster? In the city?" she asked. "No, never mind. I don't want to know."

Some days, she wondered if she'd be better off if the Metro PD knew about the paranormal realm. At least then, they'd be more prepared for the off-the-wall stuff they encountered on a regular basis. She knew the Chief of Police would love it if the unsolved cases miraculously solved themselves. He might even prefer it over having officers chase down loose roosters. Of course, Ilsa would kill her for revealing any of it. It would put her sisters in far too much danger. They had enough to focus on as it was.

Scratch that, no telling Metro PD anything. She'd take care of things. She always did. It was part of her job, training, teaching the others, cleaning up their screw-ups, putting herself on the line when they needed to rest, heal and recover.

She'd been the first.

Her leg cramped, and she bit back a groan.

"Lady Ronin? Are you hurt?" Jace's electronic voice whispered in her ear.

"No."

"Your biorhythms shifted."

She smiled to herself in the darkness. "Yes, it's called discomfort. I'm being a baby."

"You are no baby, Lady Ronin."

She bit down on the corner of her lip to refrain from laughing. "Figure of speech, Jace. Figure of speech. Continue scanning and ignore me unless I spike into the red zone."

There were days she missed her time before having an AI focused on her every movement. Then, on the days he helped save her tail, she recanted. She shifted her shoulders and settled herself into a more natural position, one her body was used to. Her legs crossed in lotus. She closed her eyes, the sounds of the night flowed over and through her. She'd let Jace scan the streets his way. She'd do it her way. She'd been scanning a long time before she'd introduced technology to her arsenal.

She inhaled in and up, out and down. Every movement in her body slowed down. Her heart rate decelerated to mere whispers of a beat. She took one deep breath a minute and extended her senses outward.

Heartbeats thrummed in her ears. Each body in the building beneath her held a steady rhythm. The couple in 2B engaged in a heated argument, while the couple in 4D hit the sheets, skin on skin. Sexual energy rippled over her. She had enough of that rolling off Detective Calder, she didn't need it distracting her on the streets. She ignored the couple, seeking the anomalies, the odd energies.

A hint of strangeness drifted past her. Every cell in her body tuned in.

There. Her head lifted. Her nose twitched as a scent tickled her.

Had anyone been watching her, they never would have seen her move. She unbent from her pose and flowed into movement in a matter of seconds. She stood and dove off the top of the building in a single breath. She curled as she sailed through the air, and uncurled as her feet hit pavement in a solid, yet silent landing. Her hands touched down, balancing her for a brief moment, before she lifted into her full height.

Thank the universe for shock absorbent boots. Not that she wanted to run in them, but she would. Her senses honed in and the pulse of the Rissu demon flowed through her. Senses locked.

Must eat.

His hunger swept over her causing her a moment's pause. She rebalanced and shifted as his rage and gnawing in his belly took over.

She shook her head and forced her body to cooperate, ignoring the resonating pain in her belly. The empathic part of her nature, in all her years, she'd yet to block it out. Then again, it had its uses.

When she opened her eyes, the hunger retreated, and the trail lit up before her. Red lights danced and darted about the street and sidewalks. Her swords hummed against her back, vibrating all the way through to her chest.

She set out at a steady trot, staying close to the darkness and shadows. She blended, light bending, cloaking her as she followed the path. Any other time, she'd leave the natural realm to flow around her, but tonight, she didn't need the intrusion.

She needed to hunt.

Her nose twitched. Wet dog, again. Well, at least he hadn't moved further up the food chain. Yet.

She halted in the shadows of a building, feeling his energetic imprint from around the corner. She crossed her arms over her shoulders, reaching back, hand drew an opposite sword from their sheaths. Blades hissed against the leather. The hilts rested against the palms of her hands. She stepped toe to heel as she entered the sheltered alleyway. The longer katana balanced in front of her, the shorter one behind. She listened, every cell of her body attuned.

The air before her shifted. As natural as water, she flowed to the side as a clawed hand attempted to sweep over her. Instead, it fell a few inches short and in front of her. With lightening speed, she drew her sword back, and slashed down, slicing though skin and fur. A growl of pain washed over her. Swipe at her again would he? Her stomach still tingled from where his claws ripped her open the night before.

Not many things sliced her and lived to tell about it. Sisters excluded, of course.

As her arm slashed down slamming into the demon's collarbone, the other cut horizontally, the gleaming tip disappeared as it buried itself in the Rissu's stomach. Satisfaction arced through her at the subsequent sound of a snap and rip. His howl echoed in the alleyway.

Thank the universe most humans couldn't hear the

otherworldly battles. If they could, she'd have an audience.

He lurched towards her. She danced aside, pulling her swords from his sizzling flesh. Blood, black as night, dripped from his body and the shining metal. Shia whirled as he lunged for her. Her left sword swept upwards, speeding toward his jaw and slammed his head back. She pulled the right one back and sent it smashing into his chest. Sheer speed allowed the blade to penetrate bone.

Crack.

The demon's eyes flared. His mouth opened wide and rage poured forth in an unearthly keening sound. His claws clamped down, too late, around the blade lodged in his chest. Then, his body stopped. Everything about him stopped. She stilled, leaving the blades where they were. There they stood. One demon. One semi-human. Cracks raced across his dark skin as it ripped open, peeling away.

She watched as she always did—impassive. The demon's body splintered and shattered and shed. Her body was still, her weapons steady.

When the Rissu's final parts became dust, she re-sheathed her swords.

Ashes to ashes. Dust to dust.

She nodded to herself and turned on her heel. The dead weight of exhaustion attempted to creep over her. She forced its silence. She'd rest when she returned home. The streets pulsed around her as she darted through the darkness. She needed, no, craved the safety of her home. She shivered as steady weight settled in the middle of her back.

Too bad she knew that weight wasn't from the swords.

CHAPTER FIVE

The blinking cursor on his screen taunted Ryan. He stared back down at his desk, re-reading Hector Gonzalez's last statement and examining the photos submitted by the private eye. He was missing something. He knew it. He was trained to find the unknown, the tiny facts that chose not to be found. He cursed, lifting the cup of cold coffee to his lips.

His phone chirped to life, demanding his attention. He lifted the comm to his ear. "Calder."

"Well, Detective," replied the cheerful voice. "I hope I haven't caught you in a tough predicament."

Ryan choked down the taste of shame. His impulsive response was self-serving and arrogant. That was no way to answer the call of a Holy Man. "Father Munoz, I apologize for my tone."

"Please don't, Mijo. You wouldn't be you if you did."

Ryan closed his eyes and did all he could not to bang the receiver against his skull. "How can I help you, Padre?"

The priest responded with compassion. "The church is very thankful for your foundation's generous donation, Ryan, as we are every year. As you know from our newsletter and our calls, the annual Gala is this Saturday night."

Ryan fought the urge to curse under his breath.

"You're one of our most generous contributors, Ryan. I would appreciate it if you would join us."

"Padre..."

"Ryan, your efforts have meant a great deal to the children we've assisted. I don't want to intrude on your professional or private life, but the church is looking forward to recognizing you at this year's celebration."

Ryan held the receiver against his temple. "I don't want to be recognized for..."

Father Munoz hacked through his weak excuses with a machete. "Fantastic, Mijo! I speak for the entire congregation when I say we anticipate an unprecedented attendance this year."

"Padre..."

"Save it, Ryan," Father Munoz replied with the tone of a Drill Sergeant. "As you know, it's a black tie affair, so dust off your one good suit." The priest seemed to lose interest before he spoke up one final time. "And for Heaven's sake, Detective, find a suitable date this year. We've overlooked a few of your last-minute candidates in the past. We are hoping you bring a well respected partner with you."

The line died in his hand, and Ryan dropped the phone into the cradle. He swore under his breath in three languages, including neighbor-turned-amnesiac Espanol. Father Munoz was a priest Ryan trusted and respected. Where the hell was he going to find the priest's prescribed "suitable partner?"

The lines of the digital display faded from black and white into a blurry storm. Ryan realized they were numbers, but he couldn't recall if he was staring at a clock, or a bomb. He closed his eyes, exhaled, and rubbed his neck. When he glanced back up, the microwave counted down in solid black digits. He yanked the scalding hot mug out and set it on the counter, cursing under his breath.

He shook his hand a few times, half-pissed at his stupidity and somewhat grateful for it reviving his energy level. He paced for a several minutes, watching his coffee cup the way a panther stalks its cornered prey. He dared once again to grab a hold of the molten liquid container, scowled as he lifted it, and headed back to his desk. His head was swimming. His hand hurt like hell, and none of it seemed to matter.

Ryan sat the cup of coffee down on his desk, unknowingly setting it atop the circular stain established by its thousand predecessors. A voice still echoed in his head, and for the first time in recent memory, it wasn't Joe Cocker. It was Father Munoz. The Holy Man seemed pushier than usual about the annual gala. Ryan hadn't been prepared for Munoz's call. If he had been, he wouldn't have spent feeble attempts at an alibi

Ryan sipped at the coffee. Finding it somewhere between molten lava and tasteless truck stop filth, he slugged down a full gulp. Munoz's invitation meant plenty. He'd have to arrange a backup contact for his informants if they called in and ask for leave for the first time in recent memory. His suit needed cleaning, and that meant a long conversation with Mr. Bak, the neighborhood chatterbox who believed he was as valuable to the cops as every badge on the force. Ryan could already hear the white noise of the man's broken English. He sucked down another mouthful.

His fingers traced over the contact database. He tapped a few buttons and the professional, networking, educational and community programs left the query. The single filter remaining was marked "personal." Ryan cringed before checking the results, ashamed at the limited numbers of names showing on the list.

Once he began to read through the names, the tightening in his gut worsened. Ana. Six-foot, two inches of Swedish bodybuilder he'd met in the gym. She'd been his date a few years back. She hit on a priest and was politely escorted out. Father Munoz had chewed Ryan out behind closed doors. The detective remembered several uncharacteristic phrases that escaped the Padre.

Brittany, the bartender aspiring to be an actress, a bottle blonde, among other fake things. Six glasses of wine, plus whatever she smuggled in. During a bleary-eyed dance number, she hit on a nun. Ryan broke it up when Brittany copped a feel on the stunned Sister. Munoz hadn't even known about the incident before Ryan managed an impromptu escape with his sauced date. Some creative damage control kept Ryan in the so-called good graces of the local congregation. Digging out took him more time and more money than he thought.

It didn't have a purpose other than to help him bridge the idealistic world of the religious and the streets filled with pushers and pimps. He hated them both, but this job had him trapped in between. The alphabet game was senseless. Ana. Brittany. Charity. Denise. Elana. He knew each name, and every one of them was an absolute zero.

He took another pull from his black coffee and returned his gaze to the list of names still highlighted in front of him. Maybe he would hire a "date" this year. He'd pay extra for a warm body that would be polite and courteous and shut the hell up.

He cursed again and ran a hand through his hair. Why was this situation such a challenge? He dealt with disasters and lost lives on a daily basis. The list was evidence enough. His love life was a homicide.

Homicides and Lost Lives. It was catchy. Ryan chuckled. Perhaps he'd write his memoirs someday when he was retired and rich. Focusing thirty years down the road didn't solve his formal gala dilemma, but it gave him a brief escape from a laundry list of bad dates and religious devotees. One taste of lousy coffee and it all came back. Maybe he needed a better distraction. The first thing that came to his head was Mrs. Bradbury's missing pooch. Ryan hit the point where he pictured the mutt pulling off a fantastic karaoke version of "You Are So Beautiful."

He shook his head and reached for the coffee, but paused, the dead woman's image overrunning the image of the smiling dog on Mrs. Bradbury's newsletters. Joe the Rottie might still be out there, but Ryan had put in his time looking for the canine. He stared at the folders piled up on the desk, and Abigail Huang's name stuck out like a neon storefront. He clamped his jaw shut, reigniting the particulars of the case, right down to Hector Gonzalez's multiple calls to the police.

Shia glared down at the papers in her hand as if her abilities allowed her to will them into an alternate dimension. She didn't want to deliver the report. She hated inefficiency. It slowed her down. Paper was inefficient. Her walking it to the Chiefs office was inefficient. At least, nowadays.

She'd slept fitfully. The other realms had taken over her life, when she wasn't supposed to be covering for them. Instead, she wanted to corner one well-built, eccentric Detective in a few dark corners and get this overwhelming fire out of her body. She was surprised she could feel again. The last time human emotions flowed through her...oh, she couldn't remember the date, must have been before she'd died. The first time.

The paper crinkled in her hand. Self-preservation kept her from crushing it. She forced herself to uncurl her death grip, instead fantasized it bursting into flames. She took a deep breath and released it. No, the paranormal activity stayed far away from the precinct. She didn't want to explain it any more than she wanted to deliver this report. She'd had to do too much creative writing with this one. It sounded far-fetched, even to her. She knew just how far fetched they could get.

She'd already sent it via email, but for some reason, their beloved Captain demanded a paper trail as well. Maybe it was his age, still used to the old ways of doing things. Hah, she was far older, but even she still had managed to keep up with the times. Then again, the department didn't have her unlimited source of funds. If they did, the DC Metro area would be a different place.

She rubbed the corner of her eye and yawned. Instead of overseeing Shellie's area and South America, she landed smack dab in the middle of being active and having to hunt down the Rissu. She'd rather be hunting down that sexy Detective. He kept stumbling into her way, and it didn't bode well for his longevity in the physical realm. People who drew to near to her, well, they end up demon food, downside of the job. She'd learned through the years, she couldn't save everyone.

She mentally shook herself. This need to cry...the last time had been...She didn't remember.

She should meditate. Sleep. Something to get her focused again. Sidetracked by a human. Bested by a

Rissu. Rissu sightings cropped up every night the last few nights, in thirteen different cities no less. She wasn't the teleporter of their group. There's no way she'd make to that many cities that fast. She'd let Raisa handle those. Besides, DC, well, they had more than their fair share of demons. With three sightings here, she preferred to stick to her own turf and see what she snared. She'd killed one, and she'd place good money on the odds the creator originated here, with the most sightings being in the nighttime hours.

"Oh!" The air slammed out of her. Papers crushed into her chest. She reached out to steady herself and encountered a hard wall of muscle beneath a soft white shirt. A large hand steadied her at her waist. Warmth stole through her.

Ryan.

Her body melted, and she couldn't do a thing about it. Something about his hands on her.

"You should look where you're going." Ryan's deep voice set her heart vibrating.

"I was looking where I was going. You shouldn't sneak around corners." She needed her hearing checked. No one should startle her as much as he did. No man should send this kind of fire through her body. Had all her years of meditation and training gotten thrown out with the dishwater in the alley from last night?

She glanced up and realized she shouldn't have. His dark eyes gleamed down at her, a half smile on his face. He appeared to be happy to see her. He shouldn't be. She'd been mean and rude to him, brushed him off and tried to avoid him at all costs. So none of it explained why he pulled her closer when they were in the middle of the hallway, albeit a deserted one at the moment?

He'd backed away, but didn't let go. A spark crossed his eyes. "I wasn't sneaking, I swear. I've been pretty distracted myself." He grinned. He glanced down at the empty mug in the hand that didn't have a hold of her and then back up. "Ran out of coffee. Downside of the job."

Coffee. She focused. Coffee? The man was addicted. She closed her eyes and tried to reorient herself. With his hand still on her, she struggled to remain centered.

How could this human, this man, be such a detriment to her mental balance? This was getting ridiculous. Yes, he was good-looking, sexy to boot, but she'd met men over the centuries who had been far better looking. Yet, none of them made her heart race the way this one Detective did. She'd gone out of her way to avoid cops and detectives with the superior chips on their shoulders. She'd learned long ago that most of them couldn't deal with her schedule or her fighting abilities. She sure didn't need a man in her life. And why she was thinking of life, instead of something shorter...her brain waves had to be short circuiting.

Her hand curled, and the papers crinkled again. With a soft huff of frustration, she forced herself to let go. She didn't need to reprint and escort the file back to the chief's office a second time. Not because she'd made the mistake of running into Ryan.

"No, you weren't sneaking, but you weren't looking any more than I was. What has you so distracted?" She wrapped her arms around her report close to her chest, trying to ignore the hand still latched on to her.

Ryan smirked and rolled his eyes. "I opened my mouth before I rebooted my brain. I have this charity..." He stopped, stared into her eyes and started over. "Let's just skip the long version. I have a good friend, with a deep conviction, who is using a position of authority to make certain demands of me. It's more than a bit uncomfortable."

"Oh, how so?" She couldn't believe anything made

the detective uncomfortable. Seriously, he lived and breathed his job, much like she did. They, at least, had that in common.

"Well, it's just that he's made a request that's a little out of my regular scope of, um, night life. I'd rather not talk about it."

Her eyes widened, "A charity made a request outside your regular scope of what? It is a charity, yes?" She was an idiot, an intrigued idiot. Something to make him so awkward...was worth pursuing.

"It's a little thing, something I do on the side. I'm hardly ever involved. I just sort of send checks and things happen. You know, good things, for kids. Like I said, I'm hardly involved. This is one of those times I'd prefer to be completely not involved. But, there's this certain person who won't settle for 'not involved' as an answer." He raised an eyebrow. "Does that make sense?"

She had to laugh. "Yes, it makes sense. I have some of those people in my life as well. And, you can't ignore them."

"Well, he's not the kind of guy you say 'no' to. Normally, I would, I'd have an excuse, or an emergency, or maybe even wreck my unmarked car, but I've sort of run out of alternatives here."

"'Not the kind of guy you say 'no' to? Ryan, what kind of trouble are you in?"

"No, wait, it's not like that! He's a priest!"

"He's a ... you have a priest who's holding some ultimatum against you?"

"Well, it's not that simple. It's got a lot to do with the last few times I showed up at this particular event...and the company I brought with me." Ryan practically turned green as he finished his sentence.

"What kind of event? What is it this mysterious priest

is asking you to do?"

Ryan swallowed. "I need..."

"You need?"

"...a date..."

"...a date?"

"...and will you please accompany me as my guest to the Calder Foundation formal gala fundraiser and awards ceremony this Saturday night?"

"Formal gala?" She blinked. Had he asked her on a date? Who asked her on a date? Drunk guys who didn't know better, random homeless people, and apparently, one handsome detective. "You're asking me to go with you to a fundraiser because your local priest guilted you into it? What kind of dates have you been bringing to this event?"

Ire snaked through her at the thought of some other woman on Ryan's arm, quickly surpassed by sheer curiosity and stupidity. She didn't have time to date. She had demons to hunt.

"Dr. Shia Ronin, you can ask me many things under many circumstances, but, please, please, don't ask me to give you the details of my past dates at the Foundation's annual event. They'd give demons nightmares."

She bit back a smile. He wouldn't know a demon if it snuck past him in a dark alley, or if it ran past him in a dark alley. These dates must have been entertaining.

"You're not scoring points here, Detective." She nibbled on her lip. She needed to track down the source of the Rissu creations. She shouldn't even be thinking about going on a date to a gala with him. She should be patrolling, hunting, tracking. She couldn't believe she was even considering this. "And just what does one do as your date to this event?"

Ryan rubbed his neck and glanced past her, down the

hall. "Well, if my past escorts are any indication, you try to make out with Holy men and women, dance on tables, and generally make a world-class ass out of yourself." He turned his eyes back to hers. "If I had the ability to rewrite history, I would invite a classy, soft-spoken, intelligent, focused woman in a simple but elegant black dress, understated high heels and beauty that turned every head in the place. That's where you come in."

She smiled. Classy and understated she could do, but she thought she'd refrain from telling him about being heavily armed to boot. She hadn't been on a date in well, forever. Her training schedule never allowed for it, and then life never allowed for it. Yet, here she was, gravitating to going out with a co-worker, when she had a million and one other things to get done.

She tilted her head at him. "What time are you picking me up, Detective?"

Ryan stared at her, a thousand questions flashing across his face. "You'll go?" Laughing, he hugged her against him. She refrained from pushing him back as he crushed her. She didn't need to break his solar plexus and truth be told, it was nice being curled up against the hardness of his chest. She ignored the press of the empty mug against her back.

"Holy...I mean..." He released her, nodding while trying to regain some semblance of professionalism. "I will pick you up at 8 p.m." She let go of the breath she'd been holding when he set her back on her feet, not realizing she'd been doing so. He was like an exuberant puppy, yet a hint of danger coiled within.

She inhaled and smoothed out her report in her hand. "I'll be ready then."

After a long meditation session and a common sense talking to. It had to be good to be out among the people. Perhaps someone had seen something the last few nights.

At least, that could be her excuse if she was questioned about it.

She'd dropped off the deep end. "And I'll try to be appropriately dressed."

"I'm not sure of many things in life, Dr. Ronin, but I'm sure you'll be amazing."

CHAPTER SIX

Ryan tapped his fingers on the steering wheel of his unmarked Impala. The opening vocal harmonies of Kansas' "Carry on, Wayward Son" replaced Jethro Tull's "Locomotive Breath" as his playlist cycled through random music. Upbeat Kansas songs always helped on a stakeout. He loved "Dust in the Wind," but on a dimly lit cul-de-sac at 3 a.m., even he had issues staying awake when it played. He gave himself a mental reminder to create a "Stakeout: No Slow Stuff" playlist when he had a few free minutes.

He stared at the neighborhood in front of him, and then gave the mirrors a cursory check. The Georgetown suburb was still nearly lifeless, as it had been for the last few hours. Other than a couple of dog lovers out with man's best friend, the place was a ghost town. Two lights graced the Huang residence, one over the front porch and one on the ground floor. Ryan had checked the model floor plans. The inside light filled the space over a sink in the kitchen. The only thing different at the Huang residence? One more plastic-wrapped newspaper by the door. If Charles Huang had returned, he hadn't left a trace.

Two other teams of officers were on shifts watching Charles Huang's workplace, as well as his mother's home in southern Maryland. So far, they shared Ryan's lack of productive updates. Huang had disappeared. Ryan scoffed. Hardly the behavior of a grieving husband. However, very common among people who went over the edge, did something stupid, and panicked afterward. Part of him wanted to watch Charles pull up, if only for the chance to bring the mysterious man downtown to sit down for a few polite questions. An equal part hoped Charles would put a gun in his mouth and save the taxpayers a whole lot of appeals money.

The opening guitar riff of the Rolling Stones' "Satisfaction" came to life in the car, and Ryan laughed. "Alright, Mick, you made your point. We can't have it both ways."

Ryan rubbed his neck, wondering why he paid an exorbitant mortgage on a small place when he lived in his car. The low rumble of a diesel engine crept into the far corners of his head, and he lowered the volume on the radio. The diesel was coming closer. Ryan pushed a manila folder of paperwork against the dashboard and covered any light coming from the car. Headlights illuminated the street sign, then the sidewalk.

A huge white delivery truck turned the corner. Its lights filled the interior of the Impala before it moved on. The vehicle stopped briefly in front of the Gonzalez house, and after a few seconds, started again, stopping in front of the Huang house. It skipped the next house, stopping at the fourth for a moment. An arm emerged from the passenger side and flung something at the two-story home. The truck continued on, passing the Impala and heading out of the cul-de-sac. Ryan took a quick glance at the Huang's house and exhaled. Nothing had changed except one more plastic-wrapped paper on the doorstep.

The Detective cursed and shook his head. Jumpy wasn't productive. Jumpy got you killed. He pulled the folder off the dash and tossed it on the passenger seat. He took in a deep breath and started picturing the long list of places he would rather be right now. The first image that filled his tired head was one gorgeous medical examiner in the classic "little black dress." A smile tugged the corners of his mouth. He reached for the radio and brought the music back to life. The Eagles were singing "One of These Nights."

Ryan nodded, grinning at the blue display of the radio. "One of these nights...very, very soon."

"You still can't locate the source?" Ilsa asked.

Shia gazed at the open screen on her laptop. In one corner, Ilsa's beautiful Nordic face, lined with fatigue and concern studied her. Beneath her window, Celeste's green-eyes stared at her in quiet elegance, worry deep in her eyes. The dark haired Parisian princess from centuries ago always managed to appear calm, cool and put together no matter what issues they faced. She even fought with grace. In the last window, Raisa fidgeted. The Russian beauty barely restrained herself most days, the fact she'd been put back on active duty had to have finally made her happy. She seemed ready to pounce, which had nothing to do with the knife she had out, using it to clean her nails.

"I'm confident the demons are originating from DC. I've had two new sightings in the last 24 hours. First sighting was three or four days ago. Shellie still hasn't checked in, but we know she's on the trail of the Rissu who made off with a child," Shia said. She hated that one of her sister's hadn't been able to contact them.

"Aureline and Iniko checked in. They commented on

sightings of lesser demons, no Rissu in their respective territories." Celeste said, her French accent lilting.

Raisa nodded, stopped her fidgeting and leaned forward into her cam. "Da, yes, Yvaine, Taji, Christelle and Maya are all accounted for as well. A Rissu here or there, but they dispatched the demon dogs. The hunt still progresses for the portal they came through."

"So, Shellie and I have our hands full here in the States and Canada," Shia stated. She minimized her sisters on screen and pulled up several others. A tracking map lit up the majority of the screen. Her gaze darted quickly around the map, looking for a pattern, letting her vision expand and then narrow. Technology was both a blessing and a curse. She had an expanded view nowadays.

"Europe is not quiet," Ilsa reminded her. "Raisa, send Maya and Christelle to the US. Tell Yvaine and Taji to come to me here. We'll reallocate for a while and locate the sources."

"Oui, and the others?" Celeste asked.

Shia frowned at the various blinking dots on the map in front of her. There was no rhyme, no reason, no pattern. There was always a pattern. She clicked another button and shared the sight with her sisters. "Keep them monitoring and hunting. The infestation will likely spread before we can contain it."

"Shia!" Ilsa scolded her.

"No, Ilsa, I'm being honest. This is the same pattern that started the Plague. At least then, we could hide the body counts. Right now, we need to come up with something to feed the media about all the recent canine deaths." She never wanted to revisit that particular incident. The tiny flea-like demons had killed thousands in Europe before they'd figured it out and systematically done a metaphysical sweep. The first time they'd all fought together as a team with them having newly found Raisa in Russia, and the fight had been against demonic fleas of all things.

"It is dogs this time and one child," Celeste commented. "The dogs, they are of less importance than the humans. And the child…can be explained away."

Raisa laughed, "Celeste, don't let Taji hear you say that. She will cut out your tongue."

"Taji cannot hurt me. Let her try." Celeste sniffed. "I am simply saying this is far easier to cover up, no?"

"Neither are a laughing matter," Shia stated, her chin tilting up and shooting them both a look over their digital connection. Two sets of eyes flicked away and then back. "And, so long as we catch them before they realize they like the taste of humans more than dogs." Shia clicked off the map. "Enough, send Maya to Chicago and Christelle to Quebec. We'll be able to cover this sector better and spread out the search. Someone is playing with the dimensional portals. We will find the pattern. Shellie is dedicated, I hope, on retrieving the child, which would be of utmost importance since the other attacks have only focused on the canines." She would have said more, but Raisa and Celeste were both alike in caring little for the humans they protected. The Russian preferred the hunt, the action, while Celeste was more concerned with power and accumulating wealth in anyway possible.

"I'll research the pattern. Puzzles always intrigue me," Ilsa said. "You guys track and destroy. If I find anything, I'll let you know."

Shia titled her head in acknowledgement. Ilsa was the best at managing the maze of business and life. She'd love the research for finding the portals.

"Keep your cell phones near and on at all times. We don't know what's happened to Shellie, and we don't want anyone else disappearing." Shia glanced at each of her sisters. "Stay safe."

As one they bowed their heads. A whisper of matching voices echoed across the Internet, "Walk softly, remain aware, and fight fierce."

Ryan stared at the bored face staring back at him. The mirror never lied. He needed a shave, a vacation, a stiff drink, and lessons in patience. Naturally, he didn't have the time for any of those things. He had a suspect on the lamb, pressure from his boss, and two tickets to a formal gala with one of the most beautiful women he'd ever met.

In his finer moments, he would find a way to turn even that into a negative. He'd been eyeing Shia Ronin from the moment they met. Two years ago his senses had gone on high alert when she'd been introduced to the department during a debrief. Since then the sexy ME haunted his vision daily. He'd never seen her focus on anything other than work.

Something had changed when he'd run into her in the alley the other night. She was finally seeing him, not another detective, but him. In a moment of insanity, he'd asked her out. Now that she was willing to accompany him to an event...not a date, of course...he was finding ways to ruin the date and stress out before they'd even walked out the door. He wasn't much of a dancer, and there was bound to be dancing. He was awkward with the overly polite, religious crowd. He was going to say the wrong thing to Shia, and then to some blue-haired parishioners.

Why not keep the miserable track record alive?

He dropped his face into his hands as the tinny speakers in the shop belted out a muzak version of Fleetwood Mac's "You Make Loving Fun." The original was too sweet for his taste. This version gave him an ice cream headache. He scowled at the door the tailor had disappeared through a few minutes ago. The little man already invaded nearly every inch of Ryan's physique with the measuring tape. He left mumbling about alterations and vanished into the back room. A lesser man would have felt violated. Ryan added the little tailor's behavior to the list of annoying shit that only happened to him.

Father Munoz had been accurate when he mentioned Ryan's one good suit. That accuracy stung like hell. Ryan decided the suit represented all the previous appearances at the gala. He needed a new start, something fresh, new.

He smirked at himself in the mirror.

The new suit wasn't about his past at all. It was about his future. It was about Shia.

She deserved to be courted, given his best, new and fresh, without...history.

The curtain leading to the back room swished open quickly, and the tailor emerged as if he was on fire, nose in the air, indignation painted all over his face.

"I need one more set of measurements," he declared.

"You have the tux we discussed?" Ryan asked, having voiced the question numerous times without receiving any confirmation.

"We have several that fit what you described."

Ryan leaned down, yanking the vinyl measuring tape from the tailor and wrapping it around his fist. "We seem to have some sort of communication breakdown here. Let me make this clear. It's the Gauthier, or I walk, and you lose my business. Then, I go to every contributor to my charity and inform them of how you lost my business, and you lose theirs. The snowball becomes an avalanche. It's a small town, my friend, but it's a big one when you're living in the alley behind the store you used to own."

The tailor turned several shades of green, his eyes opening wide and his gaze leveling for the first time Ryan could remember. He nodded, and his voice cracked as he replied, "We will have the Gauthier, as you requested."

Ryan smiled and handed him the measuring tape. "So long as we understand each other. What do you need to measure next?"

The detective's phone rang before the tailor responded. Ryan gave the phone an annoyed glance and picked it up. Once he saw the number, he cursed, closed his eyes and dropped his head.

"Agent Simone...to what do I owe the pleasure?"

CHAPTER SEVEN

Ryan scoffed and turned down the radio. It was way too early for this crap.

No, this would suck any time of day and night.

At least he'd been summoned to Adams Morgan during the brief period between the happy hour crowd and when the chopper boys took over. He managed to find a parking spot two blocks away and registered plenty of evil glances as he stepped out of the Impala.

Cops weren't very popular in DC.

He figured a few corner boys would call the bigger fish and report his presence. None of that mattered. He hadn't shown up for a drug bust. Although, manhandling a couple of well-armed thugs sounded like a good idea.

He crossed 18th, continued down Columbia Street and pressed through the myriad of scents: stale beer, smoke, pizza ovens, and perfumes. He stopped outside the Grill from Ipanema. He stared at the green lettering above the door and ran his tongue across his teeth. GFI had fantastic food, and his stomach began to remind him of how long he'd gone since breakfast. He shook his head, took one last look around at the tourists and bar-hoppers and headed inside.

The Grill from Ipanema boasted a decades-long reputation for its menu and service. The Brazilian steakhouse never failed to provide a wide variety of meats, and its Sunday Champagne Brunch rivaled Stingy Lulu's, without the transvestite entertainment.

Ryan walked in and gave the place a visual sweep. He counted the number of white-shirted waiters and well-tailored meat servers. His eyes darted over to the pair of bartenders shuffling about, filling drink orders for businessmen and young couples. He sensed someone looking at him before he wanted to be noticed. He knew she'd spot him the second he walked in. He would have preferred a quick drink first, but apparently, it wasn't meant to be.

Ryan turned and noticed her right away. FBI Special Agent Felicia Simone wasn't someone to be spotted and forgotten. Every man in the room had her in their sights, and they weren't hiding their interest.

She smiled at him above the rim of her martini glass. Her full lips glistened with a light red lipstick. Her hazel gaze seemed inviting. She'd left her brown hair down, resting on her shoulders, a section flopping over one eye. From what he could see, her tanned, toned body brought out the best in the blouse she sported. The first few thoughts flashing through Ryan's mind were neither productive nor professional, and he juggled with the idea of going to the bar anyway. He knew that wouldn't fly. Instead, he turned and walked toward the agent's table.

"Ryan," she purred as he neared. "I'm so glad you could join me." She pushed the chair opposite her toward him with a high-heel. He pulled the chair out a little more and nodded.

"Agent Simone, I'm so glad you called."

"Agent Simone? Oh, come on now, Ryan, I'm not some prick in a suit and dark shades from IA. Lighten up."

Ryan sat down, staring at her. "You called me about a case, not Churrasco con Pebre. As I see it, this is a business meeting, and even then, I'm not exactly sure why we couldn't talk this over on the phone. I'm busy, and I know you are, too."

"How about a drink? Are you hungry? I'm buying." She titled the menu towards him.

"Agent..." he drawled.

"Felicia." She lifted a perfectly groomed eyebrow.

"Felicia..." he said. In all his history with her, he'd never won an argument. Why had he expected this time to be any different?

"See, was that so hard? Christ, Ryan, what the hell is eating at you?" Her smile widened, and she took a sip of her drink. "Relax. It's just me."

Ryan shook his head, feeling defeated already. "Yeah, that's what I'm afraid of."

A tall, dark-haired man in uniform came by with a skewer of beef and a knife. "May I serve you?" he asked through a thick accent.

"Gracias," Ryan replied. "Pero yo quiero el pollo en vez del carne de vaca."

Felicia smiled. "Can you send over the waiter?" She shook her empty glass. The man nodded and left quickly. She turned her focus back to Ryan. "Your Portuguese has gotten better. Been practicing?"

"A result of the times, I'm sure. I have a lot of bilingual cases recently."

"I remember when you were still trying to iron out your languages, but you had a few phrases I can recall rolling off of your tongue...so to speak."

Ryan slapped an open palm on the tabletop. "You called me, not the other way around. You have questions about my case, so let me answer them and get back to work."

Felicia stared at him through heavy eyelids for several seconds. She shook her head, though Ryan couldn't tell if it was in sympathy or disappointment. She cocked her head slightly to the side. "You wanted the chicken, right?"

"What?"

Felicia's gaze darted to the right, and Ryan followed. The waiter and another uniformed man holding skewered chicken stood to his left. He motioned without a word, and the man with the skewer began slicing several cuts of chicken breast onto a plate. The waiter took his order for a double Maker's Mark on the rocks, and they both disappeared.

Ryan rubbed his face before attempting to look back at his FBI counterpart. She had sidetracked him several times already and had him so focused he was vulnerable to everything else around him. She managed to pull his strings with no effort, a talent of hers since the first time they met and were assigned leadership of a task force to bring in a serial killer. She made good use of her skills when they went undercover to stop a human trafficking organization, and once more when they'd had to catch a woman trying to hire a hit man to make her rich husband disappear. Whenever Felicia had a case in the Capitol, she made certain Ryan was her man.

He leaned back in his chair. "I'm still pursuing persons-of-interest in the Huang case. I don't know why its come to your attention."

"Oh, that is too easy. You have a suspect."

"No," Ryan countered. "I haven't charged anyone. I'm still investigating."

A sly smile and bedroom eyes challenged him again. "No, you simply haven't found your killer yet."

"Yeah, that's what I said."

"Your vic's hubby is still on the run. Must be frustrating."

Ryan scowled. "A bit, yes. Thanks for your sympathy." How the hell did she know so much about his investigation?

"Still singing along to classic rock songs in the Impala while you wait to make an arrest?" She asked, spearing her fork into her plate.

"Okay, Felicia," he replied with an edge. "I'm done with the sweet talk. Why did you call me?"

She glanced to her right again, as the waiter returned with their drinks. The small man departed faster than he'd appeared. Felicia raised her glass in a toast. "Here's to working with my favorite detective in the MPDC again."

"What the hell does that mean?" he demanded.

She replied with a smile, "Charles Huang is on the run, and the Bureau believes he's crossed state lines. Simply put, Detective, this is now a Federal case, under the jurisdiction of the FBI. I look forward to our work on this case together." She tipped her drink towards him.

Ryan took a long, stiff drink. Busting Charles Huang was at the top of his to-do list. He was suddenly very uncomfortable with the price he would have to pay to make it happen.

"Lady Ronin."

"Yes, Jace?" She tunneled further into her closet. When had she last worn a dress? Did she still have dresses? No, wait, she'd worn a dress…she shook her head. The only way a dress hung in her closet was because…

"The dog breeder is approaching the door with a rather large dog in tow."

"Well, that's what he was paid to do, right?" Ah, hah! Her hands landed on silk. All the way in the back. Figured. He would have hidden her finer clothing deep within her closet. She made a mental note to add a few programming fixes to Jace's next update.

"Yes, but, our house is not equipped to deal with a four legged creature of his size and...potential destruction tendencies."

"He's not staying, Jace. Make sure Mrs. Bradbury is home." Since when had her AI become such a prima donna? Not part of his programming. She scowled to herself, perhaps he did need a software update.

"She's gone to get groceries this week, posted more fliers, checked on Detective Calder, and has been home mostly, listening to her music, according to the cameras and audio you planted in the building."

"Good. We shouldn't interrupt her if we bring her Joe back tonight, correct?" she asked.

"No, Lady Ronin. She's up all hours because she seems to be missing her companion."

"Understood. This dog better be worth this."

"I did all you asked. He should be as an exact match as we can get."

A knock sounded at her door.

When she swung the door open, an overly large, military cut man started back at her, his hand latched onto a strong leash. "Ms. Ronin?"

"Yes. Mr. Hamic?" She stood her ground, feet braced, well aware the man outsized her.

"Yes, ma'am." He nodded and tilted his head ever so slightly at her stance.

She glanced down, shifting so she wasn't as ready to attack as she seemed. Something about his energy and automatic authority caused a shift in her energies. She would revisit it later. Now, she needed the dog. "This is Joe?"

The Rottie sat on his haunches gazing up at her, tongue lolling out of the side of his mouth, eyes bright. He looked intelligent. Too bad Taji wasn't here, communication with the Rottie would fare far better with her special talents.

"Yes, ma'am."

"Come in." She so rarely let anyone in her apartment, but this was a unique situation, as unsettling as he was.

Hamic and Joe stepped a few feet in and both stopped. Joe sat without asking.

"Mr. Hamic, I hope my assistant informed you of the circumstances?"

"Yes ma'am, Joe is trained specifically to cater and deal with the elderly population while keeping them safe. He is also trained to find the panic button and trigger an alarm in any way possible."

Interesting. She wished she'd thought of the request. "Any way possible?"

"Yes, ma'am. We have trained him with security remote systems and the keypads. He can trigger them with a pen in his mouth or his paw, depends on the situation. He will, in fact, seek out a way to activate the trigger."

"Gentle and fierce?"

"He will be gentle as a lamb with your mother, but she will need to use a trigger word ...We've trained him to respond to 'family' for those he is to accept. I explained you were family before we entered your home and space. He knows friend, someone to keep an eye on. Everyone else, he will put himself in the line of fire and defend."

"Good." She couldn't fault him on any of it although, she briefly let her mind travel down the path of teaching the dog the correct techniques. Shaking her head at herself, she refocused. "How is he with unknown things?" Not that she wanted to pit him against a Rissu. His predecessor hadn't fared too well with the creature.

"Ma'am?" The man tilted his head at her.

"Is he adaptable?" she asked.

He shrugged. "As far as I know, but you'd have to give me a scenario."

Jace sent out one of the cleaning bots. The bot whirred and hummed happily doing its job as it rolled across the hardwood floor.

Joe jumped between the bot and Shia, lips pulled back, teeth showing, growling deep in his chest. His claws clattered on the floor. He'd dropped his head.

"Perfect." She smiled. The bot stopped. Joe maintained his stance.

Mr. Hamic raised an eyebrow as he back at her. "They're not trained to deal with tech, ma'am."

"No, but neither am I, and he responded exactly the way I do." She grinned.

Mr. Hamic nodded.

"I'll take him." Shia smiled at the dog. "Stand down, Joe. Bots are friends, mostly."

The dog whined and sat back on his haunches, glancing from her to the creepy bot.

"Yes, I know. I've killed a few. We might play some."

Mr. Hamic shot her a funny look, and Shia smiled at him. Let him wonder. So long as the dog protected the old lady...that's all that she asked for.

Joe stayed, and she paid Mr. Hamic and let him out.

"Jace, anything else you can add to him?" She and the

dog stared at each other for a moment. The Rotties chocolate gaze watched her with alert readiness. She'd never kept a creature before. Her horses didn't count. He stared at her as if he expected her to do something.

"Well, he could be programmed to return to you if anything happens."

"How does his ability to return to me help?" She didn't correct the AI on programming a dog, but if Jace thought he could do it who was she to doubt him.

"It might not. But his programming might save the old woman and keep you safe."

"I'm never safe."

"True."

"Fine. Do it," she said. "He goes to the old lady in ten. I've got a party to get ready for."

Ryan's eyes darted to the clock on the bottom of his screen again. He reassured himself there was plenty of time before he had to pick Shia up for the gala. Besides, it wasn't like he had ever made it on time before. Why should he start now? He shook his head. This year was different. He was determined this year would mean something. Shia meant something. That thought alone was frightening.

He stared down at his case notes and traced along the screen to find where he had stopped. This whole exercise was tedious. Agent Simone had asked him for a transcript of his interviews regarding the murder case. Ryan wasn't certain if she did so just to re-establish her credibility as a self-serving bitch, or if she had information that might actually lead to an arrest. Knowing her as he did, he was willing to bet it was a little of both. He typed a few extra notes, wrapping up several of the street interviews. He flipped the page and stared at the notes he had taken while interviewing Hector Gonzalez.

The detective cursed under his breath, eyeing the clock once more. If Charles Huang hadn't pulled some Harry Houdini tribute, he might get to the gala...and Shia...in time. He was better prepared than in the past. The garment bag housing his tuxedo was hanging in his locker, and the station had enough amenities that he could get showered and shaved without a trip back home. Going home wasn't an option with D.C. traffic the way it was. Tourists, construction and the occasional motorcade made for far too many uncontrollable variables.

Ryan typed along through his interview notes, silently reinforcing his original opinion of Hector Gonzalez. The portly neighbor may have been enamored, even infatuated with Abigail Huang, but there was no murder in his eyes. In cases like this, the husband was usually near the top of the suspect list, and Charles's untimely disappearance wasn't helping his case. Ryan stared back down at his notes, recreating the series of questions and answers. He smirked in annoyance when the phone on his desk buzzed to life.

"Calder."

"Hello, Detective."

Ryan rolled his eyes. "Good evening, Agent Simone. Can I help you?"

"How's your investigation going?"

"You didn't ask me to investigate. You asked me to type case notes. That doesn't exactly mean I'm working leads. I'm rehashing what I already know."

Agent Simone sighed. "I need to make sure that all the information is coordinated between our agencies. You understand that, don't you?"

"Yeah, I get it, Felicia. Now's not the best time. I have plans tonight, and the sooner I get done this secretarial bullshit, the sooner I can get to that life I allegedly have away from the station."

"Hmmm," she replied, and Ryan was sure she was pursing her lips. He'd seen her make that face plenty of times. "You're going to hate me, then."

"For what?"

"I need the motor vehicle records for both Charles and Abigail Huang."

"What?" Ryan stood, pushing off of the desk with an open palm. "What for?"

"I looked over the autopsy report. We need to know if Abigail had any traffic incidents that would account for some of her injuries."

"Get a probie to pull that shit. You don't need me to do it."

Agent Simone paused, the last reaction Ryan expected. "Just kick off the search and export in the system, then you can go do...whatever it is you have planned."

Ryan tapped the phone against the side of his head. The department had given up pen and paper reports years ago, but the systems responsible for the archived data were old and slow. Even kicking off the search would take the better part of an hour.

"Fine," he said, hoping to get off the phone before the FBI agent started asking for family trees, "it's on its way."

"Thank you, Detective," Felicia replied with an artificially sweet tone.

Ryan hung up without a response. He cocked his fist, debating whether or not to destroy the phone on his desk. He gritted his teeth, exhaled and turned his eyes back to the screen once more, and to the little clock in the corner taunting him. He was going to be late, for sure.

He tapped through his contact list and found Dr. Shia Ronin. Angered at being delayed, he hit the green "call" icon. Seconds later, he heard the artificial ring tone of her phone. The tone repeated several times before Shia's voice filled his ear. "This is Dr. Ronin."

"Shia?"

"I am unavailable to take your call..."

Ryan listened to the rest of the recorded message. He left a short apology in response, hoping he could meet her at the event. He slapped the phone down, ending his recording and returned to the keyboard. He entered several more lines and then stopped, looking at the phone. Cursing out loud, he picked up the phone and dialed Shia's number again.

CHAPTER EIGHT

Ryan ran the towel roughly through his hair several times. He could've stayed in the hot shower all night, if he didn't already have somewhere important to be. Entering the data query into the system should have been routine, but the "intelligent" software managed to turn a simple process into total chaos. The system kindly auto-completed Charles Huang's last name as "hung", "hang", and "Juan" before allowing Ryan to discard its suggestions.

He brushed his hair and reached for the well-tailored tuxedo shirt hanging off of his locker. He buttoned the shirt, put the cufflinks on and tied the silk bow tie. He then grabbed the hanger holding his tuxedo coat and inspected the jacket. He looked it over twice, then picked up a roll of tape and wrapped the sticky side out around his fingers, removing the few offending pieces of lint and hair that remained.

He gathered up the garment bag and hangers, leaving the locker room. He checked the screen as he passed his desk, to make sure the database query was actually running and hadn't decided it needed more qualifying information or a response to the inevitable "Are you sure you want to run this?" confirmation.

"Hunk of junk," he grumbled.

As if in answer, the phone on the desk came to life. Ryan stared at it through three rings, everything in his body screamed to leave it alone and to get out of the station. He picked up the receiver halfway through the fourth ring. "Calder."

"Ryan, Agent Simone."

Ryan shook his head. He should have let the call go to voicemail. "How can I help you now, agent?"

"Cancel your plans, detective. I need you in Little Falls Park."

"Little Falls Park? What's so important about Little Falls Park?"

"Charles Huang is no longer missing. Two joggers found what's left of him an hour ago."

Shia paused at the edge of the double church doors. The old stone building hovered between past and present. Memories threatened to creep up. She pushed them aside. Now was not the time to bring back the centuries. On closer inspection, she realized the stones in this century had bits of technology imbedded in them. A small security panel blinked on the wall next to the door. She glanced further into the church. Tiny white holiday lights danced across the rafters. Laughter flowed from another set of doors. Greeters urged her forward past the pews and into the reception hall. Food overwhelmed the buffet tables. She smiled when she caught sight of the chocolate fountain.

She should be annoyed. Ryan left several messages

while she'd showered. Jace hadn't bothered to interrupt her, he'd waited until she'd dressed to inform her that Detective Calder had gotten stuck on the Huang case before meeting her here. She didn't fault him, work demanded attention. She should have used the same excuse to bail on the entire night.

Her curiosity won out. She wanted to see the people he interacted with, the ones he knew outside of the precinct. She wanted to see something more than death and destruction. Churches had a way of setting things right bringing some measure of calmness.

There were so many people. Alive ones. She toyed with the idea of darting back out the door and waiting for him in her car, but she'd had to park behind the church in the alleyway. She wasn't too caught up in the thought of hanging out in the back alley in a short cocktail dress and heels. She was a little less than dressed to her normal regalia. She dropped a hand to check the small purse she'd thrown over her shoulder. It wasn't much, but held her ID, cell phone, a lipstick, and a switchblade.

She felt naked without her swords strapped to her back, but her dress hadn't left her much room to work with. She'd had to sheath an ancient dagger to her stomach. There would be no slow dancing with Ryan tonight. She'd hidden the blade well with the folds and drapes of the dress, but it would be noticed if someone were close enough to her.

"Can I help you, miss?"

Shia started and turned her head to find a wizened old man in priest's robes and collar standing next to her, a smile on his face. Even his eyes beamed at her, they crinkled up at the edges. He had his hands tucked into his sleeves.

"Father Munoz?" Shia asked. Based on Ryan's description, she would have recognized him anywhere.

She held out her hand. "I'm Dr. Shia Ronin. I'm supposed to be meeting Detective Calder here tonight. He got stuck on a case, but said he'd be here as quick as he could."

"Ahh, what a delightful surprise, m'dear." Father Munoz took her hand in his and bowed. "Please, Dr. Ronin, come in and join us. Have you ever visited us before?"

Shia allowed him to tuck her hand in the crook of his arm and lead her into the mass of people milling about and chattering. She couldn't take issue with the Father as much as she preferred having her hand free. She started when a few children shrieked and ran past playing chase amongst the adults. Music lilted and echoed throughout the church. In the center, a few couples danced in brightly colored cocktail wear.

"Please, call me Shia. And, I'm sorry, no. My work keeps me fairly busy. My down time is spent running errands." She smiled. Or hunting demons, but the padre didn't need to know about that one. He had enough to deal with tending his human flock.

"Well, welcome. We're a small space of peace and tranquility in the chaos that flows around us." He led her over to the buffet table. "Please, eat."

"Oh, thank you." She picked up one of the small plates when the priest released her arm. She wasn't hungry, but she'd nibble so her hands remained free should anyone else seek her out. "Ryan mentioned that you host this event every year."

The Father smiled as a few wiggling bodies darted around him. "Yes, we do. Our annual fundraiser raises money for the families we take care of throughout the year."

"Oh?" She selected a strawberry and bit into it. Flavors exploded in her mouth. Perhaps she was hungrier than she'd thought. "How many families do you help?"

"We have four that live on site while we help them get back on their feet. Getting their job skills updated, providing childcare, helping out in any way we can."

"That must be rewarding, Father."

"Very much so. And how do you know Detective Calder?" Father Munoz asked.

Shia smiled, her eyes darted back towards the church doors. "We work together at the precinct."

"But, you are a doctor..."

She shifted her stance a bit to keep a better eye on the door and the people around her. "Yes, I am the medical examiner."

"Oh, bless you for helping those souls find peace."

Shia started and gazed at the Father, trying to see the energy patterns around the older man. "Excuse me?"

"Your job must be difficult. Seeking out the answers to a death."

"Challenging." She nodded. "But rewarding when we catch the bad guys." She smiled. She'd sensed an undercurrent to his question, but then it flitted away.

"I shouldn't keep you all to myself," he exclaimed. "Let me introduce you around to a few of our congregation and some of the families."

Shia nodded and trailed beside him. She smiled and made small talk with people as he introduced her. She couldn't keep her eyes from straying back to the doors, waiting for Ryan to walk through them and save her from the well-meaning questions.

If he was going to be this late, a cancellation or a rain check would have been nicer. She had a demon to track, not bonding with people she watched from the streets in the dark of the night. More connections she didn't need.

An hour in and she gave up. She made her way through the church, back toward the doors. This was getting her nowhere. She needed to make better use of her time tonight. If Ryan got caught up in a case, it could be morning before he'd remember where he was supposed to be. Since her cell phone switched to E, she knew she wouldn't be getting any calls from within the abbey.

"Father Munoz, I wanted to thank you for a lovely evening." Shia stopped next to him. She wouldn't leave without saying good-bye to the old man. "You are blessed here."

Peace permeated the entire building. She understood what drew the families, Ryan, to supporting their cause. She'd have Jace wire some money to the church when she got back to her condo. They were trying to help make a difference here. She'd help the way she knew how, by sending funds over.

"You're leaving so soon?" the father asked.

"Yes, Detective Calder is caught up in his case, and I suspect they're going to be calling me in soon as well if they haven't tried already. But thank you. The families you have here are wonderful people."

"Thank you, m'dear. Are you okay getting back to your car?" He glanced around the room. "One of the men..."

"No, thank you. I'm quite safe." She smiled. "Enjoy the rest of your party."

She stepped past him and out the doors before he protested. She didn't want him sending someone after her. No one else needed to be out and about on the streets of DC with the Rissu roaming around.

She pulled her keys and her cell phone out of her purse. The thing still wasn't re-synced and back online. She couldn't tell if anyone had tried to call her. She'd been off the grid for an hour. She turned left at the end of the sidewalk and stepped into the alleyway.

She strode through the shadows on sure feet even in three-inch heels. She was going to be so glad to kick them off when she reached the car. She should have thought to bring a change of clothes. Instead, she would head back to the condo, change and head out again.

The growl gave it away.

Shia stopped, listening. She dropped the keys and the phone, her hand dipping into her dress to pull out the blade. She palmed it. Her gaze adjusted to the night as she kicked off her shoes. The pantsuit and boots would have been a better choice. Live and learn.

"Here kitty, kitty. Nice Rissu. Let's come out to play," she whispered into the night.

A hiss and a claw slashed through the darkness, grazing her arm. Pain ripped across her bicep. She danced to the side and sliced back. The knife glinted in the shadows. Whoever called these creatures into being needed to be sent on a vacation to the nine depths of hell—forever. Kill one, three more show up. Ilsa said she'd find the source. In the meantime, it left too many roaming the streets at night.

She crouched, looking for the red haze, the giveaway. She cried out when the demon raced at her, slamming her body into the stonewall on the backside of the church. The stones trembled with the force of their bodies as they hit. Her head cracked against a rock, pain lanced through her skull. The Rissu growled in her ear. She wrinkled her nose at the rank of his breath. One clawed hand latched around her hand with the knife. The other sunk into her shoulder.

"Get off me," she snapped. She lifted her feet and kicked out with all her might. Fire flowed through her, and the Rissu flew back, into the dumpster, a loud clanging as the spikes on its back clashed with the metal.

Shia landed on both feet, panting as she forced the

pain to take a backseat. She knew she couldn't go on the attack with just her knife, but her weapons were far out of reach. The Rissu snarled and lunged at her again. She darted to the side, under the fire escape and cursed when its clawed hand ripped right through the metal, pulling it off the wall.

"You're causing a lot of damage and making way too much noise." She dove at it, knife flitting out, striking where she could. The world swayed, and her vision swam. She tried to right herself in time, but couldn't.

The Rissu's claws slashed down on her in rapid succession across her face and then her stomach. The knife slipped from her hand. She doubled over. Her hands clasped against her abdomen attempting to stop the flow of blood.

"Cào nǐ zǔzōng shíbā dài" she muttered. She fell to her knees trying to focus on her breathing, willing the pain to retreat.

Voices echoed through the darkness. The Rissu twisted and snarled. Light spilled into the alley. Shia shut down as the voices drew closer. Her head dropped into a puddle. Somewhere, her subconscious winced.

She knew she'd bleed out if someone didn't get to her soon. Her body shut down. This was going to cause a hell of a resurrection. What a graceful way to die, death by Rissu.

CHAPTER NINE

"This is Dr. Ronin. I am unavailable to take your call at the moment. Please leave..."

Ryan hit end. He didn't need to hear the rest. He had it memorized, her very professional instruction to leave a message. He'd left a message. He'd left six during his drive from the station to the park entrance. He slapped the phone back into its case in disgust. The Impala came to a stop in the gravel, and Ryan shifted into park and set the brake.

The alternating blue and red lights created long shadows on the pathway from the parking area down to the shining beacon of the crime site. Uniforms were on the scene, along with members of the forensic team. Yellow crime scene tape hung across several of the trees like streamers from yesterday's birthday party. Ryan grabbed his flashlight and checked his holstered pistol.

The path down to the site was slick, and Ryan moved slower than he wanted. His dress shoes provided zero traction on the combination of rocks, dirt, roots, and leaves. He slipped twice, caking his slacks with mud. Spitting profanities, he finally reached the bottom of the trail. He ducked under the garish yellow tape and caught a glimpse of Agent Simone in conversation with one of the forensics team.

Simone wore a padded black leather coat, with the letters FBI in stark white. Her slacks fit like they were painted on, with not a speck of dirt anywhere on her. Ryan eyed her with disbelief. Even in this miserable environment, she managed to remain flawless. He shut off his flashlight as he approached. Simone glanced over at him and hardly stifled a laugh.

"Detective Calder...wow, what ran into you?"

"Thanks," Ryan snapped in reply. He had left the tuxedo jacket in the Impala along with the bow tie and cufflinks. His sleeves were rolled up, allowing him to make something out of the tux that wasn't restricting and nearly suffocating. "Where's Huang?"

Simone gestured, and Ryan followed. "Snazzy clothes. You did have plans tonight."

"Yes, I did."

"You never change, Ryan, such a creature of habit."

Ryan stopped and took a breath to refrain from screaming, sucker punching or shooting the FBI field agent. "You care to elaborate?"

"Silly boy," Simone grinned over her shoulder. "You're still letting the old priest guilt you into prettying yourself up once a year?"

"What the hell does that have to do with this case, exactly?"

Ryan sensed her gloating, even as she turned back away from him and walked ahead. "Tsk tsk. Strike a nerve?"

"Let it die, Felicia."

"Like him?" She stopped, pointing down at the corpse that resembled the pictures from Charles Huang sitting in Ryan's case file. Unlike the still shots, this version was missing a sizable chunk of his head, and blood and mud covered most of his body. He wore black boxer shorts and dress socks. Simone raised her eyes expectantly toward the detective.

Ryan glanced over the remains of Charles Huang and the surrounding area. "Lividity says he was killed here."

Simone nodded. "Spatter pattern seems to confirm that, blood and other remains on the leaves, and even a patch that hit the Dogwood a few feet over."

"The primary wound is the exit wound, indicating a close-range gunshot to the head."

She nodded again.

"Gun in his mouth?"

"Based on the burn pattern and the missing left top incisor, it's a likely scenario. We'll know more when the D.E. analyzes the nitrate levels."

"Stripped to humiliate him and then forced to suck a gun barrel. I'm going to rule out robbery gone wrong here."

Simone crossed her arms, watching him recreate the scenario in his head. "There is something that doesn't exactly line up with our initial analysis."

"What's that?"

She pointed a gloved hand at Huang's head. "You would think that someone going to this degree of humiliating him would've chosen a superior position, right?"

Ryan took a few steps around the body. He glanced at Simone, catching her eyes on him. He reversed his path, still studying the fallen form of Charles Huang. The man he had pegged as a loose cannon and belligerent, possessive husband was now hardly more than a dead Asian male in his underwear. Someone had gone to great lengths to ensure Huang died in a position of submissive humiliation. "The trajectory is wrong. The shot went upward, not downward."

"Right. He was standing."

"And taller than the shooter."

Simone nodded. Ryan knew she was processing new information. Maybe she'd finally overlooked something. She smiled as she replied, "Huang isn't exactly a starting center for the Wizards. What's he, five foot nine?"

"DMV lists him at five eight, but his license is a few years old. Maybe he grew an inch."

"Or he's got lifts in his cute little dress socks." She smirked.

"No chance we found any shell casings?"

Simone shook her head. "I wish. Our luck wasn't that favorable, at least, not yet. Once our boys move him back to the morgue, we'll have a better idea about the specifics of his injuries."

Ryan examined the body and the surroundings. "The real question is why here?"

"We still don't have enough information to tell. We know Huang was shot here, but not what brought him to the park. He might've been hiding out here and been discovered."

"Ok, that's reasonable. He's a few miles from his Georgetown residence, but this isn't a suicide. Screams to me of a targeted killing. I'm thinking he was picked up and brought here at gunpoint."

Simone nodded. "Sure, or he agreed to meet someone here and things went wrong. Like I said, we still don't have all the information we need. We'll know more once my techs analyze the crime scene, and our recently deceased suspect."

"Actually, Agent Simone," Ryan countered. "I'm not sure we'll require their analysis."

"Excuse me?"

Ryan checked at the clock on his phone and pointed to the moon. "It's not even 9 p.m., and there's the moon," he replied. "That means we're on the Eastern bank of the Potomac."

"And?" Simone asked, playing along with his new wrinkle in the game.

"Not only are we still in D.C., Agent Simone, but we are in District 2. As much as I value your insight and assistance, this is not a Federal case. You're devoting resources to a local crime. Isn't there some form you're required to fill out to justify pointing this many resources to a crime too small to fit your jurisdiction?"

Simone shot a glance around before settling back on Ryan. "A moment, detective?" She gestured to a small, unmanned area between cameras and crime scene inspectors. Ryan followed her, stopping a few paces outside of the floodlights.

Agent Felicia Simone spun on a heel, her gaze piercing right into him. Her whisper was loud enough to hear back at the crime scene. "What the hell are you trying to prove, Ryan?"

He offered a slight smile before he dropped into a monotone he reserved for press conferences or peer-to-peer reviews. "If we're going to tie Charles Huang's death to his wife's, as we agree we should, then this is still a D.C. Metro case. Both Abigail and Charles Huang died within the second district covered by the MPDC. I hate to let you down, Agent, but this case isn't something to be considered national jurisdiction."

Felicia smiled back at him with equal parts fire and

frustration. "You can't push me out of this, Ryan. I've been assigned to this case. Don't think you can wish me away with some creative paperwork."

He returned her gaze. "Felicia, I've tried for a long time to wish you away. I'm hoping some creative paperwork is step one. I'll figure out the rest as I go."

Felicia stared at him, but refused to reply. After several long, silent moments, she turned and walked away. Two separate technicians moved out of her way as she strode back toward the well-lit staging area.

Ryan reached to his belt and pressed the redial button. Several seconds passed as he waited.

"This is Dr. Ronin. I am unavailable to take your call at the moment..."

The golden warhorse shifted beneath her. Sweat dripped between her breasts under her armor. The katana on her back started to weigh down hours ago, but she had no intention of leaving her shift. She and her horse remained on the edge of the cliff. Her gaze glued on the horizon. Her master ordered her to take first line of defense. She knew she held a unique position in their society. She took pride in the honor bestowed on her. She would not falter or fail. The men behind her stood strong and proud.

She waited.

As the sun began to set, she caught the reflection off a war helm in the distance. She lifted her bow, notched a long feathered arrow, and took sight down the lines. Whispers of bows being drawn and fitted sounded around her.

She waited.

When the approaching invaders crested the hill, she

let the arrow fly. Sure and true, it lodged between armor pieces, toppling a man from his horse. Around her, arrows shot through the air.

She raised her bow high and gave the signal. Warriors behind her flowed down over the edge of the mountain, drawing swords and firing as they pounded towards the oncoming army. She and her horse shifted and turned. She secured the bow and unsheathed her katana, and leapt in with her men. Cries echoed across the battleground. She spun around, looking for her master's steed, knowing he'd been in the second wave to ride into the fray with them. Wave after wave of the enemy flowed onto the battlefield. Their warriors held their own the best they could, but sheer numbers began to overwhelm them.

She fought her way to her master's side, never wavering in her intent, merely continuing to swing and dodge the attacks of her enemies. Her smaller form allowed her more freedom of movement. She turned barely sidestepping the battle axe aimed at her head, ducked and slashed her sword, taking the attacker's head from his shoulders. She shifted back, in time to see her master take a blade to the stomach. She cried out and forced her way to him. She reached him in time enough to keep him from sliding off his horse.

"Run, woman. We're outnumbered," he commanded her.

She shook her head. "No, I'll not leave you here." He'd rescued her as a child, raised her to fight and think. She refused to leave him to die.

"That was not a request, woman. Leave. I will not die on the battlefield next to a woman." He pushed her away and righted himself on his horse.

Her heart pounded, and she reared back as if he'd struck her. "Master?"

"I said leave. Find safe haven with my brothers." He

grasped the reins in hand and kicked the steed forward, leaving her in the midst of the battle, chaos swirling around.

Ryan tapped the six-digit code to his alarm system as he entered his apartment. The confirmation chirped at him that the theft prevention systems were now disarmed. He kicked the door closed with the heel of one waterlogged Forzieri leather dress shoe and walked inside. He hung the garment bag holding his tuxedo coat in the closet, and continued straight through the living room to the small laundry area. He stripped off his mud-spattered tuxedo shirt, slacks, socks, and shoes. He dropped his tank top and Under Armour shorts into a separate pile and turned back toward the main living area. He stopped long enough to turn on the shower and grab a towel before he picked up his phone and put it on the charger on the coffee table. He'd managed to run the battery down completely between calls to the morgue, the station and Shia's cell.

The steam wrapped around him like a lover when he stepped into the stall. He welcomed it into every pore. He ached right down to his bones, and his stress levels were through the roof. He leaned his forehead against the porcelain tile and let the hot water course over him.

How the hell had everything come off the rails so quickly? A few days ago, he was working a case with no pressure, and no one in his small social circle laying claim to his life. Like that, he had been goaded by Father Munoz and pulled every which way by Felicia. What had it cost him? A few hundred bucks in dry cleaning, and the single chance he had to get to know Shia Ronin outside of a cold, cramped lab complete with an audience of dead people.

Shia hadn't answered any of his calls. First, he made

her drive to the event. Then, he stood her up. At least she belonged at an event like that--radiant, classy, and demure. Maybe it was best that he hadn't made it, after all. He'd be the one dragging her down, instead of the usual roles he played with his past dates. He lifted his head and let the water strike his face. He'd make it up to her. He had to. Next time he saw her, there would be no bullshit, no games, and no Joe Cocker.

He turned, letting the water pound his back, washed his hair and body, and shut the water off. He grabbed his towel and began drying off, letting his mind wander. Felicia had been jerking him around most of the evening, but the body in the park was no game. Charles Huang, prime suspect numero uno in his wife's murder, was found dead, half naked alongside a jogging trail. Powder burns confirmed it wasn't a suicide. Where did that leave the investigation?

Ryan threw on some loose boxing shorts he bought when he first began Brazilian Jiu-Jitsu and walked to the bar he kept well stocked for nights like this. He filled a tumbler with Glenmorangie Scotch. Turning the chair away from the TV, he watched as the faint rays of dawn over DC filtered through the curtains. Tonight had been miserable. Tomorrow had to be better.

An annoying sound buzzed in her ears, Shia shook off the remnants of memories and struggled against the heaviness flowing through her body. The beeping grew louder. What? She let it all come back, second by second, the gala at the church, and the fight in the alleyway.

She took a deep breath and realized there were needles and tubes attached to her arm. Hospital. Someone had gotten to her in time. Well, they could have left her in the alley. She would have eventually come to on her own.

She'd done it before. She'd do it again.

Her stomach hurt. Her head ached. She opened her eyes to the harsh hospital lights overhead.

"Dr. Ronin?"

She tensed at the whisper. Her senses righted. She turned her head. She recognized the form of Father Munoz.

"Why are you here, Father?" she asked.

"I found you in the alley, bleeding badly. The paramedics didn't think you'd make it to the hospital, but you proved them wrong." He smiled. "I confess, I used my position to remain at your side through the night, praying that you would be saved."

Shia forced herself up, ignoring the slight tilt the room took before righting itself. The beeping on the machine next to her went haywire. She wrinkled her nose at it and ripped the IVs from her arm. The small holes in her skin healed over quickly.

"Dr. Ronin!" Father Munoz gasped. "I've watched a miracle occur here tonight. Please, go slowly."

She knew she had moments before the nurses swept in, unless they were on rounds. She wasn't going to take any chances.

"Father Munoz. Return to your church. Keep yourself and the families inside after dark. I am not a miracle, but I thank you for your faith and your diligence in staying with me." She swung her legs over the edge of the bed and bit back a cry at her instability. She needed to stabilize and fast. She'd been off the grid for too long. Ilsa and the others would descend on DC if she didn't check in and quickly.

She glanced around the room. Her dress and her shoes lay in shattered ruin on the hutch. She needed clothes. And her phone, she surveyed the room again.

"My dear, I cannot let you do this." He reached out to help her. He looked up at her in surprise at the smooth expanse of her forearm. "You cannot…"

Shia laid a hand over his and stared into Father Munoz' eyes. "Father, your flock needs you. I am not one of them. I appreciate your staying with me, but now, I need to get back to my job. I shouldn't have been at your event. I'm sorry, now I must stop what was started."

Father Munoz released her hand, "I witnessed a miracle this night. Here, take my coat. It will at least keep you covered."

Surprised, she smiled at him. "Thank you, Father." She slipped into the jacket and stuffed her dress and her shoes into the large pockets. She'd lost her phone and her knife in the battle. Her keys jingled in the toe of her shoe. Thank the Universe for small favors.

She turned back one last time when she reached the door. "Stay indoors at night, Father. There are things darker than you know in the shadows."

"May God watch over you, child." He crossed himself and bowed his head.

Shia didn't look back a second time. She'd lost too many hours, too much time. She willed herself to pass through the halls unnoticed. Blend in. It was harder to do in broad daylight, but it could be done.

Whatever being in the universe who watched out over her finally paid attention to her request. She sulked into an empty office and closed the door quietly. She needed a phone. Clothes would be a bonus. She darted across the room to the desk. Using the edge of the coat she picked up the phone. A quick dip in her pocket, she pulled out her keys and used the end of one to tap out a series of numbers.

"Lady Ronin, you were off the grid." If the AI could have taken an accusatory tone, she would swear this was it.

"Yes, I need a pick up at GW Hospital. Car is at the church."

"Routing a taxi your way, outside the West entrance."

"Great, I'll be back in a few. Alert Ilsa and get me a new phone. Mine's gone."

She made it to the outer doors without incident. She'd left the Father with more questions than answers. She'd been negligent in her quest to learn more about Detective Calder. She knew better. Draw close, get burned, and grow careless.

It could have been an innocent. Better that it had been her.

CHAPTER TEN

"Before you ask, I'm fine." Shia dropped down in front of the computer. Ilsa's fair visage scowled at her across the Skype screen.

"You ended up in the hospital," she said. Papers shuffled on her desk. "You're slipping."

Shia knew it. She'd berated herself on the way to her car and the entire drive home. She knew better than to engage in anything other than her job. She'd let Ryan sidetrack her. The man might be good at his job, but he could never handle hers.

"Won't happen again. I've called into the office. Told them someone totaled my car with me in it, so they're pulling in another ME for a week. Gives me seven days to get rid of this problem."

Ilsa glanced up from her paperwork. "You think the Rissu are originating from DC?"

"Yes," Shia said. "Whoever is causing this infestation is manifesting them here. They show up locally first, and then use the portals or another means to move to the different areas."

"Makes sense." Ilsa nodded.

Shia pulled up the map on screen and shared the image so it appeared on Ilsa's as well. She pointed out the hotspots. "The energy flared here, here, and here, then faded. When the portal popped open in Toronto next, one left, one arrived."

"The one who attacked me was new last night, not in full power."

"Yet, he caught you."

Shia glared at her. "I didn't have my swords on me. I'd like to watch you take down a Rissu with a knife and bare feet and live to tell about it."

Ilsa's lips twitched. "Only a knife and bare feet? Nice. You should be dead."

"Probably was." She hadn't stuck around to find out what the records stated. She'd set Jace to the task of removing all accounts of her being at the facility. She couldn't erase memories, but she'd made sure her records never appeared again. "I'm going to relocate back to the warehouse. I don't want the Rissu trailing me here and attacking any of the neighbors."

"You shouldn't have moved into the high-rise to begin with. No room to train," Ilsa commented.

Shia smiled. She wondered if Ilsa realized their bodies were so programmed to respond now that training seemed moot. She'd moved into the condo to be closer to people. She worked with dead bodies with the occasional visit from a detective or family member of the deceased. She trained on her own. She lived by herself. The AI didn't count. She'd grown tired of being so remote and wanted living, breathing people around her.

She did better working solo. She'd have to start going to a park to be around others instead. Putting them in mortal danger wasn't part of her code.

"I'll lock down the condo and have Jace purge everything. Won't take me long. Jace's main housing is in the warehouse anyway." She gathered her feet under her. What few things she had here would be boxed up in a matter of seconds. The furniture sold with the condo.

Behind her, the soft whirl of the bots sounded as Jace put them to work.

"Check in when you're settled. I'll check in with the others and relay the message," Ilsa said. "Shia?"

"Yes?"

"Stay safe, sister."

"Stay warm, sister." Shia responded before killing the connection. She snapped the laptop shut.

"I'll take care of shutting down the condo and listing with a local agent." Jace's voice flowed over her. "I'll need to move your clothes and your weapons cabinet."

"Use the same company as last time. They're discreet and won't require a human presence to move the items."

"Of course."

Shia stepped over the bots flitting about the floors. "This place should be clean in thirty."

"I'll try to make it less," the AI droned.

Shia smiled. She figured he would, but sometimes it was fun to play with the intelligence system. She hadn't stumped him yet.

She changed quick, dropping the hospital gown on the floor in a heap. Fitted black cargo pants, black sports bra, followed by a black long sleeve knit shirt. She sighed in pleasure as the fabric flowed over her body. This is what she should have worn to the gala. Then maybe the Rissu wouldn't have gotten the drop on her. She pulled on her boots and her holsters for her swords. The blades collapsed into themselves with a quick flick of her wrists,

94

and she settled them in their places.

Never again. Next time, she'd watch the event from the darkness. Safer all the way around. Ryan would understand. She wasn't of his world. He'd never fathom hers.

She drew her jacket over her shoulders. "Jace, I'm heading out."

"See you at the warehouse, m'lady."

She strode back over to her desk and emptied everything into the flack backpack. Good thing she'd gone digital years ago, made moving so much easier. She had a few stops to make. She reached the door and took one last scan of the condo. So much for trying to mainstream.

The ring of his phone made Ryan jump. His head shot forward, and he squinted at the sun. He cursed a few select profanities, realizing that he had fallen asleep in the living room chair, and had spilled whatever was left of his Scotch. Rising on weary legs, he walked across the room and picked up the phone.

"Calder."

"So, you are alive, Mijo."

Ryan shook off the cobwebs. Father Munoz was the last voice he expected to hear on the line. "Padre, how...I mean...is everything alright?"

"I must speak with you regarding your companion for the gala last night."

"Shia?"

Father Munoz's tone was calming, slow, and compassionate. It drove Ryan nuts. "Si, Mijo, your friend, Shia. There was an incident after that gala. She was taken to the hospital."

Ryan instantly mapped out events in his head. Holy Unity Catholic Church was close to several hospitals. Shia could have been taken to Georgetown University Hospital, but Father Munoz hadn't said she was taken from the actual gala. She could have been heading home. What hospitals might have been on her way, Sibley Memorial?

"Are you still there, Mijo?" the father asked.

"Yes, yes, I'm here."

"They took her to George Washington University Hospital. I have been with her all night."

Ryan was already heading to his room to get dressed. "What happened? Is she alright?"

"Breathe, Mijo. She was attacked outside of the gala."

"Attacked?"

"She had severe lacerations and lost a lot of blood."

Ryan half-dropped the phone, catching it and cradling it on his shoulder as he slid on a pair of jeans. "I'm on my way."

"Mijo, there is something you should know…"

"I'm on my way. Thanks, Padre." Ryan killed the conversation and dropped the phone onto the bed. He threw on a tight dress shirt, socks and shoes, and finished with his belt and shoulder holster. The phone was ringing again before he grabbed his jacket and hit the door, but he was focused on the fastest path from his apartment to the Emergency Ward at George Washington.

The Impala glided into the parking spaces reserved for law enforcement, and Ryan exited before the engine was silent. He armed the alarm and walked quickly up the sidewalk, pushing the automatic doors apart when they didn't open fast enough for his patience. He strode past a variety of waiting patients who needed everything from stitches to anti-itch cream, and straight to the desk clerk in charge of processing. By the time the young Latina girl acknowledged his presence, she was staring at his badge.

"Good morning, I'm here to see a patient who was admitted last night."

Her eyes were glued to his badge as she asked, "Of course, sir. What is the patient's name?"

"Shia Ronin, First name: S-H-I-A, Last name: R-O-N-I-N. She was brought in via ambulance last night."

"Yes, sir, let me look."

"Gracias, Consuela," he replied after stealing a glimpse at her plastic ID badge.

She smiled. "De nada, señor," she answered with a calmer demeanor. She turned back to the screen and furrowed her brow. "There seems to be a problem, señor."

"What kind of problem?" Ryan asked through gritted teeth.

"Your friend, Miss Ronin, is gone."

Ryan stormed out of the hospital. The Impala disarmed its doors and stared its engines at the touch of his thumb on the keypad. Annoyed, he looked around, opened the door, and dropped into the driver's seat. His hand was on the shifter when the guidance system chirped to life. He snapped out the address of Shia's apartment and received the artificially cordial confirmation from the overly British voice programmed into the GPS.

He was barreling up Wisconsin Avenue when he hit the button on his cell to speed-dial Shia's number. "This is Dr. Ronin. I am unavailable..." He killed the line again. When he finally got Shia back in his arms, the first thing he was going to do was to make her change her outgoing voice message. All right, not the first thing, but it was on the top ten list. As he swerved through traffic, he dialed again. After several rings, he managed to get Father

Munoz's voicemail. He ended the call and snapped the phone into its charger on his dashboard.

A few minutes later, the Impala came to a screeching halt alongside a fire hydrant outside of Shia's apartment building. The meter maids in Washington, D.C. were vicious, but they knew better than to play with Metro D.C. detectives. He dashed up the steps three at a time, stopping once he reached the eighth floor. He walked to the end of the hall, halting at 803, the apartment number where he should have picked her up 12 hours ago. He gripped his pistol with one hand and knocked on the door with the other.

He knocked again, and a third time. No response. He weighed the option of kicking her door in, but he knew such an impulsive move never got the right results. He took a step away from the door, looking down the hallway for anyone he might have woken up. All remained quiet and still. The feeling reminded Ryan of the morgue, and he hated every second.

Eight flights of stairs later, he fired up the Impala once more. The polite GPS voice began to address him.

"Holy Trinity Catholic Church." He cut the system off. The GPS began its calculations as Ryan gripped the gearshift of the Impala and moved into the flow of D.C. traffic.

Getting to the church was a miserable cocktail containing every ingredient that sucked about D.C. There were lane closures for road paving on Reservoir Road, an animal rights protest near Collins Animal Hospital, and a homeless, alleged veteran asking for change regardless of whether the light was red or green. Ryan was waiting for the inevitable motorcade, and while it never came, there was a ten-minute delay while everyone going his direction slowed down to rubberneck the fender bender in the oncoming lanes.

When he got close to Holy Trinity, he slapped the police credentials on the dashboard and pulled the Impala up next to a fire hydrant. He had been delayed enough. Spending another thirty minutes to find a vacant spot along the street would have driven him insane. He shut off the engine, exited the car, eyed traffic in both directions, and headed across the intersection to the place of worship.

He reached the bottom step when two of the large, wooden doors opened. Father Munoz held one of them open as a young man exited, saying "thank you" several times to the Pastor. The man skipped down the stairs several at a time, stopping when he looked up and found Ryan directly in his path.

"Whoa...excuse me, Detective."

Ryan raised an eyebrow. The younger man had light brown hair, parted on the side. He wore tight jeans, white sneakers, and a baggy gray sweater. A camera with an extended lens hung around his neck. A faded backpack was slung over his shoulder. He was slight, but not scrawny, and pale. Ryan had seen him before, but couldn't put a name with the face and voice...not yet.

"It's alright," he gestured to his left. "Mosey along. There's nothing to see here."

The kid stopped, and Ryan placed him. He was a journalist, probably going to whip out his press credentials on the spot. "Are you here to investigate the events from last night?"

Ryan leveled his gaze at the reporter. "What's your name, son?"

"Chris Weitzel, from *The Washington Insider.* Do you have a statement regarding the alleged assault that occurred here last night?"

Ryan glanced down both sides of the street and then back at Weitzel. "Official? No. However, off the record..." He looked each way again and then beckoned Weitzel to lean forward. The reporter obliged. With his lips a few inches from Weitzel's ear, Ryan whispered, "Off the record, go fuck yourself."

Weitzel's face tensed for an instant, and then he smiled broadly. "I look forward to hearing from you, Detective. I can't wait to hear your take on this one." He moved around Ryan, walking away and holding his smile. "In the meantime, keep chasing dead immigrants!" He waved and managed to cross the street before the light changed.

Ryan stared at the nosy reporter over his shoulder, watching the younger man half-walk, half-jog down the sidewalk. There was something he didn't trust about Weitzel, even deeper than his distrust for most reporters. He made a mental note to keep an eye out for that kid.

"Are you going to stand out in the cold all day, Mijo, or come inside?"

Ryan shifted his gaze to Father Munoz, who was still holding the wooden door open. He walked quickly up the stairs, addressing the priest before he reached the top. "Thank you for your patience, padre."

Father Munoz smiled, though his eyes and his grin betrayed hints of exhaustion. "My strength isn't what it once was, Mijo. I can't hold this door open forever."

"No, padre, nor would I expect you to." Ryan caught the hint instantly.

"Come inside. We have a lot to discuss." Father Munoz let Ryan hold the weight of the door as he turned and entered the warmer, darker sanctuary of the church. Ryan stole one last glance back over his shoulder, looking for the nosey, young journalist. Weitzel was nowhere to be found.

"Come, Mijo," Father Munoz called from deeper within the church.

With a final scan around, Ryan stepped inside. The door closed behind him with an ominous boom. The detective didn't flinch. He locked on the form of the holy man and followed him past the parishioners. Father Munoz had told Weitzel something about last night's events. That meant he could tell Ryan what happened at the church, at the hospital, and to Shia.

At the thought of her name, Ryan quickened his pace, following Father Munoz to his private quarters.

Father Munoz's office was humble, like the man himself. A mahogany desk stood in the center of the room, with a matching chair facing the door. A pair of matching bookshelves lined the wall behind where the pastor sat. Two plain, comfortable chairs faced the desk. A toy chest sat in the corner with its lid open, resting atop a three-by-three square of carpet dyed like a train track. A doll with unkempt hair and a smeared face stared up from the box of toys.

Two windows centered the wall to the right. Long shadows filled that side of the room, cast by the iron bars blocking the priest's office from any robbery attempts. The opposite wall hosted a plain, white cross and a painting of the Holy Trinity. Father Munoz walked past the desk and sat in the chair facing the door. Ryan followed, making his way to one of the chairs facing the pastor. He shifted the chair slightly. Even in churches, Ryan hated having his back to the door.

"You come here curious, but also angry, Mijo. That can be a dangerous combination."

Ryan nodded, shooting another glance at the door. "This isn't the first time I've mixed those two feelings. It's not even the first time in this office. I understand that you're upset with me for missing the gala. I had a murder case to work."

"Do not raise your voice to me in the house of the Lord, Mijo. 'Oh Lord, correct me, but with judgment; not in thine anger, lest thou bring me to nothing.' "

Ryan exhaled instead of speaking on impulse. He studied the painting of the Trinity, trying to slow down his thoughts.

"We should pray together," the pastor offered.

"Padre," Ryan replied, suppressing his annoyance, "you know I don't believe any of that...what you believe. I know you want to save my soul, but right now, I need to know what happened here last night."

"I am not certain I can answer that question, Mijo."

"It sure seems like you answered it for that kid from the *Insider*. He was grinning like the cat that ate the canary."

"I cannot tell you what I told him."

Ryan stood, his anger stomping all over his etiquette. "I have done more for this church and for those children than that little cockroach could ever do in this or any other lifetime. Why would you tell him something and not tell me? Why does that parasite get your trust and I don't?"

Father Munoz took a deep breath. "He doesn't have my trust. He has what I told him, which is different then what I will tell you."

"Why?"

"Sit, please," the pastor continued with a soft, knowing face. Ryan reluctantly followed instructions.

"I told that reporter what he wanted to hear. I will tell you, Ryan, not what you want to hear. I will tell you the truth."

CHAPTER ELEVEN

Ryan followed the priest out of the large, wooden doors and down the steps exiting the front of the church. On instinct, he shot a glance across the street to make sure the Impala was still parked. It rested in its parking spot, looking almost bored at the time away from the detective. He followed Father Munoz to the end of the sidewalk, and then into the alleyway.

The alley hardly provided enough room for a compact car to navigate between the buildings and the dumpsters sitting at each end. Fire escapes graced each side. Dirty water filled potholes-turned-puddles. Halfway down a back alley opposite the church were parking spots for tenants of the apartments. Ryan knew the area well. The building on the far end was a run down tenement; a HUD project the landlord bought and barely put any money into. The apartments on the near side were slightly better, though few tenants were out at this hour.

He studied the details, walking forward a bit to the sewer grate on the church side of the alley. Mud, trash and oil in the water meant detecting blood with any accuracy was going to be difficult. The water fled downward from the alley to the darkness of the city sewers, where rats and outcasts ran rampant. Father Munoz didn't witness the attack. He recreated his account from what he had seen, and from what Shia had mumbled during her time in the hospital. Ryan paced down the alley slowly, scanning from side to side. He stopped when he reached the fire escape bolted on to the side of the church.

"You have some kind of accident with a trash truck, padre?" he asked.

The priest hobbled slowly down the alley to the spot stopping next to Ryan. He raised his gaze and looked at the area where Ryan was focused. The steel of the fire escape was split. Half of the ground floor ladder hanging on the bent skeleton of what was left.

"The fire inspector was here two weeks ago. He was a fine man, about your height, but not as big, or as brash. If he saw this, we certainly would not have passed the inspection."

"Any ideas if this happened last night?"

Father Munoz coughed before answering. "No, I don't routinely walk through this alley. It's recent, but I don't know if it's a result of last night's event."

Ryan studied the damage. His first thought was the forklift blade of a trash truck severed it. There weren't many things able split steel cleanly, even with momentum. A rush of energy passed through his body. He shook it off and scratched his cheek as he studied it. He stepped closer, inspecting the metal for any trace of transferred blood, or shavings from whatever had managed to slice through the metal. He exhaled. He'd stood up Shia, and then chewed out the priest for all the wrong reasons. Even if this wasn't related to last night, the least Ryan could do was to help Father Munoz with the insurance papers.

Ryan made a mental note and continued down the alley, scouring the grounds and the walls for details. He traced back and forth three more times before he stopped, looking over to the priest. "All right, you told me to come out here and take a look. You said Shia claims she was attacked here, and she had very real injuries. Then you followed the ambulance when they took her to the hospital."

"She did not claim anything. This is where I found her, unconscious, bleeding, on the ground. You're standing where she was."

Ryan shook his head. "I would not, in a million years, dream of calling either you or Dr. Ronin a liar. You know that, right?"

Father Munoz nodded with a soft smile. "Yes, but..."

"I don't have enough to go on here." Ryan exhaled a half-laugh of frustration. "There's a reason this isn't a crime scene buzzing with MPDC cops. There's nothing here. If something did happen, at best, and I mean the absolute, please-listen-Mr.-District-Attorney-I-swear-I-have-something best, we would have a he-said, she-said situation." He threw his hands in the air and began pacing. "What am I supposed to do with this, padre? There's nothing here...nothing."

Father Munoz's reply was soft, steady and slow. "She means that much to you?"

"What?" Ryan asked, confusion stemming the tide of anger in his head.

"This isn't about closing a case, Mijo. This is about her." The priest smiled when Ryan nodded. "Good, then you will listen to what else I have to share with you. You will listen. Come, Mijo," he continued, pulling out the key to the service entrance of the church. "I will tell you what I learned in the hospital."

"I know the answer, even before I ask, but I will ask regardless. Do you believe in miracles, Mijo?" Father Munoz rested again in the chair behind his desk. He had a hand-woven blanket around his shoulders. On the desktop before him was a steaming cup of tea.

Ryan leaned against the wall opposite the pastor. "Other than the Lake Placid game where the U.S. kids beat the Russians, not so much, padre."

"'Then those men, when they had seen the miracle that Jesus did, said, This is of a truth that prophet that should come into the world,'" Father Munoz recited with closed eyes. He reached forward and took a sip of his tea. "John 6:14. My faith has always been a part of me, as your pessimism a part of you. I wish you could approach things with the open mind, and open heart, that guides my journey to God. I understand simple words won't make this happen, Mijo. Let me, then, tell you all I know of your Shia, and what occurred last night."

"Shia...Dr. Ronin as you referred to her earlier, was, beyond the shadow of a doubt, the most delightful and personable female companion who has ever attended our fundraiser on your behalf. She is a special woman. I knew it from our first introduction, and the feeling was shared by many of the event coordinators and attendees. I dare say only my title kept several patrons from asking me about her. However, I will say I saw her redirect several advances, all the while maintaining her posture and demeanor."

"The only off-balance portion of her behavior were her repeated glances to the entrance, but I will not beleaguer the point. You explained your absence, and your job requires your attention." The priest took another long pull off of his tea. "This church is an old facility, but you know that. I've watched you in the past attempt to call the local taxi companies on behalf of your companions, and every time, I've seen you walk outside to get any type of reception. I fear any calls you made to Dr. Ronin were not received while under our roof."

Ryan nodded, leaning his head against the wall. "I can't even count how many times I called her. I blew the battery on my phone." He reached to his hip and cursed under his breath. "Hell, I left it on the charger in the Impala."

"Eventually, Shia realized you were not going to be in attendance. She made her rounds, politely excused herself, and left." Father Munoz sighed, blowing the steam from his tea into a broad pillar floating upward. "Minutes later, we heard screams from the alley. One of the hostesses from the waiting staff found Dr. Ronin, bloodied and battered, lying outside the service entrance to the church. It took us seconds to dial 911 and alert the local Emergency Medical Services."

"We are four blocks from the local fire station, Mijo. They were here in a matter of minutes. I joined Dr. Ronin in the ambulance once they had her stabilized and prepared for transportation. I provided as many details as I had, and the EMT's initiated life-saving procedures. At that time, I truly believed Dr. Ronin was on the brink of death. She had deep cuts on her stomach and arms. And, I believe head trauma from being thrown into the side of the building, from what the EMTs were saying. I prayed the Lord's prayer. I prayed Matthew 4:23; 'And Jesus went about all Galilee, teaching in their synagogues, and preaching the gospel of the kingdom, and healing all manner of sickness and all manner of disease among the people.'"

Father Munoz leveled his gaze at the detective. "I have no explanation for what happened next."

"I am a man of faith, Mijo. I believe all things are

possible through the Word of the Lord, and I believe in my heart I witnessed a true miracle," Father Munoz continued, more animated than he had been earlier. "When I followed Shia Ronin to the emergency ward, I feared for her life. I prayed for the salvation of her soul. I stayed by her bedside, and I prayed as she dreamed. An hour before sunrise, she sat up, stared at me, and swung herself off of the bed. She removed her IVs and gathered her items, and she left."

"What?" Ryan took two steps toward the pastor. "That doesn't make any sense."

"Psalm 107:20 says 'He sent His word, and healed them, and delivered them from their destructions.' This was an act of the Father, Mijo. Shia has a strong faith, and it rewarded her tonight."

"Really, because she believed something hard enough, padre? I believe child rapists should be electrocuted on pay-per view television, but that doesn't make it a reality. People see things in a different light when they're in shock, or emotionally pressed. With all due respect, I...maybe you're interpreting what happened differently than I would in the same situation."

Father Munoz nodded. "You can reason away many things, my son, but do not insult my faith and the power of the Holy Father. This is His home, and you are free to state your opinion, but not to disrespect myself or my Lord."

Ryan ran a hand through his hair, shifting his attention out the window instead of voicing the first few responses that came to mind.

"My God is a merciful and loving God, Ryan." Father Munoz smiled softly. "I know she is different. I know you care for her, perhaps more than you realize yourself. Maybe this time, He is looking out for your interests, even though you are not interested in Him. Find her, Mijo, and find your answers."

Ryan's anger deflated as he recognized how hard-headed he had been to the pastor, hours after screwing up the gala, and possibly destroying any chance to develop a relationship outside of work with the most amazing woman he'd met in years. He exhaled and met the pastor's gaze. "Maybe you're right, padre. Maybe there is something outside of my own little world. If you're right, I hope it's on my side in this one."

CHAPTER TWELVE

Shia kicked off her boots the minute she entered the door. Her bare feet relaxed on the smooth concrete floors. She loved the look of the polished floor and enjoyed the coolness against her skin even more. Some days, living was all about the textures, the feel of things. It made her remember she was alive. Sort of.

Home.

A ripple of relaxation flowed over her. She'd forgotten how much she missed her haven. She should have known better than to move into the city. Closer to people? Who needed them?

Well, there was one person she'd like to be closer to. She tramped down on the thought before it could take hold. One sexy, crazy detective didn't need to keep intruding on her thoughts.

"I've started the shower. You can wash the stench from the hospital off since you neglected to do so before leaving the condo," Jace said.

She ignored the AI. Instead, she wandered into the office, trailing a light hand over the cherry blossom wood that made up her desk, a memory from her homeland. She set down her backpack on top of it before walking back into the entry way.

She took a deep breath in, taking in the clean, cool air. The warehouse was sparse. The floor plan open. She'd made it that way on purpose. She always preferred wide-open spaces and simplicity of design. The first floor housed her office and a conference room for when her sisters arrived en masse. The kitchen and gym hidden from the main entry were tucked around the corner. The central staircase led up to her private domain, which was a mixture of textures, wooden stairs with black metal railings. She'd left the ceilings open, showing the ductwork. Skylights allowed the night sky to shine through in every spot she'd been able to place them without damaging the structural integrity of the building. Bedrooms made up the top floor. She'd built her personal area separate—a large, luxurious bedroom and bathroom—and added in rooms for her sisters to crash when needed. Each one had their own space, small though it was, for themselves. Most of them left some personal effects in each room. They shared a communal bathing space with baths, showers, and a sauna. And on the roof, a zen garden, outdoor training deck, and hot tub to relax under the stars.

Home. She'd created a training ground reminiscent of her growing years. For over a hundred years, each new sister trained here. Yvaine, Shellie, Maya, and Christelle suffered under her training for a few years before moving on to their respective homelands to help defend against the dark things in the night. She couldn't be sure as to how many more would be adding to their ranks. Perhaps it was a good thing she'd purchased the surrounding warehouses as well. After waiting for over 200 years for Ilsa to show up, she'd added six new sisters in the last 100 years. With the rate things were going, she'd be finding more in the near future.

Thankfully, Jace's main components remained housed here, hidden in layers of cooling space and protected floor beneath her feet. It would take an army to unearth his circuitry. He'd managed to migrate the annoying cleaning bots as well. They'd swept the place clean before her arrival, not a speck of dust remained.

"M'lady, Detective Calder has been leaving a message every hour." Jace interrupted her musings.

She frowned. "He can wait. I'm off duty from the precinct." It wasn't exactly true, but she'd taken medical leave for a week. Technically, he could deal with the ME who'd stepped in. She'd had Jace upload all her pertinent records, relevant enough for the department. Her personal notes remained hers. Now, to keep the Rissu from hunting said detective since she was certain the demon targeted his trail as well as hers.

"Jace," she came to a quick decision. "Warm up the training room. I need to stretch these kinks out. There is no way the creature should have gotten the better of me, barefoot and unarmed, regardless."

"Yes, Lady Ronin." Halls lit up as she strode through them. "Would you like me to register you a sparring partner?"

She sighed. "You've been programming again, haven't you?"

"I do many things at once," he answered.

She shook her head. "Fine, I'll tussle with your beta program after I've gone through drills. Have you wired the place for sound too?"

"Of course. You may have music anywhere, any kind, any era. There will be few that you won't find in our database."

Wouldn't the musicians around the world love that?

"I hope you paid for it all."

Jace didn't bother with a response.

Shia stepped into the training room and relaxation flowed over her body. Built similar to the hall she'd trained in as a child with hardwood floors and rice paper walls. Well, three of them. Concrete and mirrors lined the back wall. Weapons racks, benches, kettle bells, and dumb bells edged the walls.

"You've upgraded more than the sound system," she commented.

"Yes, I had a sense you'd return sooner than you'd anticipated. I've added in weapons for partner training as well...should your sisters visit."

She lifted an eyebrow. Had she detected a hint of hesitation in his comment? Who else but her sisters ever visited?

"Put on something pop so I can warm up for ten and then switch it to the Yoshida Brothers' 'Rising'--I'll flow into my drills with that one."

Black Eyed Peas kicked into high gear and echoed around the hall. Shia closed her eyes and let the music wash over her. She rarely used music, but to fuel her workouts and maintain her focus, she'd learned the benefit of the different beats to help her improve her reach and range.

Truth be told, the Rissu demon had done a number on her. Her ribs ached. She hadn't been down like that in centuries, and the last time she'd been outnumbered four to one. The fact that one demon had been able to break her, it bothered her more than she'd let on to the priest. A Rissu rarely moved fast enough to catch her. They were cumbersome creatures, more power than finesse, more animal than humanoid. She ruled out wearing dresses in the foreseeable future. She could figure out cocktail wear in battle style if need be.

She shifted into a lunging stretch, working with the muscles in her legs to loosen and warm.

"Jace, notch the heat up to 110 degrees," she said.

The temperature climbed, and she deepened the stretch. Her one foot flattened against the floor, the other angled and relaxed down. She closed her eyes and flowed into a series of yoga poses, working on flexibility and strength.

Ten minutes in, when Jace shifted the music, she moved with it. Her eyes snapped open and lit on an imaginary foe. Her body surged in rhythmic movements, a flurry of motion, punches, kicks, and elbows, using only her body, her personal power to defend herself. She worked in the space she was given, moving for the entire length of the song. As the last of the notes echoed throughout the room, she dropped to a knee, panting. Her heart raced. Energy swept along her nerves.

"Do you require air, m'lady?" Jace's electronic voice sounded concerned.

She closed her eyes and lifted her head toward the ceiling. Anyone looking at her would see the delight etched into her face. Sweat trailed down her cheeks.

She smiled. "No, I haven't danced like that in ages."

She would be working on that more often. Oh, how she'd missed making the energy move. That is what had been missing from her fight with the Rissu. Focus, determination, she'd cut off her power.

She stood. "You can ready my shower now, Jace."

Never again.

Shellie Adams rubbed her eyes with her fingertips partially from sleep deprivation and partly as if she could get the violent images out of her mind's eye. She set her gear down in the chalet's living room. She'd fled the scene in the dark of the Nevada night knowing her best chance of finding the child meant she follow the Rissu's trail as quickly as possible. In his effort to get the young girl, he'd left a mess of the parents--limbs, clothes strewn about and their home a shambles in his wake. She offered up every prayer known to man and some not known that the girl remained living.

To die that young as a samurai would forever shift their lives. All of their lives. No child should have to endure the transition into a samurai along with an endless life of childhood.

The child's energetic pattern was faint and fluctuating, but finally settled in the general area of Mount Shasta, California. She hoped Sierra Tate was a stronger five-year-old than she looked. Shellie had taken a few things from the child's house--clothes, a picture, and what appeared to be a favorite stuffed animal. She'd left no trail for any human to find and took great care not to mess up the crime scene. She hadn't had time to call the cops, certain the neighbors would based on the screams she'd encountered when she'd entered the house. She hadn't even taken the time to check in with her sisters. They were going to be livid with her. Her cell phone had been smashed in the battle, and she'd been doing nothing but tracking for three days. At least she'd had the forethought to pick up the shattered device and take it with her.

Now, since she'd reached her destination, she could take the time to get a new phone, and perhaps, get some rest before heading out to track down what had to be one scared little girl.

Energy rippled across the nape of her neck. She shivered.

No, no time to rest or do anything else if the shift

were real. He was on the move again, but staying within a radius as if the demon dog waited for something or someone. She kicked her clothing pack further into the living room and grabbed her gear. Pocketing the key, she turned, taking in everything around her. She memorized the location of every piece of furniture and placement of the window treatments before leaving.

She stepped off the deck and took off at a light jog through the forest surrounding her isolated space. Her moccasin-covered feet whispered across the ground. Her eyes adjusted to the light of the mountainside, her ear picking up all the sounds around her. She let her awareness expand until she could feel the energetic pulse in every living being. And there, one non-living entity. She stilled for a moment, turning slowly, then turned in the direction of the pull and set off through the trees.

A shiver crossed over her neck. She should've packed some warmer weight clothing.

Ryan nodded as the waitress offered a refill on his coffee. He scarfed down his second egg and cheese sandwich with peppers and tomatoes as he scoured the messages from the last twelve hours. His phone was charged when he returned to the Impala, but the two voicemails were both from Agent Simone asking him about autopsy and transportation issues. He could call her back whenever he wanted. Felicia would take his voicemail as an opportunity to do things her way, rather than wait for confirmation.

He swallowed a bite of the sandwich and slugged down a hot mouthful of coffee. He'd skipped closer chain restaurants to park himself at the City Place Café on 17th street. He knew all of the morning shift waitresses and cooks, and they treated him well. It helped him overcome the strange feeling of being so close to the White House. The Café was a few blocks away, and Ryan could make out the snipers on the White House rooftop from his table. He didn't like being in this neighborhood. He voted against the corrupt bastard who had won the last election. The President was also the Armed Forces Commander in Chief, and Ryan spent four years in the Air Force having the importance of chain-in-command hammered into his skull. It was one of the reasons he worked so well with the ranks of the MPDC. Ryan played the game without compromising his ideals.

Taking another bite from his sandwich, he ran his finger over the biometric scanner and opened the encrypted files on his laptop. He read over the orders for the autopsy. On instinct, he reached to counter the schedule. He stopped when he realized he couldn't put a halt on Charles Huang's autopsy to get Dr. Ronin to perform the autopsy. No one had seen her since she left the hospital, and he was pretty certain, miracle or not, her next stop wasn't to punch a clock at the City Morgue.

Another new message flashed on his screen, and he clicked on the icon. A confirmation message asked if he would like to view the attached video. He double-checked his security software, which had already scanned the message before accepting it. A second later, Ryan was face-to-face with the smile of a dark blonde man, wearing a just-too-big gray sweater. Ryan groaned. He had bumped into the same face earlier, outside Holy Trinity.

"Hello, Detective," the recording began. The kid even waved. "This is Chris Weitzel from *The Washington Insider*. We spoke earlier today. Let me cut to the chase, sir. I'd love the opportunity to buy you lunch, to thank you for the fine job you do protecting our local citizens every day, and to help you, in any way I can, to identify and interview those suspects or persons-of-interest you have in your ongoing cases. I've attached an electronic copy of

117

my contact information. I can meet with you somewhere local, like Bangkok Bistro, for instance. I'll be at Bangkok Bistro at 11:30. I look forward to our discussion."

Ryan sucked down some more coffee, even if it was too damn hot. This Weitzel kid was working an angle. He needed to locate Shia, but he had no idea where, and every minute he tried to find her and failed was another minute Felicia used to steal control of the Huang case. He closed his eyes trying to focus over the general clatter combined with Bill Haley and the Comets classic rendition of "Rock around the Clock" on the jukebox.

Ryan picked up his sandwich and shook his head. "Okay, Holy Spirit guy, if you're the coach, give me an idea. What the hell am I supposed to do now?" He swiped his card on the table's register and exited the diner.

Father Munoz's God was apparently content to follow the pattern everyone else had started, and Ryan's request for spiritual guidance went to some heavenly voicemail. He swallowed a mouthful of coffee, reached down and shifted into gear, driving over roads he knew all too well. The morgue was down on Massachusetts Avenue, which wasn't far, but trying Constitution this early in the morning meant screaming cabbies and belligerent commuters, and that didn't even factor in the tourists. Ryan took a few side streets instead, arriving as Sting was wailing away the closing chorus of The Police's "So Lonely."

Ryan entered, showed his credentials and bounded down the stairs to the medical examiner's office. He tapped twice on the door before stepping in. He looked around, surprised by the sound of rockin' country music playing over tinny speakers. He made out the figure of a male M.E., chatting to himself while prepping a body for the Y-incision on the corpse on the table. The man wore a full-length white lab coat. His face protected by a plastic mask, and a synthetic material covered his hands up to his elbows. As Ryan drew closer, he realized the man wasn't mumbling to himself, he was recording the autopsy findings into a remote computer on the other side of the lab.

Ryan cleared his throat, and the ME looked up, startled.

"Pause." He lifted the plastic face shield. "Wow. Dude, you almost gave me a heart attack!"

Ryan tilted his head in a half-apology. "I'm sorry. Who the hell are you?"

"Oh, yeah," the mortician replied with a grin. "I'm Cicarelli. I'm here on loan from southeast. You guys had an M.E. call in sick, and the roster's pretty thin. So, they called me in for a little OT. Happy to oblige."

Ryan knew without looking it had to have been Shia who had phoned in. She worked this shift...always had...and instead, he got some Garth Brooks impersonator as the lead examiner. "How long are you on loan, doc?"

"I'm covering the first three days. Someone else has the tail end of the week."

"The week?"

"That's what I was told. There is an open slot here for the week. Come up and make time and a half. I wasn't going to pass that up!"

Ryan walked to the tablet PC on the wall and scrolled through the mortician's case backlog. Charles Huang was scheduled for processing. He checked the attending medical examiner, scowling as he read the name. Simone had brought in her pro to take a look over his corpse. So much for letting her call go to voicemail. He headed to the door.

"See you around, Detective," Cicarelli called from his workspace.

Ryan grunted and stepped out, angrier than ever at his

current situation.

CHAPTER THIRTEEN

Ryan stopped the Impala at the edge of the alleyway, staring down the length of the space between Holy Trinity and the neighboring apartments. He wasn't certain what had brought him back here, but he knew there were stones left unturned. Father Munoz said this was the scene of Shia's attack, but as he probed into databases and news feeds, the event became less and less real. If anyone had reported the attacks, they'd dried up and blown away--no reports crossed his desk, no medical records to speak of, and no ambulance logs to trace.

Not right. And, even more suspect.

Ryan stepped out of the unmarked cruiser and began looking around. He investigated the alley, searching for signs that indicated struggle. Shia was no pushover. He measured his steps, checking for larger shoe prints, or marks that confirmed someone had been dragged. No real luck there, though he considered casting a few footsteps that looked like work boots. He laughed at himself. Those might be his footprints from hours before.

121

He continued down the alleyway. The bent steel of the fire escape caught his eye once, twice, and then enough to be annoying. He walked that direction stealing a few more glances around. He pulled out his smartphone and took some quick shots of the damaged metal, getting the confirmation message that they arrived, encrypted on his computer at the precinct. He moved closer, switching his phone from camera to microscope, and stopped. He'd swear the image rippled. He shook his head, blinked several times and refocused on the mangled metal.

Whatever had cut through the steel still moved, at least on the cellular level. He snapped more images. The element that had sliced through the metal ladder was dense, but from this angle, it appeared to be liquid at the same time. Ryan drew back from the lens, looking over his shoulder again. No liquid was dense enough to cut through steel, was it?

He pulled an evidence bag out of his pocket, along with a tiny cotton swab. The cotton was used routinely to gather samples of DNA, but it would work in this instance. If this substance was liquid, he'd be able to pick up some of it. He stared at the cotton tip, satisfied that it appeared to have picked up the strange material. He bagged the sample and scanned the area, deciding on what to search next.

A tiny hint of light caught his eye, and he stepped forward. His initial paranoia led him to believe that he'd been tailed by one of DC's infamous rogue reporters. When he saw it a second time, he realized he wasn't the target of some flash photography. He was catching light reflected off of something in the alleyway. He took cautious steps forward, losing the reflection, then seeing it again at intervals. As best as he could determine, something under the lopsided dumpster had landed in the ideal spot between him and the sun.

Ryan walked until he was close enough to smell half-eaten meals, baby diapers, stale beer, cigarette ashes, and all the ingredients of a DC alley dumpster. Sneering at the scent, he took a few steps closer. The reflected light disappeared. Ryan nodded. The object was below the dumpster, not on it or in it.

He shrugged off his jacket and dropped into a push-up, inches off of the muddy, cracked asphalt of the alleyway. From there, he made out the shape of something beneath the dumpster. He moved closer. Was that a blade? He couldn't tell from his angle. Propped up on the weight of one arm, he reached under the dumpster. His fingers gripped pebbles, dirt, and a crushed bottle cap. He drew in a breath, stretching further, and grabbed more of the same, maybe even an old banana peel.

Cursing under his breath, Ryan dropped down, pressing his chest into the muck and dirt of the alley. He reached again under the dumpster, and the tips of his second and third finger touched something solid. He struggled against the edge of the dumpster and gained no ground. He cursed and then stopped. Closing his eyes, Ryan pictured Shia as he had last seen her, off guard, staring up at him. He exhaled. Stress left his body. His fingers extended a bit further...and grabbed a hold of the item under the dumpster.

Ryan rolled to his feet, spitting away the iron taste of whatever he was laying in. He palmed the strange object. It was a knife, perhaps ten inches long overall, including the hilt. The blade was slightly convex, as sharp as anything Ryan had ever brandished. He offered quiet gratitude that he hadn't sliced his fingers open, reaching blindly for the knife under the dumpster. The hilt was basic, bronze with onyx inlaid between its layers, and comprising a simple pattern of thread. The butt offered elementary protection for whoever wielded it.

Ryan stared in confusion. This looked like a knife some maniac kid crafted in his basement, but the texture was strange. He switched his gaze from the knife back to the fire escape. This blade balanced in his hand like nothing he'd ever held before. He slid it underneath his belt.

He sat up and drew in a few deep breaths. Something about the knife made his head swim. He stopped, breathing slowly until his head cleared. Ryan glanced to his right. There wasn't much there other than the patchwork fence behind the salon. If Shia had lost her phone by dropping it from her right hand, it was at any of the six local pawnshops. Ryan had officers casing them all. He turned to his left, pondering the new possibilities.

He pulled the small flashlight from his belt. The light struggled to pierce the darkness of the sewer from this angle. He had gotten lucky enough groping around in the dark under the dumpster. Flailing blindly in D.C. Sewers was another matter. He still considered the decision when his phone vibrated on his hip.

Ryan sent a call out to the universe for some good news. He yanked the phone from his belt and read the message. "We need to talk ASAP--Felicia". Ryan dropped his head back against the pavement when an idea sparked to life inside. He switched the cell to dial and hit the number for Shia's phone.

It was distant, and he doubted he had even heard it, but an electronic chime called to him. Ryan rolled to his side, moving closer to the sewer grate. The chime repeated, louder this time, five steady beeps. It stopped, and then chimed again. After three series, it stopped completely, and a familiar voice rose in Ryan's ear.

"This is Dr. Shia Ronin."

Ryan killed the connection. He stared at the sewer grate, measuring possibilities. There was no way for him to fit between the bars. Cutting them would require an acetylene torch. He pushed himself off of the gravel, glancing from side to side. In an instant, he saw his opportunity. Ryan took a few steps until he reached the center of the alleyway.

He yanked the manhole cover off without a second thought.

Detective Ryan Calder dropped into the six inches of unspeakable liquid, Doc Marten boots splashing the surrounding walls. The impact echoed in all directions. Chittering of sewer rats answered in the distance as they fled. Ryan's thoughts went straight to a hot shower…Shia included. He held the phone in one hand. His other hand gripped the 10mm Glock semi-automatic pistol. He clenched the mini-flashlight between his teeth, for all the space it bought him in the darkness.

He took six measured steps forward, and his thumb pressed down on the "redial" button. He heard the familiar chime in the darkness ahead. He stepped forward cautiously, taking a few strides with each repeated sequence of beeps.

"This is Dr. Shia Ronin."

He killed the call, waited a few breaths and then re-dialed the number. The chime repeated, closer now. Ryan made out the actual sound of the phone from the echo in the alley. The chime resounded, and Ryan was close enough to touch the source of the sound. The flashlight revealed the reflection of the sewage.

The chime sounded once more, and Ryan reached forward on bind faith. His arm submerged in the unspeakable chemical compound that lived beneath D.C. He turned his head, and the flashlight between his teeth illuminated a screen. The screen read "Incoming Call: Detective Calder."

He stopped, as if everything that mattered didn't matter anymore. The phone died in his hand, and he blinked several times, trying to will it back to life.

"This is Dr. Shia Ronin."

Ryan stood in the grime of the undercity, staring at the phone. He pulled the LED flashlight from his mouth, putting it back onto his belt. He shook his head, staring at the cracked screen of Shia's cell phone. Father Munoz's story replayed in his head.

"Jesus, Shia," he asked the darkness around him, "what the hell happened here?"

Shia sunk lower in the deep soaking tub, sighing as the wet heat radiated throughout every muscle in her body. Muscles finally relaxed from hours on the battlefield. As tradition demanded, she'd bathed down with a cloth before entering the tub. Aiko, her front room attendant, had helped wash the length of her hair before she'd dismissed her to clean her clothes and weapons. Katsumi waited for her within the bathing area, aided her in piling her hair atop her head and offered to give an after battle massage for her back. But Shia sent her away as well, informing both attendants she only wanted to be left alone and soak, and she was quite capable of getting herself out and dressed again in time for a meal with her Master and his other samurai.

She craved solitude before joining the others.

With her eyes closed and her head back, she realized how grateful she was then that she didn't share the Sento, the communal samurai-bathing house. Her Master had granted her a space and attendants of her own since the day he'd brought her into his House. The murmurs behind her back quieted down over the years. At first they'd been hurtful, but then, as she'd grown and trained, she'd begun to ignore them as unimportant. Eventually, they died off.

She smiled to herself, proud of her accomplishments. Yes, she served tea with the best of them, yet none matched her skill with her bow from horseback. And, the battle from which they'd returned had been the worse one on record, but she'd more than held her own and saved many of her brothers. She had a feeling the battles would get far worse before they got better.

She sighed and sunk a little lower. The water steamed, heating up her face. She jumped when hands landed on her shoulder.

"Katsumi, I told you, I am fine. I want to be alone," she murmured.

"Ah, but I am not Katsumi, little one. And, you worked hard today and deserve some respite." Her Master's voice startled her. She bolted upright in the water, her arms moving to cover her chest. She dipped her head and cut him a glance over her shoulder, giving him full view of her naked back. Her heartbeat climbed up her throat. She swallowed, determined to show no fear, only curiosity.

"Master?" she asked, proud her voice remained steady. She moved her feet enough to give her leverage should she need it.

"Relax, little one. I offer only to provide that massage you so determinedly turned down. Katsumi mentioned you'd sent her away, and she didn't want to be punished for not doing her job." He gently urged her to move in the water, his hands playing across her shoulders.

Shia followed his lead leaning forward so the view remained the same. She bit back a question as to why he was the one who'd returned rather than Katsumi. He'd made the girl return on more than one occasion. Why was this time different?

She closed her eyes and expanded her senses, listening to his every movement, waiting for outside sounds of returning attendants. His hands worked magic along her back, her muscles relaxing from hours of fighting. She'd been afraid she'd torn something in her shoulder, but it released and let go, and the pain fled.

"There, see, you should not turn your attendants away next time. I have them serve you for a reason," he scolded her.

"Yes, sir," she murmured, keeping her eyes lowered. In this comprising situation, she couldn't bring herself to meet his gaze as she normally did. In uniform or even casual clothes, she always stood her ground. But no man had seen her naked, she hadn't intended that one ever would.

She sensed the heat of his stare as his soft steps carried him out of her bathhouse. She waited until his footfall was faint and the water cooled so much she shivered. She stepped out of the tub, her body shaking. She would remember to keep her attendants with her at all times going forward.

She turned to grab a towel, and the world shimmered. She frowned as a strong hand reached out and tugged her to him through the steam.

What? Her gaze darted everywhere at once, tile, light, mist surrounding her. And then she glanced up, not at all in fear of the hard, naked body pressed up against hers only the towel between them.

"Ryan," she whispered.

"Shia," he whispered back before his lips descended on hers.

She did nothing to avoid him, meeting him strength for strength. Her only hesitancy was the curiosity flowing through her body. Why did the detective want her of all people? Tall, blond, blue eyed, he had women fawning all over him. Yet, he'd set his eyes on her?

His hands pulled her closer, but she pushed back on his shoulders. She glanced up at him, a smile graced his lips as he stared down at her.

She cried out when the vortex swirled again. Her eyes opened seeing nothing but her bedroom ceiling. Surprise lanced through her. Another dream, but this time, no fear.

No fear.

"Calder."

"You know your voicemail is kind of cold and distant, right? You might want to re-think that for your activist, vegetarian crowd, just in case."

"Is there something on your mind, Agent Simone, or are you calling to torment me about my use of technology as a part of my bedside manner? Either way, I'm not sure I have the time to spend coddling to your instruction."

"Wow," Simone replied with feigned surprise. "You are neck-deep in this case. I won't judge you, Ryan, I'll let you know that Charles Huang's autopsy is being handled by my medical examiner. I apologize if this affects your normal routine."

Ryan grinned, content in his own misfortune. "No, Agent Simone, I am not impacted in the slightest. As a matter of fact, I think you and I should meet to discuss the autopsy results."

The phone was silent for several seconds before the agent replied, "You do?"

"Yes," Ryan remarked, staring at the simple blade in his hand. "Send me the details on where you'd like to meet. I'm curious to hear what your medical examiner has to say about Charles Huang's cause of death."

Ryan killed the conversation. Watching the scene through his mirrored Ray Ban shades Ryan noticed the slight man sitting alone in a booth at the Bangkok Bistro. The FBI had joined the hunt, along with one very aggressive reporter from *The Washington Insider*. Ryan studied the young man who instantly leapt to his feet, tapping into his smart phone.

Simone wanted something he couldn't give her. Weitzel wanted something he wouldn't provide. Still, they were both hell bent on using him as an angle to promotion. Ryan maintained his smile, but growled behind his façade. Abigail Huang was an innocent, young woman, murdered for her devotion to her husband. One or more than one of those he interviewed knew how or why she was killed. Yet, none of them were talking.

Ryan flipped the evidence bag housing the dagger in his palm, blade over hilt, hilt over blade, again and again. There was an answer to this, and maybe, just maybe, the key rested in his hand. He set the bagged dagger down on the passenger seat and picked up the phone.

CHAPTER FOURTEEN

Shia struggled to get out of the bed and shakily dressed, so many years without dreaming and now two in one night. First her original death, and the second…she had no name for the other dream yet.

"Shall I start your tea, Lady Ronin?" Jace asked.

She nodded, distracted, the dream playing back in her mind's eyes. She remembered the incident in minute detail, right down to the sound of her Master's footsteps retreating across the wooden floor, but she'd never, ever, encountered Ryan in a steamy shower. Her body heated up with the thought, her stomach fluttering.

Stop, just stop. Her Master's advances and then subsequent snubbing on the battlefield had hindered her focus and resulted in getting her killed. She didn't need a diversion now, especially one ending with Ryan dying. She'd resurrect. He wouldn't. She couldn't have his death on her hands. Better she stay away. No matter how much her body and mind seemed to want him near.

"Jace, status." Focus. She'd concentrate on the tasks

131

at hand, her sisters, the demons, and not one hard bodied detective.

She cursed under her breath at herself. This would not do, not do at all.

"Christelle arrived in Quebec without fanfare. Maya is in Chicago, a little more ruckus. She refused to be subtle in her arrival and caused a flurry of excitement in the Arab community."

She sighed. Of course. If it wasn't Celeste, it was Maya. The two took turns this century causing uprisings with the paparazzi.

"Give her a not so subtle hint I'm displeased, and she'd better provide a good reason for upsetting our strategy," she said making her way down the stairs after quickly pulling on her favorite black flak pants, a soft blue top and a black vest, which hid her swords well.

"Sent," he continued. "I found an energetic pulse in California I believe may be Shellie or the child she chases. I am detecting two pulses, which is why I think that's her."

Shia stopped on the second to last step. Her sister…"She's hunting down another one of us?"

She sprinted down the rest of the steps and into the office. "Pull the tracking map up, now."

Images sprang to life, lighting up the room. Red dots appeared on an overlaying grid marking demon sightings. Yellow, their deaths. Blue lights pulsed for each of the Samurai with a faint blue-green overlaying the one in California.

"When did you figure out how to track us?" He hadn't been able to do so before, or at least, hadn't hinted he'd been working on such programming.

"I decided to test my theories out on you while you were sleeping. I ran multiple algorithms against your body mass, type and heat index. Samurai temperatures are as unique as the different demons. I made adjustments based on each of the sisters and then, the mathematical calculations reconfigured themselves and actually picked up the changing signatures of the child."

She stared at the map in amazement. Shock kept her speechless for the moment. Had the AI told her they now had the ability to predict new samurai who would be coming into being, and they potentially track and protect them? She couldn't list the numbers of them she hadn't been able to sense, the ones who died, who hadn't survived because their sheer will had been stripped from them. Break a samurai's willpower and you had one who couldn't resurrect. Their spirit would refuse.

"How many have you found?" she whispered.

She'd lost several over time, so many potential ones yet to save, depending on their ability to seek them out and guide them.

"Sierra Tate is five years old, born in Reno, Nevada. Current location is northern California. The information lit up my radar when the Reno police department sent it out. I connected the dots since that's where Shellie went off the grid. I am still trying to verify the identity of one teenage potential in the DC area. Obviously, female, but with the population density here and movement, she is harder to track and pinpoint her exact location. Her energy pattern is going in and out, so she's not in any immediate danger, at least according to the current way I can trail her. Last one, a young woman, her power is more consistent, outside of Norway. She will be easier to pinpoint when I can focus resources. She follows a set schedule and does not seem to be in eminent danger, but the higher arc in her levels indicates sooner rather than later. I've been narrowing my search parameters in the last few minutes."

Her phone chimed. She commanded, "On screen."

Ilsa's visage filled up the lower left corner. "Any updates?"

Shia turned her full focus on her sister. "Oh, you're not going to believe this one. Jace open the stream to her."

She sat back letting it all register, while Ilsa started at all the data before her attempting to absorb everything.

When Ilsa finally realized what she was looking at she stared at Shia. "You know what this means?"

She laughed. "We can track our sisters, our future samurai, but we are not one iota closer to knowing where the demons are coming from?"

Ilsa wrinkled her nose at her. "Well, yes. At least we've located Shellie, and she has only one demon to deal with. She can handle him."

Shia shook her head. "Send Taji. She's in the mountains with a child to save. If the girl's energy is awakening, she's in danger, and we do NOT want one so young to change."

Ilsa was already tapping on her keyboard, sending a message to the junior samurai. Taji would aid Shellie and then return to her natural hunting grounds.

"Track the one in your area while helping us keep tabs and figure out where the portal is. I still believe the entry point is here because of the infestation."

"I agree. I'll take care of things here. Stay in touch."

Shia bowed her head as Ilsa hit end on their call. She wished she could tell Ryan.

Oh lord, she jerked up staring at the ceiling. She was further gone than she thought. She needed to increase security. She didn't want anyone finding out about Jace's technology.

Ryan watched as Weitzel stopped running his mouth long enough to eye his phone. The reporter pumped his fist in the air and then switched lines. His nasal voice stabbed Ryan in the ear. "This is Chris Weitzel."

"That would be the number I dialed."

"Detective Calder, I'm so glad you called. Are you going to be able to meet with me? I saved a table. I can order something for you if you think you're going to hit traffic."

"I don't think I'm going to hit much traffic, kid. I'm staring at you from across the street."

Weitzel turned and stared out the window, catching Ryan's gaze. He laughed, still talking into the phone. "Great! I'll save you a seat."

Ryan killed the connection before engaging in some awkward back and forth goodbyes. He waited until the light changed and crossed at the signal. He was still almost crushed by a taxi driver slamming on his brakes.

Ryan shot him a disapproving glare and pointed at the digital sign that read "Don't Block the Box: $200 Fine."

The cabbie rattled off something in a dialect Ryan only half-recognized. With a grin, he flashed his badge, and the man changed skin tone and demeanor. Ryan turned away, finishing his life-threatening walk from one side of Prospect Street to the other.

Weitzel was holding the front door of Bangkok Bistro open when Ryan arrived. The detective removed his shades and stepped into the bustling restaurant. The lunch crowd was already in full effect. A myriad of voices engaged in conversations covering politics, sex lives, new apartments, changes to the menu, and the latest celebrity scandals. Equally chaotic was the blend of scents in the air.

Ryan caught a new spice with each step through the restaurant. Sweet basil, Siamese ginger, chilies, mace, cloves, turmeric, garlic, and mint all swirled in the air. He slid into the small booth, stealing a quick glance around and another at the Impala before resting his hands on the tabletop.

Weitzel dropped into place opposite the detective, his smile seeming to take up more room than his face could offer. "I am so glad you came, Detective. We've got lots to talk about."

"Do you mean an exchange of ideas and information, or did you invite me here to pick my brain and get the scoop on your competition in the more mainstream papers?"

"What? No, I mean I want you to know what I've found, and I hope you're willing to share a few things with me. I understand the ongoing investigation privacy and all. I...I think we're both after the same thing here."

"Yeah, what's that?"

"Justice for Abigail Huang and now for Charles Huang, as well."

Ryan nodded. "You have the red light on?"

Weitzel raised both hands and shook his head. "I'm not recording anything, I swear. If I am, you can punch me right in the face, and I know you study that whole karate thing." To emphasize his point, Weitzel turned sideways and feigned a series of punches.

"Whoa!" The waitress was nearing their table, carrying a tray with two glasses of water. Weitzel's impromptu MMA act nearly took her out. He glanced up, his eyes even wider than usual.

"I am so sorry. Let me help you with those."

Ryan was humored by the younger man's attempt to connect with him, but whatever research the kid had done was way off base. Ryan's black belt was in Brazilian Jiu-Jitsu, involving a lot of grabs, holds, strikes, and on-the-mat techniques, not kicking people and watching them fall down. He had discovered the art thanks to a roommate at Boot Camp, and learning close-quarters fighting had already saved his life at least three times.

The waitress allowed Weitzel to assist with getting the drinks. She regained her composure and her practiced smile and pulled out a pen and paper. "Good morning, gentlemen, would you like to hear the specials?"

Ryan shook his head, but Weitzel perked up with the curiosity of a puppy. She rattled off something about catfish. Ryan took the opportunity to steal another glance out at the Impala. The car was fine. Ryan's dreams of being behind the wheel usually involved him topping 140 mph in pursuit of a bad guy, but right now, he would be content in the driver's seat, even in the parked car.

"And for you, sir?" The waitress' tone brought Ryan back to the conversation.

"Pad See Ew with chicken, please, and some Larb Gai."

"Will that be it?"

"That will be fine, thanks," he replied with a grin. She half-bowed to their table before disappearing into the chaos. Ryan bet he would get five breaths in before Weitzel interrupted.

He got two.

"So, the official cause of death on Abigail Huang was asphyxiation from a broken neck, right? That was one hell of a header she took."

"Yeah, hard to survive a fall down a steep flight of stairs, much less those ones."

"Did you know that's exactly how the Father Karras character died in *The Exorcist*? Weird, huh?"

Ryan rubbed his forehead. "Chris, there isn't a resident or tourist who has been in DC for more than four minutes who doesn't know about those stairs.

Coincidence? No. Subconscious suggestion, maybe."

"Do you still think Charles threw Abigail down them?"

Ryan shook his head. Maybe once, but not on the trip that killed her. "That, I don't know. You know even if I did offer you information, the FBI has jurisdiction on this case."

"I heard this was Federal now. Must be frustrating."

"Actually, we're pleased to have additional resources allocated to the swift justice Abigail Huang deserves."

Weitzel grinned again. "You practice that line a lot."

"What gave me away?"

"I think it was the whole 'swift justice' thing. That's cliché, and you're not very good with cliché, detective."

Ryan smirked. "Thanks, kid."

They stared at one another in silence before the waitress broke the tension. She placed the appetizers they'd ordered on the table before them. Weitzel poured duck sauce over his egg rolls and shoved one into his mouth. Ryan put some of the shredded chicken onto his plate.

He devoured a few pieces as the reporter mounted a new strategy. "So, we all know most of the time, it's the husband. The problem with that theory is the husband was found murdered in the park. Where does that leave us?"

Ryan smiled. Chris had switched from you to us, an interesting transition. "I'll let you know once I hear the autopsy results. We have to confirm Charles Huang's murder before we start speculating on any link between his death and his wife's. For all we know, Charles killed her and ran into a random, desperate mugger in the park."

Weitzel nodded while chewing on his egg roll. He swallowed the first one and immediately dipped the second one in the sauce and popped it into his mouth. He chewed several times before he could even attempt to communicate his thoughts. With his mouth full, he continued, "I hope you're right, detective."

Ryan knew he wasn't right. He knew the hypothesis was crap, but he wanted to give Weitzel something quick, easy, and ready to print. Anything to get the ambitious kid off of his back.

"So, my question to you is this..."

Ryan stared at the reporter who seemed both full and hungry at the same time.

Christopher Weitzel, star reporter for *The Washington Insider* smiled, pieces of lettuce, onion, and other egg roll goodness between his teeth. "Did you talk to the boyfriend?"

"What boyfriend?" Ryan asked, his gaze focused on the news rat across the booth.

"That's just it, I don't know," Weitzel replied, dipping a finger into the remaining duck sauce on his plate and licking it clean. "Abigail wasn't exactly as pure as the driven snow, and Charles had anger management issues."

"If that's all you have, you made a very large, jump-the-shark leap to a conclusion."

Weitzel nodded. "Well, I have something. Look, detective, I told you, I want to share information, not pick your brain and get a headline out of it."

"Floating bullshit theories at me is a bad way to provide value, kid. You may want to regroup and revisit your strategy here."

"I'll tell you what I have, and I admit it isn't as much as I'd like. But..." Weitzel replied with a waving finger, "I have information you don't, and you have resources I don't. So, I'm looking at this as a win-win, eventually."

Ryan stared at the younger man, wondering silently how many secrets he would confess in the right choke hold.

"Does everything taste okay, gentlemen?"

Ryan glanced up. The waitress gave a recited yet uncomfortable smile at the two men. He offered a grin in response, as Weitzel chimed in about the fantastic recipe for the egg rolls and how he would love to learn how to cook them if he wasn't so clumsy in the kitchen. He swore the reporter's dialog had the same aftertaste as artificial sweeteners, but there was some substance to Weitzel's hypothesis. He smiled and played along.

The waitress departed, promising to check on their food. Ryan returned his gaze to the reporter. "Did you know Abigail Huang?"

"What, me? No!"

"Then why the interest, kid? This is a local homicide, probably some stupid lover's quarrel. Why poke your nose into it?"

Chris Weitzel leaned back and smiled. "Thank you."

Ryan shot a look across the table to remind him that breaking many of his bones was still a potential plan of action. Weitzel continued. "I told you before, you're not cliché. You're also not willing to think like me, which is very, very rare in cops. Reporters are always taught to think like cops, but cops think like, well, cops. You want to hear my angle. I love it."

"Then get to it, kid."

"I have two words, detective, Chandra Levy."

Ryan took a drink from his water, an eyebrow raised. "Levy was an intern who was killed in Rock Creek Park over a decade ago. What the hell does she have to do with this investigation?"

"Exactly," Weitzel replied, "There are over a hundred homicides a year in the District of Columbia, yet Levy's murder gained national coverage. Why?"

"Let me venture a guess. I'm going to say she was put center stage on the evening news once something came up about her involvement with a Senator."

Weitzel threw his arms up to emphasize the symbol for scoring a touchdown. "The detective is correct! Chandra Levy was another dead jogger until somebody linked her to Gary Condit."

"And eight years later, the courts decided he had nothing to do with it. What's your point?"

"I received a call six days ago, from an anonymous source. They didn't call the police. They called me. And what they told me made me pretty curious."

Ryan refrained from snapping. He was tired of playing the chess game, but Weitzel had something. Something he couldn't reach out and grab on his own. "What's that?"

Weitzel grinned. "Abigail Huang had a boyfriend, a steady on the side who she was seeing despite warnings from her jealous husband. Here's my thought on the matter, if he's a nobody, I walk away and let this case die. However, my anonymous caller suggested he might be somebody. Let me ask you this, detective…You know who is leaning into the Huang family business. I don't. Find the answer to my query. Was Abigail sleeping with someone newsworthy, or was this some suburbanite soccer mom hook-up? If it's not the new Chandra, I write one more article, and it's back page BS. However, if this is something big, and I have a hunch it is, you remember who gave you the lead."

Weitzel smiled and glanced to his side. An Asian busboy held the tray holding their entrees. The reporter grinned as he directed the silent server to put the right meals in front of each of them. "So, Detective Calder, do we have a deal?"

CHAPTER FIFTEEN

Virginia had colors DC didn't, visible even through the sprawling construction, which seemed unending. Ryan shifted into sixth, taking the Impala down Interstate 395 and out of the city. He stole a glimpse at the oncoming traffic. Thousands of cars moved feet at a time, then hit the brakes. Hybrids, electric, sports cars, sports utility vehicles, and motorcycles lined the northbound lanes as far as he could see. Washington, DC embraced many things--politics, history, sports, technology, but never the value of public transportation. The detective smiled at the misery of the army that commuted in and out of the nation's capital five days a week.

The heads-up display estimated his arrival at the FBI Academy in Quantico, Virginia, about half an hour away. He tapped a few buttons on the stereo, loaded a playlist and smiled when Billy Idol's "Rebel Yell" filled his speakers. Virginians treasured the history of the civil war, and he was certainly heading into Rebel territory. He pressed down on the accelerator and turned the music louder.

Ryan shut the door to the Impala and glanced around the Academy compound. The Academy was constructed on the United States Marine Corps base located at Quantico. He'd gone through the checkpoint, suffering severe déjà vu in the process and had made sure to keep his travel under the mandated 35 mph listed on the signs. MPs didn't take kindly to speeding. He passed through several guard gates, drove by the firing range, passed the training town known as Hogan's Alley, and now stood in the parking lot of one of the FBI's storied facilities.

Had things been different, Ryan might have gone to college, completed his degree and applied for work at the FBI. That wasn't the case. Ryan let his fractured relationship with his parents dictate his path. He'd enlisted in the Air Force, specialized in explosives ordnance disposal and behind-the-lines escape and survival techniques. He'd been an 18-year-old with a death wish. When his father died in a hit-and-run, he switched paths and decided not to re-up his time with the Air Force. Three months later, he was top of his class at the MPDC academy.

The smiling guard behind the bulletproof glass took his ID, phone and gun, issuing him a visitor badge. Hardly a minute later, Agent Felicia Simone pushed through the guarded doors, leveling her gaze at Ryan with a smile. "Thanks for coming, detective."

"Thanks for the invite, agent. I don't usually get a chance to leave my district."

Simone shoved the gate open, and Ryan stepped inside. "I wish I had some dynamic breakthrough on our case, Ryan, but I think you'll be disappointed with how routine the D.I.'s findings are."

Ryan followed her down the sterile hallway. The artificial lighting made her skin appear almost plastic. He wondered for a moment if she saw him the same way before he discarded such concerns. "Actually, that fits. I'm starting to think the real key to this case isn't a *how* question. It's a *why* question."

The pair entered an elevator framed in stainless steel. As the doors closed, Simone turned her large brown eyes to meet his gaze. "The anonymous shooter angle is off the table, then?"

"Not completely, but I don't think that's how this is going to go down in the record books."

A smile crept across her full lips. "You know something, Detective Calder. And, you're not sharing."

Ryan shrugged. "It's a theory, Agent Simone."

The elevator doors opened and she stepped out, stopping at a station to don a lab coat, gloves, and disposable face shield. Once she finished, she walked out of the far door into the lab, and Ryan entered the enclosed area. He donned the protective gear, waited for the green light and tone of approval and followed her into the lab buzzing with morticians.

Simone introduced Ryan to a short, wiry mortician named Vincent. After cursory introductions, Vincent began recounting his autopsy results. Ryan listened, but the outcomes fit closely to Simone's warning. Everything about the murder...and all signs pointed to murder...were cut and dry. Charles Huang was shot at zero range with a Beretta 10mm pistol. The gun was in his mouth at the time of his death. The angle indicated he was still standing when he was shot.

"What about the nitrate levels?" Ryan asked.

"Nitrate both inside and outside of the mouth, plus tissue damage, is a pretty clear indicator the gun was in his mouth. Based on the exit wound, we can confirm the shooter was slightly to Charles Huang's right, which is consistent with the missing left incisor. The blowback from a handgun would be enough to uproot his tooth."

Ryan shot the mortician a glance. "Did we find the incisor?"

Simone tapped her finger a few times against her touch screen and shook her head. "Negative. I can send a team back on site with that objective."

"Go for it, but I'm not sure it will do any good." Ryan stared at the corpse of Charles Huang. A thousand theories occupied his head.

"What are you thinking, Ryan?" Simone asked, studying him.

Ryan traced circles in the air with his gloved hands. "Let's flip the coin and start thinking differently. Remove Abigail from the equation completely. Say this was someone out for Charles. Maybe Abigail was the reason, maybe not." He stared back at Agent Simone. "If I'm going to kill Charles Huang, why am I going to do it in Little Falls Park?"

Simone took a moment before replying, "This place is special to us. It's where we met, or where you first kissed me, or where you asked me to marry you."

Ryan turned away, cursing under his breath. He stared at the wall for almost a full minute before replying. "I'll go do some digging on the Huangs. I'll find out where they met, or where they were engaged."

He glanced over his shoulder at Agent Simone. Her gaze was distant and distracted. Without another word, he left the FBI Academy morgue.

Ryan took several steps toward the Impala. He drank in the faint rays of the sun as he crossed the parking lot. Donning his Ray Ban sunglasses, he smiled. He would certainly fulfill his promise to investigate the Huang's dating history, but before he touched that information, something else needed resolution.

He tapped in a few variables, analyzing the resulting

contact list. Hector Gonzalez tracked every step of her last couple of weeks. He had even referenced a private investigator. Chris Weitzel had his nose in the case. Charles Huang had his own eyes on the case. Ryan stared at the still pictures taken by a private eye. His next chore was to find out where the shamus was, and who was funding his investigation.

"I told you, we need to increase security and yet, you're giving me a live, running feed of Detective Calder's whereabouts and conversations?" Shia's fingers tapped on the desk in an uneven pattern. The screen on the one side detailed everything, right down to how much he was sleeping or wasn't as the case may be.

"You asked if he had any breaks in the case, and you refuse to answer his calls."

"I reserve that right, he is not helping me hunt demons. Even so, that does not mean I want to know what he's doing every living breathing moment." A name popped up on the monitor. Who the hell was Agent Felicia Simone?

An image flashed on screen as if she'd asked the question aloud. Oh stars, she hadn't had she?

"FBI Special Agent, Felicia Simone. Height 5'8". Weight 147 pounds, brown hair, and brown eyes." Jace said.

Shia glared at the picture of the beautiful woman Jace provided. Skinny, if you asked her. She'd need more muscle to function as a samurai.

"She is of average in vision, hearing, physical, and mental testing according to FBI tests. Holds certifications in Arms and Defensive tactics. Her father is the deceased Energy Sciences mogul, Harrison Schechter. Her mother, alive, an actress. She has one sister and two brothers in the arts. She worked on several cases with Detective Calder in the past. The first case…"

Shia held up a hand. No, no, and no. "Stop. No, I don't want to know about past cases. I only want to know why is she involved in this case so I know how much clean up I'm going to have to do. And, stop streaming Ry—Detective Calder's actions."

The screen slid to a halt, with Agent Felicia Simone's face staring back at her. Great, just great. If she told him to turn it off, she'd never hear the end of it. She'd swear the AI had done it on purpose. That would teach her to fiddle with technology. Who knew a thousand year old samurai had mad programming skills? Whenever Ilsa asked, Shia retreated behind strategy and communications discussions to which the Scandinavian blonde quickly started to ignore her.

"Her records currently indicate she has declared Charles Huang was shot at zero range with a Beretta 10mm pistol in a Federally maintained space, which now makes it a joint investigation."

"She's reaching," Shia snapped. She tracked over the maps. No way the man had died outside their jurisdiction. The Agent wanted more and pushed her limits. Wonderful, so now she had to contend with the FBI and demons.

Many would say the two were one in the same.

CHAPTER SIXTEEN

"This is Dr. Shia Ronin. I am unavailable to take your call at the moment…"

Ryan cocked his arm and prepared to throw the phone across his apartment. He paused for a minute when her inflection changed, and he thought she'd joined the call. His hopes died with the same, routine message about a call back.

He was juggling too many chainsaws to be comfortable. Shia had come to his aid, and he had ditched her. As a result, she had been jumped and almost killed, and subsequently nowhere to be found. FBI agent Felicia Simone had invited herself back into his world and smack in the middle of his homicide investigation. Abigail Huang had taken a header down the Georgetown Exorcist stairs, but the primary suspect had eaten lead a few miles away in Little Falls Park. Ryan had nothing to work on, save the autopsy, a promise from a tabloid reporter, and instinct. He shook his head, tearing away from the video feed on his monitor.

Apparently, keeping track of women in his life, work or otherwise, was a stretch. He had a better track record with the dead ones. And, that wasn't saying a lot.

Ryan tapped the keyboard and pulled up the Huang file. He began going over the police reports previous to Abigail's death. The couple had a long history of verbal fights, and one particularly nosy neighbor. There were several photos, credited to a private investigator named Carl MacAdams. Ryan had reached out to the officers who had reported on scene, and they all had confirmed the reports. Gonzalez may be a fan of blowing things out of proportion, but the Huangs certainly could fight. He picked up the phone and called the third officer listed in the case file.

"Talbot."

"Hey, Jason, this is Detective Calder. We chatted a couple days ago about Abigail Huang."

"Sure, I remember, detective. Something come up?"

"Actually, something went down. Her husband was found dead from a gun shot wound."

Talbot made a hissing sound. "Damn. He was top of the suspect list, right?"

"Yeah," Ryan replied. "I would have liked the chance to ask him a few questions. Since I can't, I'd like to talk to anyone who had eyes on our loving couple."

"I'm happy to answer anything you'd like, detective. I've got several things on my desk. Court tomorrow."

"Thanks, and it's Ryan. I think we can skip the formalities. I didn't have too much to pick your brain on, except these pictures from the private eye. You remember those?"

"Yeah, though not well enough to comment on them without them in front of me."

"I have them. They're professional, and there are

several of the two fighting. Do you know who hired the guy?"

"My first guess would be the neighbor. We didn't actually talk to the photographer. The pictures were emailed in to us. We only traced them back to that Mac guy because he watermarked his shots. I guess he didn't want anyone else getting credit for his field work."

Ryan chuckled. "So much for the private side of private investigator, huh?"

"Yeah, I deal with the guy on too many occasions. He makes himself memorable, that's for sure."

"How so?"

"He's a real sleazebag. Think used car salesman without the moral code."

"Great, he's my next call."

"I figured. Save yourself some time afterward. Once you talk to this guy, you're going to want a shower."

The dingy office of Carl MacAdams was located in what appeared to be a condemned apartment house. Ryan parked the Impala in the lot of the adjacent auto parts store, noting the barred windows. The place was on H Street in Northeast DC, a few blocks from the Rock n' Roll Hotel. Ryan knew the area well enough. Every block had a Pho restaurant, a pawnshop, and a tattoo parlor.

Ryan stepped out of the Impala, set the alarm and checked his gun, his baton, and his pepper spray. With a quick glance around, he headed toward the two-level brick building. The windows had bars, exactly like the neighbors, and several on the ground floor were covered with plywood. The fire escape looked like it wouldn't hold a pigeon, and trash piled up against the walls, killing everything but the most tenacious weeds. Ryan opened the door to the lobby, which housed a staircase and a set of mailboxes. A hallway led into the dingy recesses past the stairs to a dentist's office and a nail salon. Ryan didn't need to investigate to know that both were probably ghost businesses acting as tax shelters for slumlords.

He glanced at the mailboxes and found the one he wanted. Office 202 listed MacAdams Investigation Services. Ryan walked up the stairs, down the hallway and stopped at the wooden door marked with the same inscription. He tried the knob, but it was locked. He knocked, but no one answered. He took a glance each way before dropping to a knee and pulling a small, black pouch off of his belt. He opened the pouch, prying out a few small pieces of metal. He put one between his teeth as he set two others into the lock. Seventy-three seconds later, he was inside office 202, tools in hand.

Ryan placed the lock picks carefully back into their designated slots. He walked into what he assumed to be a waiting room with four mismatched chairs and a stack of magazines nearly six months old. A small desk sat at the far end of the room. A blonde rubber doll with an O-shaped mouth wearing a red silk dress occupied the chair behind the desk. The nametag on the desk read "Lola Suckallyavitz: Director of Oral Relationships". Ryan stopped, glancing around for the candid camera that would indicate he had been suckered by his co-workers.

He passed the sex doll sitting at the desk to the lone door behind her. The door to Carl's office was open. Ryan walked in, struck instantly by the odor of stale cigarettes. Full ashtrays sat on the desk, the two filing cabinets, and even the small table separating the two visitor's chairs. Carl MacAdams was a smoker, and a slob. Papers lined his desk, and a set of folders over a foot deep rested next to the keyboard for his computer.

Ryan circled around the desk. He grabbed a couple of tissues from a dusty box atop one of the filing cabinets and used them to shield his fingerprints as moved the mouse. The monitor sprang to life, complete with a screen saver of Hollywood starlet Vivian Valenzcova in lingerie. The pop up blinked to life, looking for a biometric match, or a password. Ryan didn't have enough to go on to guess at Carl's passwords. He glanced at the ashtray, formulating how to engineer a fingerprint from one of the recently smoked cigarettes.

A woman's voice stopped him cold. "Don't move. I have a gun, and I have been known to aerate intruders like the greens on a private Country Club."

Ryan gritted his teeth and raised his hands. A stout, short woman dressed in a kimono filled the office door. Her face was shielded from view by an Oriental peasant hat. Her left hand extended toward him, holding a Beretta.

"I'm here to see Carl MacAdams," Ryan began, trying to get details on the figure in the door. "He's working on a case I'm assigned to. I want to ask him a few questions."

The Asian woman stopped. The revolver leveled at Ryan's chest for several long seconds before the figure lowered it. "Why didn't you say so," the Kimono-laden stranger replied in a thick, deep, New York accent. "Sit down. Let's talk." The stout figure raised its head, and Ryan stared face-to-face with Carl MacAdams, private investigator and owner of MacAdams Investigative Services.

"Why the hat and Kimono?" Ryan asked from his spot in the visitor's chair across from Carl's desk. He took a sip from the bottle of Sapporo beer Carl had offered him.

"I was working a case in Chinatown. I had to pretend to be a woman working a cart selling fish heads. That's not easy, trust me."

Ryan nodded, and then raised an eyebrow. "What about the mustache?"

Carl pointed to the mustache he had penciled in with mascara. "Well, I wasn't sure when I'd need to be an Asian guy, too."

"What?"

"You know. Asian guys are short. I figured I could ditch the robe and make do with the hat."

Ryan stared at the shorter man and then shook his head. "Your website lists you as a former linebacker with the Jacksonville Jaguars. I'm going to go out on a whim here and say that's a load of crap."

Carl laughed out loud. "Wow, you went to my site? I should pay you. No one goes to my site. I hardly even get spam. That Jacksonville stuff? Come on. No one has followed the Jaguars since they were brought into the league. Why not post something no one will ever check? My marketing guy said it was pure gold...before I fired him for his rate."

"I played ball in high school, MacAdams. JV linebackers are bigger than you."

The private investigator raised his finger in warning. "Easy, there, detective. I might have been a great linebacker in my day."

Ryan shook his head. "You've never tackled anybody bigger than the Marlboro Man. Give up the marketing bullshit and let's talk about Abigail and Charles Huang."

Carl MacAdams stopped. He opened the top drawer of his desk, opened up a case of baby wipes and wiped the black mustache off of his face. When he finished cleaning up and removing his disguise, he was a short, stout snoop with a million ways to explain everything away. "Wang? That was the couple in Georgetown, right?"

Ryan nodded. "She was murdered. Every indication points to the husband."

"Well, it should. He was a jealous bastard. I think I have shots of him slapping her around. It makes sense he would go off the deep end and kill his flirtatious little flower."

"Flirtatious?"

MacAdams nodded. "Abigail Huang had something on the side, while her ambitious husband was off climbing the corporate food chain." He slid a few photos across the desk. Ryan flicked a quick glance at the spread. They were the same photos he had already seen in the case file.

"You're wasting my time, Carl." He said, standing. "I've seen these already, complete with your watermark."

The sneaky private eye smiled up at the detective. "So, what you've seen is every ounce of what I was paid to discover. Abigail and Charles Huang weren't exactly the picture of a content family in modern day America. They had issues."

"So, where's the rest?"

Carl leaned back in his chair. "I like you, detective. I'll make you the same offer I made my client. Double my fee, and you can have the pics I took that I haven't shared." He crossed his arms. "I am a business man, after all. I have information you will certainly find worth the investment. Now, make the investment."

Ryan was on his feet before the smirk ever left Carl's face. He reached over the desk and grabbed the shorter man, pulling him around the side of the desk and knocking over an ashtray. "Hey," Carl shouted, but Ryan didn't stop. He shoved Carl through the open window leading to the fire escape. The private eye struck the wrought iron, and he let out a grunt. Slumped against the rail, he raised his gaze. "You're an idiot. I offered the old man the same deal, and he begged he was out of money. I know what you want to know, and now you decide you're gonna take the tough guy route? Don't be stupid."

Ryan followed Carl out onto the fire escape, stealing a glance downward, wondering if it would hold his weight.

"Don't worry. It's stronger than it looks."

"Had a lot of fires in this building, Carl?"

The P.I. grinned back. "No, but I have had plenty of angry clients banging on the front door. This isn't my first trip down the back way to the alley."

"I have mace, a baton and a pistol. I can use any of them to ensure you start talking to me about your clientele before you hit the ground. Let me ask you, Carl, how do you want to play this?"

MacAdams stopped, wiping ashes off of his shirt. "I found you breaking and entering into my office, and then you assaulted me, and are now harassing me for information. You can go find a polite judge this time of day, and get them to issue a warrant, but by the time you do, me, my computer, and all the information on your dead Asian girl will be long gone and far away. So, let me repeat my offer one more time, detective."

"Pay me, or the information on Abigail Huang goes bye-bye forever."

CHAPTER SEVENTEEN

Ryan raced back west through traffic, picking up a little more road rage with each block. The Scorpions' "Blackout" filled the Impala interior with the electric guitar sounds of Schenker and Jabs, and Klaus Meine's piercing vocals. The smart thing would have been to put on something lighter, but Ryan was working on a string of making the wrong decisions. This was just the latest.

He tapped his shirt pocket, which held the encrypted thumb drive he'd bought from Carl MacAdams. Ryan hated extortion, and he would certainly make Carl pay for this in spades, but right now, the chubby investigator was the only thing between Ryan and the reason for the murders of Abigail and Charles Huang. At least Carl tried to haggle a bit. Ryan made the sneaky bastard show him some of the supposed 200 additional photos before paying him. He considered calling the credit card company and claiming identity theft.

The Scorpions gave way to Jethro Tull's deep cut, "Fat Man," and Ryan laughed. Sometimes he wondered if the Impala had a mind of its own. If he was going to believe that, he might as well consider that Father Munoz's miracle claims were real. He shook his head and stepped on the accelerator.

He reached the station about twenty minutes later and tried to call Shia again before going inside. The cell phone he had recovered died. He hoped she'd replaced it and would pick up when he called. When the familiar delivery of her voice mail reached his ears, he tried a different tactic. He left a message apologizing, again, but mentioning he'd heard she was under the weather and offered to pick up any groceries or medicine she might need. He killed the phone, checked for his messages and headed into the station.

He poured a cup of coffee on the way to his desk. The label on the pot read "Kona," which meant Hawaii Bill was in the office. Thank God for a small miracle. This stuff was potent and actually had a taste other than tooth decay. He sat in his desk chair and noticed a blinking message light on his phone. He picked up the receiver, tapped the pass code, and listened.

"Hey, killer, it's Felicia. I was thinking about some of what you were saying today. I'm going to have my people speak with Huang's co-workers and maybe go over his desk. I know you're working your angle, so I'll work this one. Loser buys dinner. Winner picks the place. Ciao!"

Ryan hung up the phone. Felicia Simone's contests were mandatory. She determined the rules, the spoils, and had yet to lose one, which meant she either already had information, or she figured he was working a dead end. He was back up to deductive reasoning 101 with his theory, but maybe he had an ace in the hole in Carl's photos. He reached into his pocket and plugged the drive into his laptop. He stole a sip of coffee as the files scanned for malicious code, cursing under his breath when it burned the roof of his mouth.

The security software finished its scan and presented the pictures. Ryan clicked on the first, and the slideshow began. He leaned forward, blew on his Kona coffee, and studied each scene as it unfolded. The first dozen or so were shots from the same events as the photos he had already seen. The next thirty were more pictures of the Huangs arguing, at home, at a class reunion, and at a friend of Abigail's engagement party.

Ryan's desk phone rang, and he paused the slideshow. He looked at his phone, but it displayed "Unknown Caller." Never promising. He picked it up. "Calder."

"I wanted to thank you for doing business, detective. I understand we didn't exactly hit it off, but I'm glad we could come to an agreement."

"MacAdams, why don't you go back home to whatever bridge you live under and stick with your career of scaring small children."

The private eye laughed loudly, and Ryan pulled the receiver away from his ear. "That's good, detective. I may have to steal that one. I have this old lady client right now, worried her pet parakeets are speaking with aliens. Shit, I should write that down."

Ryan gritted his teeth. "What do you want, MacAdams?"

"What do I want? Oh, nothing, I read somewhere the fortune is in the follow-up, and I wanted to call to follow up."

"Carl."

"Yeah?"

"Be careful next time you try your fire escape. You never know when something might give out on you." Ryan slammed the phone back to the cradle. He ran a hand through his hair and reached for his coffee. For a moment, he indulged in the idea of pouring a steaming hot pot of Kona coffee on Carl MacAdams's head. He sighed, content with the commitment to remove a few bolts from the fire escape.

Ryan took a sip of coffee and started the slideshow again.

The pictures covered one more fight in the front yard before switching again. This time, the scene remained the same, but the cast changed. Abigail was still in the frame, but the man was different. He was thinner than Charles, dressed in a dark suit. His back was turned from the lens, and with the night vision, impossible to determine his skin and hair color. The slide show covered nine pictures from that rendezvous, and then more day time photos of Charles leaving for work and Abigail waving from the window.

"Damn," Ryan cursed, flipping through several more shots. After another twenty, Abigail and the man in the dark suit shared the frame again. She was leaning out of the side door, wearing a robe. The strap of a fire engine red bra was visible on her shoulder. The man wore the same black suit, and the light revealed he had black hair, too dark to be natural. Two more pictures, and the man turned, his face clearly noticeable in the frame.

Ryan nodded, clicking open the facial recognition software. "Alright, you mysterious little bastard, who the hell are you?"

Ryan spent twenty minutes on the video analysis, zooming and adjusting the camera focus to capture the facial view of the black-haired man in the shot. When he was satisfied with the results, he saved the image and clicked export. He entered the isolated shot of the man's face, tapped in his credentials and began running the image against the Violent Criminal Apprehension Program, ViCap.

The program started its pattern match, and Ryan

walked away, returning to the break area to refill his cold coffee mug. He had seen the man's face before. He needed the computer to confirm he'd seen the man during a previous bust. He returned to his desk as the program sorted through tens of thousands of mug shots.

He wanted to call Shia. No, he wanted to talk to Shia. He'd called her more times than he could count. Instead, he dialed Father Munoz. The pastor picked up after one ring. "Hello and blessings, this is Father Salvador Munoz."

"Hey, Padre, how are you feeling today?"

"I am well, Mijo. I have been in prayer much of this morning. Your ears must be burning."

"I'm glad you're looking out for me. You haven't heard from Dr. Ronin by any chance, have you?"

The old man sighed. "If you are asking, then you have not spoken with her either. I am sorry that is the case."

"I went to see her at work. She's out for the entire week. I left a couple...well, a bunch of messages, and I haven't heard back from her. You sure she was all right when she left the hospital?"

"Of that, I am certain, Mijo. I cannot explain how, but Shia's wounds were almost gone when she woke."

"It's...I deal with death every day, Padre. I hope you're right. The thought of her having some sort of internal bleeding relapse or passing out...there's too much out there, you know?"

"I know," the pastor replied in his friendly tone. "Ryan, you're a detective. Be a detective. You can find her if you try."

Ryan chuckled. "Alright, alright, I get the hint. Thanks for the advice, Father."

"Be well and be blessed, Mijo!"

Ryan hung up the phone. He shook his head at the old

man's words. "Be a detective." He enabled notifications on the computer. If the system found a match for his new person of interest in the database, he'd get the details via a text on his phone, and the computer in the Impala. Grabbing his coffee, Ryan pushed away from the desk and returned to the hunt.

Shellie stirred out of the darkness as a soft rap sounded at the chalet door. Sleep had finally overridden her desire to continue the hunt for the child. She'd started misreading signs and almost stumbled upon a momma cougar protecting her cubs. She'd quickly retreated to rest knowing she was doing the girl and herself no good in her current state. She'd left telltale traps to help her indicate the pattern of the Rissu's movement.

The knock echoed again, more insistent this time. She shook her head to clear it, glancing at the clock, quarter past eleven, at night. Who the hell?

"Shellie, open this door before I do so with my claws." A familiar hiss sounded through the oak.

She darted out of bed and across the chalet in a blink of an eye, her hands unlocking and swinging the door open. "What are you doing here? How did you find…?"

The tiny Asian girl darted into the room and closed and locked the door behind her. "Shush, there are eyes watching you. What took you so long?" The girl shoved a backpack at her. "Here, this is yours."

Shellie reached out automatically to grab the pack although her head clouded with sleep from moments before. "Eyes on me? How did you know where to find me?"

"Jace, Shia." Taji nodded to the pack and walked over to peek out the windows. "Why is there a large shifter trailing you?"

"A large what?" Shellie shot her a confused look.

Taji's almond eyes cut her a glance. She was always amazed at how such a small woman could convey so much expression with her face and body.

"Like me, only larger, and male."

She hadn't stumbled into a male in her tracking, only the female cougar and her cubs. Were they shifters too? She moved over to Taji's side.

"He's up in the tree and dark, very dark. You might only be able to see…"

"I see him now." Shellie stopped her. She stepped back and blew at a stray strand of hair. "I wonder how long he's been out there."

"I followed his trail from the state line then to another chalet." Taji turned from the window and closed the drapes before dropping into a nearby chair. She kicked her feet up over the side and leaned back, fitting her tiny form almost perfectly into the cushions.

Shellie bit her lip and turned back to the coffee table, sitting down on the couch. "We'll figure him out later. I haven't had time to reconfigure or check in."

"So we noticed. New cell phone, new laptop." Taji cracked her jaw. "New tracking device, which might even show your new buddy out there." She flicked a thumb towards the window.

Shellie shook her head. "I have no idea who he is, so long as he isn't Rissu and after the child too. Hopefully, he'll stay out of my way and I his."

"You mean our way." Taji kicked her foot back and forth, a smile deep in her eyes.

"Good, you can help me get the demon away from the girl. He's dog-like, maybe he'll like your cat nature better." Shellie slanted her a wicked grin.

Taji stuck her tongue out. "Perhaps he'll like your big shifter more."

"He is not my...."

Taji winked at her. Shellie closed her mouth and went about setting up all her new gadgets.

"Going twice...Sold!" The auctioneer put gavel to base with a smile. "The winning bid is $550,000 to bidder number 1327. Thank you for your generosity."

The bidder, a burly man in a cowboy hat too big for him and a suit jacket a size too small smiled a big smile at his trophy wife. She smiled back and patted his chest. The pearls would go great with her Alexander McQueen knit dress. So, she'd have to trade sex for treasure with the big cowboy. She'd learned a long time ago how to play the game.

Near the back of the room, a man in a dark Zanetti suit lowered his bidding number to his lap and watched the couple through dark sunglasses. He made a quiet comment to the large man next to him, who immediately rose and left the auction room. The auctioneer began speaking about the next item, an original portrait of blues legend "Blind" J.J. McClain.

The over-sized cowboy put his feet up on the glass coffee table, grabbed the remote and searched for SportsCenter. "I can't believe how lucky we were tonight, sweetheart," he called over his shoulder to the bathroom. He pictured his sweet young thang in the bubble bath and smiled wide. She'd made him promise no peeking, but that meant plenty of peaking once she was in the mood.

"I know," she replied. "They handed you everything

163

you wanted tonight!"

He laughed in reply. "Not quite everything."

"You bad boy," she called back.

He grinned. That wasn't what he had meant, but if she had her mind on something fun, who was he to correct her?

A knock at the door interrupted his adult-themed daydream. "Room service."

"About fuckin' time," he muttered as he stood up. The fancy hotel set made a lot of sense for business posturing, but it certainly left a lot of little pleasures off the list. He knew he would have to arrange a "special order" for a simple 12-pack of his favorite beer, Austin Lager, even though the valets were probably drinking it in the back of the parking garage. Whatever, he was rich, and had oil, art, horses, and women. Paying a little more for a smooth beer never killed anyone.

He opened the door as the knocking began again. "Hold your horses, goddammit."

A big man in a suit stood outside his door.

"What the..."

The large man punched the cowboy in the mouth, knocking him off his feet and back into the room. He stepped in, drawing a polished, high caliber revolver from his shoulder holster. He raised a finger to his lips and smirked.

The cowboy rubbed his jaw, forcing himself up to an elbow. "What do you...?"

The bruiser kicked his leg and again raised a finger to his lips.

"What do you want?" he replied in a whisper.

The bruiser walked past him, stepping to the bathroom door and pulling it shut quietly. A smaller man in a dark, expensive suit stepped in to the room, closing the door behind him. "Good evening, Mr. Conrad."

"Who are you? What do you want?"

"I came to congratulate you. You were quite successful at the auction this evening." The smaller man tugged on his lapel, straightening his jacket.

"Is this about something I bid on? I'm sure we can work out a deal. I ain't unreasonable." He pushed up to one knee. "Hell, call off your muscle there, and we can negotiate all you like."

"I like that idea." The dark man smiled. He gestured with an open palm.

Buck Conrad, sixth generation cowboy and ranch owner, rose to his feet. "So, who exactly am I..."

His voice died in mid-sentence, cut off by the tight grip around his throat. He flailed his arms at the bruiser behind him, but couldn't find leverage. He tried to find balance, but the giant simply tugged him wherever he wanted to go. He stumbled backward. In front of him, the dark man followed step by step. "My name is Alexander Spiros, Mr. Conrad. You purchased something tonight, something I believe I own. I simply hate it when someone claims ownership of things that are mine."

The dark man smiled a sinister grin. "That's bad for business. You understand, of course." He nodded, and Buck Conrad left his feet. He heard the sound of shattering glass before he recognized the tears in his face and across his skin. And then the falling...the falling.

He screamed.

CHAPTER EIGHTEEN

Knock, knock.

Ryan took a step back from the door to apartment 803, getting no response the first two times he knocked. He wasn't expecting much with the third. No footsteps, music, electronics, or other signs of life sounded from the apartment. If Shia was home, she was quieter than the residents in her morgue. He knocked one more time, then reached the pouch on his belt housing his lock picks.

"Are you here to view the rental property?" Ryan glanced over his shoulder to find a small woman with a big smile and bigger hair approaching him. She extended a hand in greeting. Her false eyelashes fluttered up at him. "I have a couple scheduled to come by and see it, but they're not due for another 45 minutes. I came over early to freshen the place up a bit."

Ryan raised an eyebrow and shook her hand. "I'd love a look inside, miss...?"

"Miss Rachel Mae Mickens, Lone Star Realty. What's your name, darling?"

"Philip Marlowe. I'm looking for a place with a little space."

"Well, how precious," she replied in a Southern accent so tangible Ryan could chew it. "Are you new to the area?"

"I'm returning, been overseas. Government stuff." He faked a grin.

Rachel Mae unlocked the door, and it swung open. "Well, let us check out your new abode, Mr. Marlowe."

Ryan took two steps in and scanned the place. It was clean, beyond clean. It was empty. "This place been empty long?"

"A few days."

"Looks brand new, like nobody ever lived here."

The Realtor chucked, even as she stepped to the small table by the door and shuffled through the stack of her competitors' business cards. "I must say the previous tenant did a wonderful job of cleaning up."

"Yeah, real professional job. Somebody get killed here?"

"Excuse me?" the Southern belle replied with a wide-eyed stare.

"Oh, I saw this thing on TV where these guys come in and make a crime scene look like a new place. Real shoot-em-up stuff." He accented his story by pointing his fingers forward like guns.

"Oh, no," she said, disarming any concerns. "Nothing like that, I assure you."

"Cool. I like the layout. I know my band is going to love jamming in the big room with the windows."

"Your band?"

"Yeah, Mikey Mayhem and the Rocking Rebels. Ever heard of us?"

Rachel Mae whitened a bit. "Well, there is an, um, noise ordinance in this district. I don't know if you'd be able to have a full band performing in here."

"Shoot, it doesn't bother the dogs too much."

"Dogs?"

"Yeah, our huntin' dogs, Butch and Mongo. Want to see a picture?" Ryan reached for his back pocket.

"No, no, that won't be necessary," she replied, hands in front to shield her. "The owners have a strict 'No Pets' policy here, Mr. Marlowe. I think you would have to find other shelter for your hunting dogs."

"What? No music and no dogs? Next you're going to tell me I can't throw my Friday night swinger parties here!"

Ryan wasn't sure he had a word to describe the color of Rachel Mae's shocked face by the time he left. Part of him wanted to stick around to watch her show the house to the next couple, but pressing business won out over sadistic fun. Shia's apartment was a few blocks from his, and he had a designated space at his place. He walked to her place, rather than fight for a parking spot or listen to residents moan when he parked next to the hydrant.

The thoughts in his head bounced back and forth between Shia's sudden disappearance and the mystery man in the Huang case. Weitzel's hunch turned out to be right, but MacAdams had said he had offered to sell the photos to the old man. Weitzel hadn't hired him. Odds were it was Hector Gonzalez, but Ryan had been too pissed at MacAdams to ask him.

Shia had taken a week off from work, but her apartment was completely worked over. Was that her work, or someone trying to cover up abducting her? Did she know the people after her, and did they know where she lived? Was any of it tied into Father Munoz's bizarre account of her quick exit from the hospital? The only way to find out was to find her.

He rounded the corner back onto his street and started as something bounced his way. He realized it was a tennis ball and managed to grab it before it went into the street. He turned to see where it had come from and was greeted by an over-sized Rottweiler. Off-balance, Ryan tumbled to the ground beneath the weight of the big puppy. The dog licked at his face, and then began chewing on the ball, trying to get it out of his hand.

A woman's voice called from halfway down the block. "Joseph! Joseph, you get off that man right now!"

Ryan tried to formulate a thought, but getting tackled on the concrete made clarity a distant dream. He let go of the tennis ball, and the dog grabbed it in his teeth and trotted back in the direction he came. Ryan turned onto his side, leaning on his elbow as the world stopped spinning.

"I am so sorry. Please forgive my silly Joseph. He gets so excited. Oh, my stars, it's you, Detective!"

Ryan squinted one eye up and stared face to face with the woman from apartment 4-G. "How are you, Mrs. Bradbury?"

She reached down to help him up. He felt like a ton of wobbly bricks as he found his feet. "You got your dog back."

"Yes. He's been so happy to be back home. Please do thank your girlfriend again for me. She was so sweet to bring him home. He even has his collar!"

Ryan rubbed the back of his neck. "My girlfriend, Mrs. Bradbury?"

"Yes, yes, that lovely dark-haired girl, she said you

two work together, a very nice woman."

"You mean Shia? I mean Dr. Ronin?"

"Doctor? Well, I don't know about that. I don't recall her ever saying she was a doctor. I assumed she was your partner, or maybe a yoga instructor. She's so tiny. Anyway, she was very kind to bring Joseph back home."

"When did she do that?"

"Why, Saturday, it was Saturday, she was elegantly dressed, like she was going to some formal event, maybe one of those ribbon-cutting things? I thought you would know. Don't you two see each other every day?"

Ryan sighed. "It's complicated. I'm glad you and Joe are back together. I can't wait to hear the two of you at our next neighborhood karaoke tournament."

She laughed and patted his arm. "You're so funny, detective."

"Thanks, Mrs. B. I do my best."

He walked her back toward the apartment building, half-listening as she talked about some upcoming super box set that had previously unreleased live concert footage. He'd been out chasing Shia, and she had been right under his nose. He watched Mrs. Bradbury walk Joe into her apartment before turning away with a scowl.

Shia couldn't have gone far. She had taken a week away from work, not a transfer, so she must have intended to stick around. She'd even managed to find Joe and returned him to his number one fan. If she was willing to go that far for the old lady, maybe she'd risk checking up on her and the pooch as well.

Ryan walked the stairs toward his apartment. "Alright, Dr. Ronin, I don't know what you have up your sleeve, but I plan on finding out."

Shia tapped an answer on the keyboard. The music fell silent throughout the warehouse. "I see Taji made record time." She'd wanted to get her evening rounds started, but needed to wait until they had Shellie officially back on the grid.

"Thank you," The healer-tracker sounded embarrassed. "I lost my phone during the fight with the Rissu in Reno."

"It's a frequent occurrence with this particular outbreak." Shia smiled. She couldn't fault the Irish sister. "Did Taj explain the situation?"

"Yes." Taji's image appeared behind Shellie's. The petite Asian wiggled her fingers over the red head's shoulder. "We have everything set up here, and it looks like I can track both energy signatures much better from the closer range."

"Good, exactly what we were hoping." Shia started to shut down the other screens around her. "That means I can get back to my tracking."

She stopped at Shellie's silence. "Yes?"

"Well, there's a male shifter here too. I'm not sure who he's tracking." Shellie frowned.

A faint, "He's tracking Shellie." Came from the background.

Shia stilled. "He's tracking you?"

The other sister shook her head. "No, I mean I don't know. I stumbled onto a mother panther and her cubs, perhaps he's guarding them. We'll be careful. With Taji here, I can always send her out to talk to him."

"She hasn't already?" Shia asked.

"He's not wanting to talk to me. Pretty sure, pretty boy is only going to talk to her," the voice called out again.

Shia ran a hand over her face. Sometimes, the shifter

samurai could get a little too playful in her antics. She blamed her cat like nature.

"If it's safe, find out what the male wants. They rarely approach us. But more importantly, find Sierra and get her to safety." Shia stared hard at the healer who nodded and bowed her head.

"It will be done."

The video clicked off.

Shia sat back in her chair and took a deep breath. One homicide detective, an untold number of Rissu, three potential new samurai, one of them a child to keep safe, the FBI and now a shifter? Someone ripped open the fabric of time and space and decided to dump it all in her lap.

She needed a moment, too bad she couldn't take one.

"Calder." He answered on the first ring.

"Still burning the midnight oil on behalf of the Huangs, Detective?"

Ryan shook his head. "Yes, Agent Simone, I am. You wouldn't believe the stupid paths this case has me running down."

"Anything dirtier than ruining a tuxedo walking through mud in the park?"

"Much dirtier, thank you."

Simone replied with a laugh. "Care to tell me over dinner?"

"I would love to, Felicia, any night but tonight."

"Ouch. You're a real tease sometimes, Ryan."

"I have something I have to do for a neighbor. It's lame. I don't even want to explain it, let me make it up to you." He squeezed his eyes shut the moment the words left his mouth.

"Well, that at least sounds promising." Felicia took a breath and changed topics. "Had any luck chasing the case history?"

Ryan exhaled away from the phone, grateful to be talking shop. "Actually, I may have something. I'm running some info through the databases now. If I get a hit, I'll let you know where to buy me dinner."

"Oh, getting cocky, are we, Detective? Which databases?"

"If I tell you that, you'll know what I have, and that is cheating."

She feigned offense. "That's not cheating! That's using my resources."

"I've got a few things I need to do tonight. If I get a hit, I'll call you and gloat. If I don't, I'll share what I have with you first thing in the morning. You can use your resources then."

"I'd rather be using them tonight."

Ryan shook his head and bypassed his first few replies. "Tonight, if I get something. Tomorrow, if I don't."

"First thing."

"First thing, yes." He agreed.

"I'll be waiting."

"Goodnight, Felicia."

He could sense her smile in reply. "Good night for now, Ryan."

Ryan hung up the phone. Talking with Carl MacAdams had made him want a shower. Talking with Felicia? He wanted a cigarette. He slugged down the remaining half-can of Rev3 and checked his watch. He didn't have the timing mesmerized, but he knew Shia would be by soon, unless she was hurt, and unable to complete her nightly run. It was a chance, but it was one he was willing to take. He grabbed his jacket and headed for the door.

CHAPTER NINETEEN

Shia slid the heavy metal door to the warehouse shut as quietly as she could. She put her shoulder into the steel with a satisfied grunt. Nothing about metal on metal made her exit subtle, but since she was the only one in the old warehouse district at this time of night, she didn't mind the noise. Jace offered to restructure it, for silent closure, but somehow, the connection to cool metal and the sounds reconnected her, keeping her bound to this space and time. And the noise cut through the scurrying of rats and kept her on her toes. She needed the distraction from her dreams and all the Universe had currently put on her plate. She wanted to focus on the here and now, not the past, or what could be, or even what was going on in the western part of the continent. She trusted her sisters to do their jobs while she took care of finding the Rissu's portal.

She shivered. She never should have left her little nest here. The old warehouse hid her far away from prying eyes. Her secrets remained hers. When she had the time and resources, she made sure those hiding outside had enough food and clothes to survive the harshest of elements. A few times she'd rearranged the inside bays to allow safe haven during the storms. She didn't hide as much as she did in the condo. Those living in the shadows here had their own secrets to keep. They wouldn't betrayed hers.

No matter how often she opened the doors, they never stayed. Somehow, they respected and kept her secret. So in kind, she left out food, clothes, meds when needed. No one ever ventured further into her space. She'd have let them in, but they'd have never understood. Jace maintained a close and tight monitor on her haven. During snowstorms, he cranked up the heat and shifted the air ducts to allow those nearby to benefit. She'd restructured several vents permanently so she heated a small outside city during the winter months.

In return, she had the most unusual gifts appear.

Ilsa would kill her. She'd never mention the small homeless city to her or the others. They all had their secrets.

Tonight, soft black hand-woven, fingerless gloves nestled in the corner of her entry way, long ones, flowed up the wrist. She smiled and pulled them on. Neither warmth nor the cold bothered her, but the gloves gave her added protection, leaving her hands and fingers free enough to move.

Her shadows knew a little more than she expected.

"Thank you," she whispered into the night. She didn't care if they heard. Had her secret been in jeopardy, she'd have moved long ago. This pattern of safety, haven, established centuries earlier. She wasn't about to restructure for society's sake.

They'd build around her as they most often did. She held the land and zoning contracts on the surrounding district, although finding the records would take someone decades of digging to figure all her layers of planning and purchases. She hid her tracks.

"Careful, m'lady," Jace said in her ear.

She smirked. Careful her...never mind.

She'd been running these streets for centuries, not a twist or turn she didn't know. She knew exactly how many homeless lived in her alleyway, three families, nine singles to be exact, how many ventured in and how many left. No crime occurred on her streets, no imbalance. She didn't tolerate it, and somehow, it was known. She was good with that. She remained aware of the patrols, the surveys, the interest, and the decline. She made sure they had shelter when necessary and food when their resources dwindled.

Those who lived in the shadows of her warehouse came because of safe haven. No demon sulked nearby. Jace monitored their home carefully, as she did in her senses, in the people left to the dredges of society. She'd learned long ago where to hide. Those deemed unfit for civilization had the best otherworldly sight. They recognized her and the others.

She flipped the dark hood up over her head and shrugged her shoulders to make certain her swords settled into place. After a quick glance around to check the darkness, she set out at a steady jog. She'd had to start her route earlier since she'd moved back into her warehouse. This kept the humans in her previous building safe. Jace sterilized the entire area so no scent or trace of her remained. She didn't want some unsuspecting soul snaring the Rissu's interest. She had enough deaths on her hands because of the demons.

"You know, you may have lost your phone, but Detective Ryan keeps leaving messages?" Jace commented.

She thought about dropping the ear bud in the nearest

sewer drain. Jace was the most annoying conscience. She sighed, steadying her pace. Her gaze shifted, picking up more and more of the night.

"And?" She'd removed herself from her human life for the week. She needed to focus on the other realms. Ryan played no part in her samurai realm. He'd never get near the creatures, understand the levels of existence functioning around them. She refused to allow the insanity of it all to touch him. She'd moved quickly so the Rissu wouldn't track him. Her chest tightened at the thought of the demons harming him.

She mentally shook herself. Human emotion no longer graced her abilities. She wasn't allowed to care about one human being, she cared about all of them. She frowned. If the Rissu targeted him, she would put herself in its path as a willing victim before she would let a demonic death take him.

She hadn't thrown herself so thoughtlessly into another's path since her master commanded her to leave him on the field of battle. No one other than her sisters warranted that kind of reaction, but this one human detective, he put more thought, focus and conscience into everything he did than anyone she'd met. Well, outside her sisters.

"This time he offered to get you groceries."

Her stride faltered before resuming a steady pace. "What?"

"Yes. He's also been by the condo several times. Joe ran over him chasing a ball as well."

"And did the dog do as he was supposed to?"

"Yes, he recognized the Detective as family and drooled all over him."

"Good." She shouldn't be relieved. She was. He wanted to get her groceries? No one offered anything of the kind before, not even one of her sisters.

"You haven't acknowledged, he is still searching for you."

"He's human. I'm not." She forced herself to resume her path, her tracking. She would not let the thoughts of him derail her. She had a job to do.

"He's not going to be able to deal with my realm. You should know the calculations never work," she said. Since she wasn't trying to hide from the Rissu, and the night bent naturally around her, she wasn't worried about human detection.

"Well m'lady, …if you calculate for the chaos theory..."

She stopped on the corner of Ryan's street. She'd been on auto pilot, safe in her run, her sweep. She did not need the discussion, the sidetrack, "We are not working on a chaos theory here, Jace. We are dealing with..."

"Leaving town, Dr. Ronin?"

"By all that's holy." Her head whipped to the sound of Detective Calder's voice. He could see her? She'd bent the darkness around her, hidden from human perception. Had she been so deep in her conversation with Jace that she'd miscalculated? What else had she missed? Wait, what? "I'm not going anywhere, Detective. Do you always sulk about in the night?"

Ryan exhaled and lowered the flashlight. "If you call walking out of my building sulking, then, yeah, I'm guilty. I can't say I'm thrilled you're talking out loud to the voices in your head, but I can say I'm glad you chose my sidewalk as the scene for your conversation."

She bit down on the inside of her cheek. He'd heard had he? He shouldn't have even noticed her.

"We all talk to ourselves at times, Detective. I'm sure you've had those conversations on more than one occasion." She stuffed her hands in her jacket pockets, but kept her eyes and senses focused on the other worlds around them.

She wasn't going to let the Rissu surprise her again. Her side still ached.

He stared at her for a few long moments. "You have every right to be pissed at me. I'm sorry for screwing up last Saturday night, but you could have at least called me back and let me know what was going on."

"Called you back?" She laughed. "My phone is long gone in Father Munoz's alley. I got all your messages leading up to the gala and then nada, Detective. I'm not mad at you. The job comes first, always does. It's why we do what we do."

A sound rattled behind her. She turned her head, and then cut her gaze back to him.

"You lost your phone? Was that at the event or during the presumed assault on you afterward, or better yet, during your miraculous healing from the touching hands of God? Or was it packed away when you picked everything up and moved out of your apartment?"

Shia stepped back at the onslaught. Ohhhh, anger, of all the....she narrowed her eyes. "Hmmm, mad at me much? Let's revisit my evening, detective." She drawled out his title. "After I'd made nice with Father Munoz and his people rather than working on my case load, and all the while giving you glowing references, I left. Got beat up in the alley. Woke up in the hospital. My ribs are heavily bruised, but I need to be up and about. As for moving from my condo, I don't think I owe you an explanation for anything regarding where I live or where I choose not to live." She tilted her head down, but kept her gaze on him as another clatter came out of the alleyway. This wasn't going to be pretty.

"Lady, two separate heat patterns showing up on the

grid," Jace's voice whispered in her ear.

Ryan held up a hand as if to halt her tirade. "I'm not mad at you. I... look, I come from a job where all I do all day, and all night, is to make sense of things. I solve riddles. I put the pieces of the puzzle together. Otherwise, the bad guys never get put away. Here's why I'm having a hard time. Nothing at the hospital, there's no record of you at any of the hospitals ... ever."

He was counting the reasons on his fingers. "I crawled that alleyway on my hands and knees. Something happened there, but there was no blood, just more things I can't explain. All I have is the testimony of an old holy man and a knife made by some seventh grader in shop class." He refrained from mentioning her phone.

Her shoulder blades twitched. Her knife, some seventh grader? The blade was as old as she was, hand crafted, by her hand. She clamped her teeth shut. "There will not be a record, I erased them. I don't need the follow-up. I'm sure Father Munoz has his version of what he think happened. My injuries were less than nothing. I'm bruised and battered, not broken or cut."

Well, not now.

"And, detective...my cell phone? It was an alley way…I'm sure some street kid has it now." Not that it would be workable after the Rissu had stepped on it. Several hundred pounds versus circuit boards and wires. She knew who came out on top of that one.

Jace's voice rose in urgency through her earpiece, "Lady..."

She shifted from foot to foot. She needed to move away from him or get him to shift from her and be on his way. The crazy man was asking for trouble.

Ryan ran a hand through his hair. "That's the problem, I know something happened to you, and I hate it. I put you in danger, and then I wasn't there when something went down. Even without evidence, I know something happened. Hell, if it was anyone else, I wouldn't believe a wo..." Ryan swung the flashlight up, shining the light past Shia. His other hand drifted to the handle of his Glock. "What the hell?"

Figures. She gave into the way the Universe wanted to play things. She turned, her hands lifting to her shoulders and drawing her katana and wakizashi as she switched into fighting speed. Her hood fell back, and her eyesight changed over completely to darkness. The night lit up around her. She placed herself between him and the Rissu. "Now, now, newborn, we're not going to play. You will leave the human alone."

She hadn't wanted this here and now, and how was he even seeing the demon? She swung the longer katana blade in an arc attempting to take the creatures head.

"Lady, one more rests and waits..."

Check. Stay aware. Keep Ryan safe and figure out how to explain everything later. Right.

She danced back and to the side as the newborn swung a clawed hand at her. Oh, no. "Sorry, newbie, not falling for that one again."

Her other blade lit up from her hand and slid through the night in an upward arc. She smiled in satisfaction as the Rissu howled in pain when she hit in the general area of what would be considered his rib cage. Fine, she'd take him down piece by piece.

She cried out when the thing's tail swept out and lashed her leg.

She dropped to one knee, gasping.

Ryan watched as Shia pulled swords from her back and went into battle against some ... What the hell was that thing? It looked like one of the dinosaurs in the

Smithsonian or one of his nephew's action figures. Did something escape from the zoo?

Shia engaged the creature in close quarters combat drawing the fast moving blades from somewhere he hadn't seen. Ryan shifted his grip from his pistol to his baton. He was an expert marksman, but there were too many moving parts to this target. He couldn't risk shooting Shia, which would be a lot harder to apologize for than standing her up.

Shia sliced the thing, and rattling echoed in his skull making his teeth ache. Then, she fell. Ryan didn't think. He reacted.

He launched himself through the darkness. His shoulder struck the thing in the ribs. Using his Jiu-Jitsu training, Ryan grabbed a hold of the humanoid creature by its shoulder and shifted his weight. Its head and chest slammed downward into the ground. Ryan looped an arm under its chin, catching it in a position designed to immobilize it.

"You have the right to remain silent...whatever the hell you are."

Shia sensed the energy shift as Ryan's body went flying past her. She edged her sword straight down in the pavement and lifted up in time to see Ryan sweep into the newborn and bring it down to its back. She hissed. No, he shouldn't even be able to see the demon.

The Rissu's tail swept up again. Without a thought, her blades swung out in twin motion, slicing from two different directions and severing the tail from its host in seconds.

She winced as the edge of the katana grazed Ryan's back. Too close.

"Ryan, get out of the way. I need to take his head." She snapped. She tired of this dance. He'd been hurt, not part of the plan.

Ryan barely acknowledged the brief pain across his back when instinct kicked in. He tucked his shoulder and dove away from the thing, rolling to his feet. He watched the fluid erupting from its back and heard the horrible sound once more. She dove when Ryan rolled out of the way. She'd been watching the play of movement along his back. She leapt, blades ready as cross hairs and sliced. Finding comfort in the few things he could still explain, he continued, looking into the inhuman gaze of his enemy.

"You have the right to an attorney. Do they have attorneys where you come from?"

The Rissu's head left its shoulders. Shia had regained her footing and held a blade in each hand.

She dropped to her knees. The katana planted down, the wakizashi resting across her knee as the demon's body dissolved to dust before her, far too close.

"Are you safe?" she asked without looking at him. She stayed on the ground a moment, still feeling the presence of the elder Rissu on the rooftop.

Ryan hadn't moved, hadn't even flinched.

He pushed up to a knee. "What the hell was that thing?"

"1733 Warehouse Row, Detective," Shia whispered before standing and pulling the night around her. She still couldn't look at him. She needed to be far away. "You want answers." She disappeared where he could not follow, stepping into the realm of darkness completely. She'd pay for this later, but it had to be done. With more coming, she needed to be away from him to keep him safe.

Time to lay a false trail. The mother demon would follow her, not him.

CHAPTER TWENTY

Shia curled her leg under her and rested her chin atop her knee as she stared at the monitor in front of her. Data scrolled across with lightning speed. She drummed her fingers on the desk. Her head hurt, but she needed to run all the statistics. She should check on Ryan, make sure he'd gotten home safely. Jace assured her he had. He had to be suffering from a massive migraine. The switch from human realm into the meta realm...she couldn't explain the process even though she'd lived it. She needed to think about something other than the detective and how he was sensing the Rissu, and the ever-pressing question of why he mattered so much to her.

While the computer ran statistics, she pulled up the history of the Rissu demon on another screen. Humanoid. Spiny back. Average height six to about six-four. Mostly male, few female of the variety, none of the females on record as having been planet side. The males always pulled from an elemental plane to this one.

She drummed her fingers harder. She'd memorized the demonology, what she didn't get was why now, all at once? If she had a pen she'd be chewing on the top. Instead, she clicked a few more keys and pulled up the map she'd shown Ilsa the day before. Each evening, new red dots flared to life in the DC area, then the numbers dwindled as they appeared elsewhere around the globe. She needed to pinpoint the entry portal in the District.

"Jace, print me out a large map of the city."

"A print out, Lady Ronin? Wouldn't you rather a hologram? I updated my system." Her eye twitched. She'd swear the AI tried to cajole her. He'd done nothing but surprise her with updates for the last few weeks, why should this time be any different?

She closed her eyes. "Fine, whatever you'd like to show off, so long as it works."

She started when the image shimmered to life. She shut the laptop. Leave the computer system alone for hours a day, and he tweaked his own code. She needed to double-check her programming abilities. Or, sell them.

"Oh, new toys," she murmured. A hazy blue image of a Washington DC map sharpened. Beneath the image a red then green map shimmered into being.

"The blue map illustrates the roads, the metro system is in red, and the sewer system in green."

Shia got up to move around the map. Her legs protested a bit when she changed position. "Add in the Rissu."

A cluster of red dots appeared scattered across the grid. "No, show where they first appeared."

"Calculating." One by one, the dots merged into a single point on the map. She stared at the dot in shock, the twitching stopped. "Well, Jace, call Detective Ryan."

Ryan tried to shake his head, but every motion incited

the fire between his shoulder blades and a dull throbbing ache in the middle of his forehead. When he finally rose up enough to recognize his surroundings, he realized he was on the floor of his living room. His head pounded, his muscles seemed on autopilot, and a mind numbing pain echoed throughout his entire body.

He reached a hand up, grabbing the edge of the desk and pulled. A sharp pain cut through most of his body, but Ryan breathed through it and found a way up to his desk chair. He dropped into it, coughing several times. He raised his hand to the side of his head, gripping his skull as if somehow the pressure of his palm would stop the ringing in his brain.

After a few minutes, the world stopped whirling, and Ryan regained the ability to focus. First, a simple object like the lamp realigned. Then, the keyboard and his fingers. Finally, he glanced at the monitor. The GPS outlined a satellite view of 1733 Warehouse Row, but the software couldn't provide anything more than a two-mile radius. Ryan shook his head. His phone could give him the distance from his pantry down to the centimeter, but a two-mile gap for a warehouse? Something didn't line up with this mystery destination.

Twenty minutes later, Ryan had showered and shaved, mixed a meal replacement shake in the blender, and headed toward the address. He wore boots, jeans, and a shirt, which hadn't been sliced through, even if his skin had. The familiar chirp of his phone echoed in the interior of the Impala, and he eyed the caller recognition software. With a frown, he answered the call. "Calder."

"You owe me a photo, Ryan."

"Yes, I do." Ryan gritted his teeth at the thought of owing Felicia anything. "Let me send the image over right now."

"Thanks, I'd hate to keep you waiting on booking our

dinner reservations, loser."

"Right back at you, Agent."

There was a short pause. "Ah, I just got the confirmation message. Let me download the pic, and I'll let you know what we know."

The tone for an incoming message interrupted their dialog. Ryan glanced at the screen and saw an unknown number. "I have a call coming in. I may have to take this."

"Uh huh, call me later, killer."

Agent Simone ended the conversation, and Ryan switched over to the new call. "Calder."

"How are you, Detective?" Shia's soft voice washed over him.

He paused a moment, taking stock and wondering how such a small, lithe body packed such power. "Better after a shower, but I feel like I got food poisoning without the benefit of tasting the food. I'm glad to hear from you because I sure as hell don't understand what happened last night."

"Welcome to my realm. You should not have seen what you did."

"What is that supposed to mean, exactly? I'm at a loss here. Tell me that was a guy in a costume, and I'll be happy. Well, I won't, but at least I can understand that."

She laughed softly. "No, sorry, no guy in a costume. I wish. Then things would be so much easier. Something that usually remains in the shadows."

"Well, damn. Not that the guy in a costume thing wouldn't have explained why the best mortician in the District can suddenly pull swords out of thin air, and kick major ass in the process."

"Best? No, never mind. Yes, you weren't supposed to see any of that much less have sensed it."

"That's pretty cryptic. Look, I saw what I saw. My

189

vision may not be 20/10 or whatever, but I saw you with swords, and some biped crustacean trying to hurt you. I'm still hoping I'm out of the loop and some Hollywood studio is filming a sci-fi film around here I haven't heard about. Otherwise...well, otherwise, I'm going to need you to explain some things to me that I can't explain myself."

"Come to the warehouse, Ryan. I'll show you the best I can. If you can see it now, well, I can't keep you any safer than I have been," she said. "If you're using your GPS, use the map on your phone now. Your other maps won't work."

Ryan smiled to himself, realizing whatever the thing was from last night, it was responsible for Shia trusting him again. He was willing to take a few cuts and scratches for another chance at building a relationship with the captivating woman who seemed to pull his every string.

"Thanks, Miss ... I mean, Dr. Ronin. Look, I know I apologized, but I don't think my apology covered how sorry I am about this past weekend. You were so perfect. I've let Father Munoz down so many times, and you impressed him, even when I got yanked away for a homicide. I owe you. You won't accept that, but I hope you do. You name the time and place, Shia, and I promise I will repay you."

Silence was his answer. After half a minute, he spoke, "Shia?"

"Dr. Ronin?"

One quick glance confirmed she'd ended the conversation. He cursed at himself for being an idiot.

Ryan squeezed the cell phone in his hand when it rang, vibrating against his palm. Anticipating Shia's voice, he raised the phone to his ear and said. "Calder."

"Jesus Christ, Ryan…you don't know who is in this picture?"

CHAPTER TWENTY-ONE

Agent Felicia Simone hit a few tones Ryan had only heard out of her when she was at emotional extremes or physical ones. "Ryan, the man in the picture…damn, weren't you in the military?"

"Get to the point, Felicia. Did you figure out who he is? If you know, tell me." He realized he was tired of her games, more so than he'd thought before.

She huffed, then returned after a pause. "Check the feed I sent you. You can put me on speaker. You won't need to hear him to recognize him."

Ryan flipped the buttons on his phone and saw the icon for new messages. He hit the touch screen. Simone's feed loaded instantly. A press conference flared to life. Cameras flashed. Microphone-carrying bots hovered around the podium, and within seconds, a figure walked confidently to the center of the scene, posing for the reporters and not just any figure. The figure from Carl MacAdams' photograph.

The caption on the bottom of the screen flashed in

bold letters. Alexander Spiros, CEO, Ixion Industries.

"Oh, shit," Ryan muttered as he stared at the monitor. A horn honked behind him, and he righted the Impala, flashing a glance at the road in front of him.

"That's pretty much what I thought you'd say," Felicia practically sang from the other end of the line. "Do you realize how big this is?"

"Big."

"Spiros holds the Department of Defense contract on the satellite laser grid."

"Big."

"That company makes every Federal space-ready passenger and military ship in America."

"How the hell..."

"Ryan."

"...are we supposed..."

"Ryan."

"...to handle..."

"Ryan!"

He stopped. Her tone had lost its edge. The I-told-you-so was gone from her voice. He paused.

She whispered when she spoke again, "Ryan?"

"I'm here."

"More than half this field office is Ixion contractors."

It had been a long, long time since Felicia trusted Ryan with her safety, but fear sliced through her words. Spiros was known for his cutthroat business tactics, and several times, his competitors had disappeared without a trace. Ryan and Felicia had shared something once that something left behind enough embers.

He slid his thumb across his phone again, touching a few icons. "Encryption is valid over both our transmissions and our conversation. Find an excuse to meet me for field research."

"Where?"

"Anywhere. Charles Huang's murder scene. We never did find his incisor."

"Right. I'm on my way."

Agent Felicia Simone killed her end of the conversation. Ryan absently held the phone in his hand. She always had a plan, always in control of the chessboard. Why was this time so different, and why did he care? He shook his head. He could answer the last question himself.

Ixion Industries never bothered with the State and Local level of law enforcement. Ryan was relatively sure his official equipment was safe, and even more confident his personal resources were protected. He connected to a separate network and set up credentials on a property he owned in Rosslyn, Virginia, across the Key Bridge from DC.

Felicia could stay at one of his places for a little while, long enough for them to build a strategy against the multi-millionaire defense contractor. Or at least, until they asked him a few questions.

Ryan finished making arrangements. He would meet Felicia in person to deliver her alias and credentials. Seconds later, his phone rang again. The detective shook his head. At this rate, the day was going to last an eternity.

"Calder."

"Good morning, Detective. My name is Jace. I am calling to inform you Lady Ronin is engaged in combat and desperately requires your assistance."

Father Francisco Munoz smiled as the children's

joyous giggles reached his ears. He looked from one volunteer to another, and to the man and woman, every one of them laughing. Raking the multi-colored leaves was hard work, but repeating the effort over and over again was worth every aching muscle once they witnessed the smiles of the children. The priest and his volunteer staff had raked the leaves into piles nearly a dozen times, and yet, the sensation of each child jumping, falling and otherwise terrorizing the leaf piles made everyone even happier.

Father Munoz leaned down, feeling pain in his lower back and his shoulders as began to rake the leaves once again into a mound.

"Can we go again, Father?" asked Antwoin, an undersized nine-year-old of a single, homeless mother, who regularly visited the church for food and clothes.

Father Munoz smiled, looked once quickly at his volunteers and then nodded. "Of course, my son. We are here for you, always, as Christ Almighty."

Antwoin grinned widely, taking a run into a pile of autumn leaves the volunteers had gathered. He landed with a flurry of laughter. The leaves filled the air like a multi-colored blizzard. Father Munoz laughed with them until something at the edge of his vision demanded his attention. The leaves fell, blurry and out-of-focus. A single figure stood at the end of the courtyard, facing him directly, even though he could make out nothing but a silhouette.

"Children," he called out in a voice louder than he intended. "Children, let us move inside. We have much to learn. The next workshop is inside the church."

Father Munoz never let his gaze wander from the silhouette at the end of the courtyard, even when everything shimmered, changing form before his eyes. The children filed into the church. Each of them casting worried glances over their shoulders, but the calming words of the priest provided enough confidence that they found the sanctuary inside. Father Munoz shut the door behind them and turned, left alone in the courtyard to face the strange figure.

Leaves swirled in the air, lifted into twisting columns on each side of the large being as it approached. The grass burned away beneath its feet. The flowers that brushed against its legs wilted and died.

Father Munoz stared, realizing this thing was not human. This was evil at its core. He began to recite 1 Chronicles 28:20 – "And David said to Solomon his son, Be strong and of good courage, and do it: fear not, nor be dismayed for the LORD God, even my God, will be with thee; he will not fail thee, nor forsake thee, until thou hast finished all the work for the service of the house of the LORD."

The thing stepped closer, and the old priest turned slightly against the leaves flying past him, slicing the skin of his face. "Leave this Holy place, Abomination. You carry the stench of Hell, and you have no power here."

The figure darted forward, shifting before the old man's eyes. The skin was pure black, leathery, and a gaze that seemed to glow red. Spikes erupted from the top of its skull, down its spine, and along the tail that whipped from side to side behind its overly large body. When the being opened its mouth, a row of sharp teeth gnashed at him, its tongue lashing out quickly, hissing.

Father Munoz shut his eyes at its awful breath, but did not turn away. "Let every soul be subject unto the higher powers. For there is no power but of God: the powers that be are ordained of God," he recited, quoting Romans 13:1.

The thing seemed to grow angry at the words from the Holy Bible. It lashed out with claws that stretched from each of its hands. Father Munoz cried out in pain and stepped back. The beast's claws had cut into his outstretched hand, creating the form of the cross on his skin.

The pain surged beneath his flesh, filling his veins with liquid heat, but the priest would not admit defeat. This being was unknown in his world, but his Faith remained strong. It empowered him, even as the burning in his blood made him want to surrender. Was this the creature Dr. Ronin had encountered in the alley way after the gala? He was even more certain she'd survived only through the aid of a miracle.

Father Munoz dropped to his knees, not in surrender, but in celebration. His voice began quietly, building louder with each word.

"Our Father, who art in Heaven, hallowed be thy name. Thy Kingdom come, thy will be done, on earth as it is in Heaven."

The beast roared, its rancid breath blowing against the priest's skin.

"Give us this day our daily bread, And forgive us our trespasses, as we forgive those who trespass against us."

It hissed, the sound a combination of wild beast and enraged predator.

"And lead us not into temptation."

"I don't think so, newbie." She said as she took in the scene all in a matter of seconds. Father Munoz on his knees, the newborn Rissu leaning in for another attack. Fury arched through her entire being.

Her body coiled, and she darted in front of the Rissu's next strike. Her swords were out and at the ready. This time, she didn't hesitate. She created a whirlwind of movement with the blades. The tornado of her swords subsided long enough for her to meet the gaze of the priest.

"Father, if you can, get inside. He cannot follow you," she said.

Letting her blades restore the whirlwind of motion, she glanced at the older man. His eyes wide, but peaceful stared back her. "Go."

She turned her attention to the newborn. "Jace. Track."

She heard the priest complete the Lord's prayer behind her and the rustling of his robes. She couldn't chance a look back to see if he had run or merely backed away from them. She had to assume he was still in danger.

"Already on it. This one is also not alone. The female is on the rafters, watching. This Rissu is three hours old. He came through the portal and straight here. He spent his first hours hiding in the shadows."

"And why didn't you tell me when he appeared on the grid?" she asked.

Her blades sliced down and out, a circular motion, creating a shield. The Rissu growled at her.

She was done. Done with the demon, the hunt, and the game. This ended, now.

"Forget it," she said. Instead of a barrier, she leapt forward. It was her and the demon now. And it, it was going down.

Her arm lifted and swept in a downward while the other sliced up. The demon howled in pain at the dual strike. She darted in closer, whirling, and bringing the blades about in an age-old dance.

The energy altered around her. Another presence appeared behind her. Shia shifted, swords at the ready.

"Nice, now you decide to play too." She gauged her distance between the two. Momma Rissu sat on her haunches staring at her, demon eyes glowing.

One sword slid in front of her and one behind her. They had her trapped between them. She shifted her feet. She knew the strategy. Move the younger in the middle of them both. She needed to reposition.

She edged back, and the sword behind her flicked out and nicked the younger Rissu. He hissed in pain and danced out of her way to the left just enough for her to dart right. The Elder Rissu matched her adjustment. The young Rissu behind her was slower to adjust. It glanced back at the injured holy man, and then to the damage it had done to the church, finally focusing on her. They were no longer polar opposites, attacking her from each side. She could defend against both of them at once.

As she contemplated her strategy, a body-shaking roar tore through her skull. Both of the Rissu reacted to the same sound, shifting their gaze from side to side. A second later, the jet-black unmarked Impala drove through the trashed courtyard. The police cruiser landed halfway in the dead leaves and flowers, caught its grip among the remaining leaves and rammed the younger Rissu hard into the side of the church.

Ryan. Shia smiled. Of course. She might have to thank Jace later, after she rewired his circuits. There was no other way the Detective knew where she was.

She turned back to the Momma Rissu. Awareness dawned in the demon's eyes, and it changed direction to retreat into the darkness.

She frowned, turning to the baby Rissu.

Ryan kicked open the driver's side door of his

damaged, beloved cop car. He walked forward a few steps, looking down at the spiny figure sprawled on the ground. "You do NOT screw with a holy man in my town, you overgrown shrimp cocktail!"

The Rissu shifted from side to side, trying to right itself, but its damaged shell left it as vulnerable as an overturned turtle. Ryan snapped the retractable police baton to its full extension and drove four steady, matched, solid blows to the demon's skull. It slowed and then stopped moving completely.

"Damn you," he shouted at the beastly form. "Damn whatever the hell you are, and wherever the hell you came from!" He reached the end of his breath, staring at the thing. In a rage, he stomped twice on the carcass of the inhuman figure, grunting an animal sound. He quit taking his anger out on the unmoving form and drew in several breaths. His gaze met Shia's, and his lips shifted into an unsteady smile.

He never saw the spiny tail sweep out, striking him between his ribs, so quickly he didn't have time to react.

Shia cried out and darted forward. She caught his limp body before he dropped to the pavement. Ryan grunted at the impact of the demon's venom. Dark lines crept along his skin. His eyes rolled back into his head, and he crumbled into her like a doll without a puppeteer.

"Not nice, demon pup." Shia laid Ryan down gently on the ground. As she stood, her blades flashed in the light of the November moon. Within seconds, she'd turned towards the injured Rissu, her twin swords lit around in her in a flurry of movement. The image of Ryan's shocked look and his subsequent fall to the ground etched into her mind's eye.

Silver lit the night, and she sliced the Rissu to

ribbons, holding nothing back. She was done with this. They hunted innocents. While she was sure Ryan had much to atone for, she wasn't about to let him die by demon tail or claw.

Dust scattered around her when she finally paused.

"Dr. Ronin," Father Ryan's voice swept over her.

She stopped, panting, her swords at her side. "Are you safe, padre?" She didn't bother to turn and look at him, instead turning towards Ryan who lay unprotected and injured on the ground.

"I will survive, as the Lord has guided me." He began a prayer. It may have been for her benefit, or the children suddenly exposed to something they could never explain away.

"Good. Stay inside as I told you." She flicked her wrists, and her blades collapsed. She sheathed them before dropping to Ryan's side. He wasn't going to appreciate her for what would come next.

"Jace, prepare a space, I need to get the poison out of him."

"Yes, m'lady. Already in process."

CHAPTER TWENTY-TWO

"Lady."

"I am not talking to you right now, Jace," Shia said. She struggled with getting Ryan onto the mattress. His large body dwarfed her small guest bed, proof she hadn't had a man in her personal space, anywhere in her space, in forever. He panted as she maneuvered. He'd taken a bad hit. At least she hadn't had to try and move him up the stairs to her private bedroom. As much as she wanted to, taking care of him would be far easier for her from the recovery room off the to the side of her workspace.

He shouldn't have been there. Especially still smarting from the hit he'd taken from the tip of her katana.

She'd argued, albeit briefly with Father Munoz about calling the paramedics. What had slashed Ryan couldn't be tackled in the hospital. The Father had caved when she'd leveled a glance at him and reminded him of her healing.

"Be useful. Get me the herbs," she ordered Jace.

Her knife would've helped. She stared down at the

gash on Ryan's side. She drew her wakizashi, the shorter of the two blades she carried, in one hand and took a deep breath, holding her other one out.

"Lady Ronin, no!"

She ignored Jace and sliced down. A whisper of a hiss left her lips as the blood welled up. She held her palm over his open wound watching it drip. She flicked her wrist, and her sword collapsed. Without another thought, she re-sheathed the blade.

"I told you to get me the herbs," she said. "My patience for this is gone, especially when this is entirely your fault."

"My fault?" If AI's could whine, Jace was close.

She watched Ryan's wound begin to knit back together. "Yes, Jace, how else does Ryan know your name?"

Silence.

"Tell me now, or I will disconnect all your circuits." She held her arm steady, letting the blood flow until the gash closed, pink and puckered. She had zero compulsion about cutting all ties to her assistant since he'd put Ryan in the line of fire. She'd tolerated nothing less in her human assistants through the years. A computerized one? As much as she'd miss his knowledge and ability she'd done without before.

"Lady."

"Don't Lady me. You overstepped your programming." She placed a hand on Ryan's chest, making sure his breathing steadied and evened out.

"You needed back up," Jace argued.

"The only acceptable backup to ever send is one of my sisters. He's human."

"Well, not any more."

"What?" She checked him over for signs of demonic

changes. Would the Rissu's blood harm him? Should she give him more of hers?

"He'd already started to transition to the meta realm. You just shared your blood with him. He's more now. Not entirely human. Not yet fully immortal. He was already sensing things."

Shia closed her eyes. Why had she thought investing in artificial intelligence would be worth her while? He caused more problems than he helped.

"I am so going to disconnect you. At least with human lackeys, they shut up and stay out of my way when it's wise to do so."

"Your previous companions all died, Lady," Jace commented.

Shia's breathing stilled, her hand withdrawing from Ryan's chest, toying with the idea of ripping the main console from the wall.

"What the hell hit me?" Ryan's voice stopped her in her tracks.

"Tall, dark, spiny with a tail. He didn't like you and your police brutality," she said as she turned back to him. Jace owed the detective one, without his interruption, he'd be a pile of circuits, or his wall connection would be.

"Maybe I need to hang out with a richer crowd. At least then, I'd know how to crack open a lobster better."

Shia smothered smile. First time she'd ever heard of a Rissu demon being compared to a lobster, but somehow the description fit. "You might need to hang with an older crowd." She moved closer to him, her gaze trailing over him. His color appeared better, the lacerations beginning to heal. "I'm sure you have questions."

Ryan pushed up on to one elbow, grimacing as he did. He closed his eyes as if to keep from vomiting. "You're going to tell me, and I'm not going to believe you, but what was that thing? I hit it with my car, and it still fought back, and stabbed me in the back. Dirty pool."

"Welcome to my realm, Detective. What you met was a Rissu demon, only the very few lucky ones can sense the other realms. Somehow, you're starting to see and hear them." She sighed and glanced away. This was her fault. He shouldn't be seeing anything. She'd never run into a human male who could. She had a hard enough time explaining to the women who'd died and come back. He hadn't died. And, he was male. "Unfortunately, they now know you can see them as well."

"Think I prefer seeing them. At least then, I can shoot the next...did you say 'demon'?"

She smiled. She wondered when the term would sink in. "Yes, one of many I've fought. Right now, infesting the DC area."

Ryan studied her for a minute. "Does that make you an angel?"

Shia choked, startled. She'd never been compared to an angel, a demon, maybe, but never an angel. "Ah, no. Anything but. I am a samurai, first in my line. My sisters and I keep the world safe from the dark realms. I've done so for the longest among us."

She stood up and strode over to the hologram Jace had left up. "I died the first time leaving the battlefield when my master released me. He said he refused to die by a woman's side. Regardless of the fact I'd kept him alive for more battles than he could count. I laid down my life for him, and he rejected me. I died for his rejection."

Ryan blinked several times. "Okay, so it's not angels and demons, but demons and samurai?" He pushed up until he was sitting upright on the bed. "How long, exactly, has this been going on?"

"Many of my sisters might be considered angels; however, I've never met one of the winged creatures. I'm sure they are beyond beautiful. I died in 1157 AD. I found Ilsa in 1350." She paced. She should not be telling him any of this, but if she'd pulled him into their realm, the first male, then she had to make him understand. He wasn't going to like any of this. She sighed. "There are twelve of us in all at the moment. We're unsure of when we'll find another." Well, not entirely true now, Jace had increased their odds of finding new samurai by tenfold with his little adjustments to their tracking systems.

Ryan simply stared for a moment, then nodded. "So you're almost a thousand years old?"

She counted and gave up, "Give or take, I think. I stopped counting."

"You don't look a day over 300."

She cut him a glance ready to take offense and smiled at the mischief sparkling from his eyes. "Why thank you, Detective. Everything after is merely an anniversary." Let him try to play her. Not.

"How is your back feeling?" she asked.

"My head started spinning somewhere around the word 'demon'. Forgot completely about my back."

"Rightfully so."

"I hit the thing with my car."

"Yes, you did."

Ryan sighed. "I love my car."

Shia smiled in response.

Ryan stared at the floor. "Forgive me if I'm having a hard time digesting all of this."

She turned her head as her new phone danced across the desktop in the other room. Ilsa was the sole person who had the authority to break her radio silence right now. "Oh, I took a few decades before understanding I wasn't hallucinating. Some days, I wish I was. Excuse me, I must get this call."

She strode out of the room. Let him digest what she'd said. He wasn't going to believe a word of it anyway. She hadn't, not for a long time not until she'd found Ilsa on the battlefields.

Ryan studied the lithe figure of Shia Ronin as she flowed into an adjoining room, rice paper walls separating them. He rubbed his neck, trying to take all of it in. If Shia was insane, he was going to have a hell of a time getting out of her place. She was fast and pulled deadly weapons out of thin air. Of course, if she wasn't lying, nothing mattered. He was a dry leaf blowing off of an oak tree, crumbling away and turning to dust while she walked the Earth, hunting demons. Christ, none of it made any sense. Demons couldn't be true.

Except he'd fought twice with some kind of creature, which only existed in The Twilight Zone reruns and *House of Mystery* comic books he read as a kid. Why couldn't things go back to simple? Pimps, pushers, and pedophiles, he could handle. This mystical stuff made his head hurt. He watched Shia's form, outlined in paper, shadowed against the wall. That genie was not going back into her bottle any time soon.

He whispered, "Jace?"

The AI replied after several dark, silent seconds. His voice was barely a whisper back. "Yes, Detective."

"I don't know why I'm asking you this. You're a computer, right? She probably created you and built you to defend her story."

"Actually, sir, she purchased me at the Tokyo Emerging Technologies Summit in 2012, but she's upgraded my systems since then, which allows me to develop my own applications, as well."

Ryan shook his head. "So, you can't prove any of this mumbo-jumbo any better than I can."

"Sir, I am responsible for her communications to Ilsa, Celeste, Raisa, and all the other samurai. They do, in fact, hunt demons. I'd be happy to provide you access to the demon database if you'd like. I've been building the library over several years."

"Lucky you."

"If you say so, sir."

Ryan stopped and looked around. A holographic map of the District hung in the air where Shia had been walking, pacing. She'd disrupted it during their conversation, and he hadn't made out the details. He forced himself up and out of the bed and walked a few slow steps forward, stopping when he spotted the pattern of red X's, and a set of concentric circles, all building out from one center point.

He raised his finger to the center of the map. "You've got to be kidding me."

Shia turned and found Ryan standing dead center in her workspace. The holographic map of the DC metro area shimmered around him, giving him an eerie glow.

"Feeling better then, I see," she commented. She should never have stepped away from him to take Ilsa's call. She knew better.

He turned to face her, blinking a few times to adjust to the different light. "Your call go okay?"

She stopped, her call? Ilsa? "Ah, yes. Same issues at hand. I need to find the source."

"Hmm, I'm sorry to hear that."

"Right. And your reason for the shock at my map, Detective? Let's not pretend I can't hear across rooms."

Ryan nodded. "I won't disrespect you, and you won't do the same to me. Fair enough. Something about your map concerns me, but if you don't mind, I'd like a little explanation before I confess the reason behind my curiosity. Okay with you?"

Shia tilted her head at him…a quiet, concerned, questioning Detective. Had he hit his head harder than she'd thought? "Ask away. Jace is tracking demon heat markers for me. Why does that concern you?"

"Chalk it up to my long and well-known experiences with women who were really, really bad for me. I'm hoping you break my streak. Hell, you didn't catch on fire when you walked into the church, or set fire to it before you left. I'm considering that a minor miracle." He took a deep breath, and exhaled sharply. "I want you to tell me why this is important." He pointed directly to the center of the concentric circles on the map.

Shia stopped and coughed. "Umm, no sorry, not into setting myself on fire or the church. The church is a safe haven, regardless of denomination. Why is this important to you? I don't understand why you haven't passed out in denial."

Ryan tapped his head. "No brain, no pain. If I were smarter, I'd probably be six states over by now." He faced the hologram. "You didn't answer my question."

"Which one?"

He pointed again. "Why here?"

"We narrowed down their origination point, the portal. Why?" she asked.

"How sure are you?"

"Umm, state of the art computer system, which nothing in mankind can touch at the moment? Pretty sure. I'd be there now if I wasn't hunting two Rissu, saving Father Munoz and getting you back to health," she said.

Her shoulders itched. And add to her day, wondering just how important the FBI agent was to him. She forced thoughts of the agent out of her mind, refocusing on Ryan's gaze as he watched her.

"Getting there might be a little more complicated than normal."

She turned and looked at the map. "No, pretty straight forward, park. I know it well. Not so out in the open at those coordinates, but reachable, yet hidden in the night."

Ryan frowned. "Does your map show it's also a crime scene?" He turned to her. "Not any crime scene. Shia, that's where I was called the night of the gala, to Charles Huang's murder."

She stared at him. "By your Agent Simone?" Please, please, please don't let this be a homicide connected killing spree. She would be required to dispatch the human who'd opened the portal. She didn't want to deal with the ensuing cover up. The thought made her head hurt. "Please tell me you're kidding."

Ryan studied her for a minute. "Agent Simone called me to Little Falls Park when I was on my way to meet with you. I tried to get her off the phone, but she told me we had a murder scene. The victim wasn't any old vic. He was the prime suspect in a connected case. I ruined a pair of Italian leather shoes and the pants to my new tuxedo trying to get down to the scene," he continued. "The vic was Charles Huang, our prime suspect in the murder of his wife, Abigail, the woman you performed the autopsy on last time I met you in the morgue. Only this guy wasn't impaled or sliced or cut to ribbons. He was shot, point blank, in the face. This was no demon. This was a sadist with a handgun."

She stopped cold. "Jace, add this to the profile."

The holographic wall lit up. Shia's gaze tracked every move, every iteration.

"Lady."

"Report," she demanded.

"Rissu demons materialized on the full moon two weeks ago. The first dead human appeared here three nights after. There are several correlations around the globe matching to the portal flares since then."

Ryan remained silent as if he didn't want to interrupt her thought process.

Shia raised a hand to her temple and rubbed at it before turning to her desk. Her fingers flew across the keyboard. "Map them."

Jace spit out coordinates. She mapped them to every initial sighting.

She lost sight of Ryan as she focused. Coordinates, maps, trails lit up before her. "Did I not build you to see this?"

She hit her head with her palm. Why had she bought and perfected an AI to help her?

"There's more," Ryan said, drawing her attention. "There might be more, at least. I have a potential suspect, but I'm still gathering evidence. He might be involved. I think he is, but I need more time to confirm things."

She turned to him, "Ryan, you can either tell me now. I have more than proven my ability and desire to keep you alive. This goes beyond a single human homicide. I have replaced a Rottle. I have hunted and defended the streets around your home. I have dealt with two, yes two, human attacks, and several more non-human attacks. I've lost blood, my dagger, my phone and had to hide my steps by moving and calling in sick for the week."

Ryan stopped as if contemplating her words. Finally, his eyes met hers. "Listen, I believe you about who you are and about your sisters. This guy I have in mind, he's a big fish. He's a big, big fish. If I'm wrong about this guy,

I'm going to risk my job, and what's worse, if you're telling me the truth, I might expose you for what you are. After all you've done for me, I can't do that." He gazed at her. "I need a little time to be sure I've got the right safeguards in place in case this suspect turns the tables. I'm not asking much. Give me 24 hours. If I can confirm what my little human mind believes, I'll share what I know with you." He extended his hand. "What do you say, samurai? Deal?"

Shia glanced at his hand. "I can give you twelve hours, Detective. I can't provide a bigger window. I can't even guarantee that. I need to be on the streets. The mother Rissu is hunting, and she shouldn't be here."

Ryan paused. "The...wait, the what?"

Shia stopped and looked at him. "There is a mother Rissu here. She should not be here. She is the first I've ever encountered. She's watching and vetting her pups against me."

"Those things were pups? Damn, it gets more fun as we go along here, doesn't it?"

She smiled, "It's never ending, Detective. You think homicide is bad? Try homicide and hiding a demon kill."

Ryan turned his gaze back to the glowing hologram, focusing on the center of activity. "You've never seen one of these Mother Demon things before?"

"No, I know about them. This is the first female to venture here. The portals are never open long enough. This portal pulled her," she said.

"The portal did, or someone using the portal did?"

Shia stopped. "Something about this portal did. She's powerful. It takes a lot of death, power or decay to pull a higher-level demon. I've dealt with some in the past. But, a Rissu? It's always the males. In a thousand years, it's always been the males."

Ryan nodded. "I was afraid you were going to say that." He took a few steps toward the door with no indication he was in any pain. He grabbed his jacket and turned back to her. "I may know who your male is, Shia, and if I'm right, I'll be in touch long before my twelve hour deadline is up. We're going to need every second we can get to stop this guy."

"Go," she uttered. She only hoped he wasn't too late, too many lives hung in the balance.

"Will there be anything else, Mr. Spiros?"

"No, Ariana, that will be all. Hold my calls, please."

"Yes, Mr. Spiros." The tall blonde stood, closed the cover of her tablet and strode on Paciotti leather heels out of his office, closing the heavy door behind her perfect body. Alexander Spiros didn't even look. He was accustomed to the finest of the finer things in life. His assistant certainly qualified, but if he fired her, the line to replace her would circle the block. He sighed.

"Tint," he said. The windows automatically darkened. The DC skyline was replaced with the soft glow provided by artificial LED's from all over the office.

"Silence." With a word, his detection programs scanned to room for bugs, silencing all incoming and outgoing speakers. He turned from his desk and stood, walking toward the matching Italian leather chairs facing his own.

"Abigail," he whispered. A 3D image came to life in the center of the room. She had bright eyes and a bashful smile. She seemed happy. Alexander walked slowly toward her image; studying the sunlight against her skin, the tiny gleam in her eyes. She was so...alive.

That was how he remembered her, how he loved her.

ICHI

And that was how he would have her again.

CHAPTER TWENTY-THREE

"How's the demon hunting going?" Ilsa's voice washed over her.

Shia glared at the computer screen. Jace uploaded all sorts of data, books, and databases while she'd slept which she'd done only with the caveat that he wake her for any Rissu sightings or antics or even a call from Ryan. Now that she was awake, they were both running through all the information. Ilsa's interruption hindered their process. Her hand flattened on the desk next to her keyboard.

"As to be expected," she said. She should tell Ilsa of her conversations with Ryan, what she'd promised him, what had been going on between them or what wasn't. But for the first time since Ilsa's resurrection, she kept her mouth shut. This, whatever it was with Ryan, she was keeping him to herself, something that was hers and hers alone. She didn't want to send in Raisa to remove Ryan or have Celeste wipe his memories. He'd come into the knowledge on his own. He deserved to keep it. Even if she'd spend the rest of his days protecting him from it. And she realized, without a doubt, she would. She'd continue to protect him from her realms.

Hell.

"That well, huh?" Ilsa's visage gazed back at her over the Net. "You need backup?"

"No, just answers. Unless you've got hidden information about a Momma Rissu that I don't." Or a better understanding of human males. She wisely bit the inside of her cheek and kept the comment to herself.

Ilsa shook her head. "We've all dealt with males. Everything is in our training database."

Shia pushed the books on her desk aside. She'd pulled out the ancient texts in case they'd missed something in migrating the data. "Right. Call Raisa. I'm going back."

"Back?"

"Yes. To one of my sources. The answers aren't here. She can move me far faster."

"Of course." Ilsa's fingers moved across her keyboard and suddenly the screen lit up. Raisa and Celeste appeared next.

Ilsa's voice flowed over the connection. "Raisa, target Shia. Move her to where she needs to go."

The Russian beauty's gaze sparked for a moment, but then she dipped her head. Her screen went blank, and Shia started when her hardcore, lithe sister stood before her in a tight concert t-shirt, ripped jeans and combat boots. Her red gold hair hung in a razor cut as her green-eyed gaze narrowed on her.

"Called for a transport?" she asked. Her hands hooked in her back pockets.

Shia stood and slanted a glance at her, "Sorry for the inconvenience, Rose."

Raisa lifted a shoulder. "Da, I am not worried, you lead the game of slice and dice. I play and move at will. Where to?"

"Tibet." Shia pictured the time and space and pushed the image to Raisa.

Her sister nodded. Molecules around them popped and shifted. In a matter of seconds, they stared at the small town at the base of a mountain.

"Thank you, Rose."

Raisa dipped her head, her glance darting away and then back again. "Any other and I would have said nein. Good luck."

Shia bowed as her sister winked out of existence.

Shia started up at the mountains looming overhead, majestic in their grace. She inhaled, letting the scent of greenery, fresh water, and clean airflow over her.

It was good to be home. Or, a home of sorts.

She settled her pack over her shoulders. Her loose linen clothes would keep her cool and warm as she hiked up the trail. She'd donned more traditional garb, with a few modifications and in all black. She bent down, checked the condition of her warm mountain boots. She'd need to replace them after this trek. They'd be worn through and through. Her swords nestled against her shoulder blades. All around her, tourists flowed, snapping pictures, talking excitedly about their expedition. She half smiled. Most would exhaust themselves a quarter of the way into the trip.

She eyed the mouth of the footpath. Barring any incidents with tourists, the hike would take her several hours at best to reach the top. She tucked her phone into a hidden pocket in her shirt, adjusted her pack one more time and set out on the trail, meaning to be well ahead of the pack of tourists milling about waiting for their guide. She wasn't carrying the required permits and wasn't interested in delaying herself to get them.

"Excuse me, miss?" a voice called out.

It took a moment for her to realize one of the tourists beckoned her. She glanced over her shoulder. A college student, young, blonde, female smiled over at her. She lifted an eyebrow, but a quick look around told her no one else paid her any attention, or, more importantly, they avoided her gaze so as not to see her. Wise people.

"You wouldn't happen to be our guide, would you?" she asked.

Shia shook her head. "No, you're on local time here. They don't run by clocks. Your guide should arrive in about 10 minutes or so."

"Oh." The girl looked heart broken. "Thank you."

Shia turned back to the trail. She would not offer to take them to the top. Another day, another time, she might have. She needed to move faster than they did. Her feet fairly flew over the rough-hewn path. The monks kept the footpath clear enough for themselves to make the trek to town and back. They never made it any easier for their guests to reach them though.

She hiked in silence, letting Mother Nature's sounds flow all around her. Out of respect for the monks she'd had Raisa bring her to town rather than the top of the mountain. In the distance she could hear the rush of the waterfall. Rocks and crawling vines littered the ground, making each step tricky. She thought of each step as she took it. She neared her destination as the roar of water added to the sounds of nature flowing around her and colorful flags began to decorate the trees along the path. The fencing went from long sticks thrown together to the more ornate carved designs as she drew closer to the bridge over the falls.

She reached the center of the bridge and looked down, over the valley. Her eyes closed, and she breathed deeply, letting all the smells flow into her. Energy raced, sparked her cells. She tingled. A smile welled forth from her soul.

She should return here more often, make the trek, remind herself of what she'd once been, merely a child left to play, live and learn in these mountains.

Bells sounded. Shia turned and continued on, up the orange brick stairs and through mixture of wood and stone door way. Seven temples graced the sheer face of the mountain. This sacred space dated back in time before she'd been born. She'd memorized the history, the myths, and the legends. In all that she'd seen in the world, even she had her doubts about tigers flying Padmasambhava here on their backs. Although, tigers did roam the high altitudes.

She grinned. Next time, she'd recruit a tiger instead of Raisa.

No matter where one went in the monastery, the sounds of the waterfall reached through. She took care walking up the twisting, turning steps, stepping to the side when well meaning tourists came tripping down them, excited in their conversations.

Shia bowed in acknowledgement when a few monks laid startled eyes on her. Within seconds, they'd begun a slow, steady chant, their voice starting out low, but took on volume, echoing above the waterfall. She shook her head, but they'd closed their eyes, ignoring her.

Heads popped out of open-air windows, monks appeared in doorways. Tourists stopped in their tracks and snapped photos of the monks. Shia melted between them, moving further into the monastery, each monk she passed lifted his voice in chant as well.

So much for going unnoticed.

She gave up and headed to the main temple, the voices trailed and lifted behind her. Regardless of their chanting, the tourists remained enthralled with them, never realizing she'd been the trigger. Thank the Universe for small favors.

"You have returned to us, child." A husky voice floated out of the darkness.

Shia took a deep breath in, stopping in the center of the hall, the old familiar scents and feelings washed over her.

"You do not know me," she said.

"No, Lady Gozen. We know of you. Your image is shared among us." The old Tibetan monk stepped out of the shadows, his saffron robes whispering against the stone.

"My name changed long ago, Wazu Lama." She finally remembered the name of the lead teacher here. She'd done a quick listen. "I am Zenshi Jin Ronin, now. Shia."

"As you wish, Lady Ronin." He bowed his head. "You have need of your brethren?"

"No, I came for solitude. I require a place where I could seek total focus."

"You are battling a great darkness."

Shia started. She knew better. "It clings to me, does it?"

"It's trying to, but it cannot find a hold."

"Bless the universe for small favors," she murmured. "I will be on the roof, Lama. Please, tell them to stop with the chanting. No one should even know I'm here."

"We are all aware of your presence, Lady. We have been waiting for your return," he said. "I will have the younger monks bring you meditation pillows and build you a fire."

"No need." She lifted a hand and slid her fingers into a hidden pocket, gently, she pulled the small soft bag from the warmth of her body. "Here, Wazu Lama, this should help the winter months." The bag jingled when she handed it to him.

His hand tightened around hers for a moment before releasing her. "This is much appreciated, but unnecessary, we are well taken care of."

"Yes, I know." She smiled. She'd done a lot of the taking care of through the centuries. "Every little bit helps. I'll be on the roof."

She bowed before turning and striding directly to the hidden staircase that would take her to where she wanted to go. How did they recognize her? She'd been so careful over the years about pictures, photos, and paintings. She'd altered her looks when needed and when she could and continued to do so. This was the first century where she'd returned to her natural appearance, dark eyes, and dark hair.

Cool air hit her as she stepped out onto the rooftop. Here, she'd spent many long hours and days in silence. She found her favorite spot, center point on the highest tower. The winds would get strong, but she had the best view, the best sense of all things here.

She pulled off her pack and dropped down on the roof. Her legs folded naturally into lotus position, her back straightened. She ignored the discomfort and instead, slowed her breathing, allowing her mind to settle and quiet. Minutes, hours, days could have passed while she sat there. For a long time, she hovered in the darkness behind her eyelids, focusing on nothing more than each breath. She dimly recognized the chanting of the monks, the bells and the waterfall, but in time, everything drifted away.

When the images came, she was ready. At first they teased the edges of her mind. For a brief moment, she protested, but the thought fluttered away. Instead, the images streamed. Some things, books couldn't tell her.

More often times, they needed to be revealed. She hovered in the between spaces.

The darkness crawled, and shadows danced. A glow began in the center and expanded out. She waited. Out of the glimmering light came wraiths, shadows, and tall spiked creatures spilling through. She watched. A portal. On the one side, humanity, now rife with demons. On the other, pure evil panting, itching to be called or pulled. A set of glowing red eyes turned towards her, sensing, seeing. Shia continued to contemplate and wait.

"You will die, Samurai," the brute hissed.

Shia's otherworld self blinked. "I know death, demon. I've already met the bliss of change on more than one occasion."

Shia examined the Rissu. It was the mother one. The mother's rarely if never set foot on the human plane. No one had called a Rissu of such strength before, mostly because no one knew how to send it back.

"This time, I will end you." She'd swear the thing smiled as she stepped through the portal and into the human realm. On the other side, figures hovered, two men, fighting, then one bleeding, his blood feeding the portal.

Shia opened her eyes.

"So that's how she did it," she whispered into the night.

FBI Agent Felicia Simone stared at her screen, re-reading the last report update she'd entered. She saved the information, and then touched the screen, opening up a folder reserved for another case. There was almost nothing new to go on in her newest disappearance case, but she needed an updated autopsy from Cicarelli.

She typed a few lines into the system, received confirmation that he was still covering at the local morgue, and pushed back from her desk. "I still haven't heard from my morgue guy," she said nonchalantly to the bored man at the desk across from hers. "I'm going to go ask him in person."

The shorter, younger Asian-American male didn't even look up. "Sounds like a ton of fun."

"You want to tag along?" she asked.

He shook his head. "I don't need to be around any more corpses. Half the folks in here might as well be zombies. Damned pension chasers."

She smiled, even though he would never notice. "I'll go ahead and assume you didn't have me included in that statement."

Agent Simone slid an arm through the sleeve of her Cavalli business jacket, checking for her phone and ID as she walked to the exit. The biometric scanner confirmed her fingerprint and iris scan, and she collected her sidearm from the check-in facility before she exited the building. Something crept at the corners of her confidence the entire time, like termites devouring the foundation.

She slid into the cool leather seat of her Audi A-3000. The engine started the moment her thumbs pressed against the steering wheel. She buckled the seat belt.

This was insanity.

She had taken the Huang case as an excuse to get close to Detective Ryan Calder once more. What had that achieved? Maybe suicide. Maybe for her. Maybe for her career. Christ, they thought to take down Alexender Spiros? He was inhuman, above human, a being driven by greed and apathy.

She adjusted her mirror, and a large, black GM vehicle approached from the rear. On a whim, Simone shifted into gear. The Audi hopped over the cement parking divider and stole toward the exit. If her instincts were correct, she would need to find a space far away from Alexander Spiros and his men.

She shifted the A-3000 between lanes with practiced ease. I-95 was usually a commuter's nightmare, but at this hour, most of the traffic was heading the opposite way. She knew where the lanes merged, where construction and tolls stopped traffic. Simone took the most strategic path through each, yet a pair of black SUVs followed, seeming to draw closer at every opportunity. Simone passed Stafford, Aquia Harbor, Woodbridge, then Lorton. She was nine miles outside of DC. She called out an order to her phone and waited.

One ring. The black vehicle drew closer.

Two rings. She saw the shadow of the GM as it obscured her vision through the rear view mirror.

Three rings. The GM nudged the rear of her Audi. She squealed in fear. Spiros's men had closed the gap.

The fourth ring never came. The headlights of the GM suddenly disappeared as the truck was driven sideways. The black SUV rolled several times before landing on its roof.

Simone froze, looking back at the men who intended to kill her. The sharp pop of gunfire reached her ears, along with flashes of light outside of the SUV. She slammed on the brakes. The Audi skidded to a halt on the shoulder of the highway.

Felicia exited her car slowly. The pistol in her hands felt cold and distant. No one moved where she had been attacked. She moved her gun from person to person. They were dead, every last one of them.

Except one.

"We need to get the hell out of here right now."

CHAPTER TWENTY-FOUR

"Come on," Ryan snapped, and Felicia followed without question. She stopped as he began to run six lanes across I-95; the traffic slowed as drivers turned their heads to stare at the overturned, flaming SUV. She coughed as the acrid smell of burning rubber reached her nose. Ryan sprinted a few more steps ahead, raising his gun and firing in both directions.

Red lights erupted at the corners of her vision. His figure became less recognizable in the sudden smoke and fire.

"Felicia, come on! We have to go now!"

She ran to him on blind faith. She trusted him. She always had. She reached out, and he wrapped a hand around her waist, firing the over-sized pistol once more behind them. Horns blared. Then, the unmistakable sound of metal on metal as vehicles smashed into one another, caught up in the confusion.

Ryan gripped her tightly, leading her across the asphalt and over the fractured guardrail that separated the northbound lanes from the High Occupancy Vehicle lanes. A bright light flashed on them from the right, and Felicia raised her hands on instinct. A motorcyclist ditched his ride instead of striking them. His body skittered along the pavement as his Honda Valkyrie struck the guardrail, then launched end over end above them. The motorcycle hit the ground in a shower of sparks.

Three subconscious steps later, Ryan shoved her into the Impala. She heard the screech of burning rubber, though the sound seemed a million miles away. By the time she remembered to breathe, they were nearing the 14th Street Bridge, entering the nation's capital.

"Felicia, answer me."

She shook her head, looking over at Ryan. The detective was staring ahead, steering hard with both hands, dodging the commuters and tourists that occupied the highway entry to DC's major attractions. "What did you ask me?"

"Good enough." He tossed the steaming pistol over to her. "Reload that. The flares are in the glove compartment."

"Flares?"

"You don't think I stopped traffic with a 10mm Glock, do you?"

Felicia reached for the glove compartment. It opened to her touch, and she recognized the compact devices every officer carried for securing an accident. She halted, turning to face him. "Spiros's men?"

"Right behind us," Ryan answered. "It took as long for me to stop those vehicles and get you as it did for the second team to track you." He stole a quick smile in her direction. "We've left the frying pan, Agent Simone."

She glanced at him. "What do we do?"

Ryan downshifted, ripping into oncoming traffic. Cars

and trucks faced them. He jerked the car from one side to another to avoid them. "Spiros has his own staff targeted. If he doesn't have us, I can buy us some time. Hang on!"

Ryan took on the commuter traffic on Constitution Avenue, leaving DC before banking a hard right and driving through the heavily occupied streets of Rosslyn. Hardly a minute, and several diving tourists later, he pulled onto the Key Bridge. The heavily populated, tourist-laden section of Georgetown filled their vision.

Georgetown. The famed Exorcist stairs. Abigail Huang's murder scene.

Felicia braced against the dashboard. "What are you thinking, Ryan?"

He gripped the steering wheel and the gearshift. "Hang on."

He noticed as Felicia grabbed onto the seat. He knew he could make a car do things it was never designed to. She used to comment she loved to witness that...from the outside.

He downshifted, and the vehicle careened between two parked cars and a bike messenger. Their tires hugged the pavement, and they headed off, away from the congestion.

A few seconds later, the rearview mirrors filled with orange flame. Felicia and Ryan each turned their heads from the light and the heat. Their skin burned, and they couldn't deny the howling of human voices above the crackling fires.

Felicia finally gained the courage to open her eyes. The darkness surprised her. "Where are we going?"

She waited until he replied. She needed his voice, his confidence. They had a lot of lives on their hands. "Ryan?"

Suddenly, before she realized, his hand gripped hers.

"You remember the Solomon House, don't you, my bride?"

Ryan pushed the wool curtains away from the window, taking in all he dared in the two inches of visibility he gained into the courtyard. He eyed his beloved ride, which appeared as a rusty four-banger Honda Accord thanks to the programming of Shia's AI. Somewhere behind him, the shower subsided. He scanned the perimeter one last time before ducking behind the curtains. The light drew his attention, and he looked back to the silhouette leaving the bathroom.

Felicia's curves were undeniable, accented by the low lights of the cheap hotel room. Ryan turned away, and then turned back as she made her way to the single, Queen-sized bed. The light was too dark for confirmation, but he sensed Felicia's gaze on him the whole time. He stole a glance towards the window for a moment, but only a moment.

As he turned back, she dropped her towel to the ground, reaching out for the blanket that covered the bed. Her figure disappeared beneath the covers. Ryan let the curtain fall. He stared at her shadow, alone among the shadows.

Felicia whispered, "Come to me, Ryan."

He remembered that bed, the feeling of her lithe body pressed to his when they posed as a newlywed couple here two years ago. He closed his eyes, temptation whispering in his ear. He was exhausted, and it would be so easy to give in, like he had in the past.

Ryan opened his eyes tempted to move back to the window. Nothing was like it always was. This was no longer only about him. He was in a fight for his life. Everything he believed about the afterlife was shot full of holes, and every time he closed his eyes, Shia Ronin's image filled his skull. Her dark, straightforward gaze, her jet-black hair, her petite, powerful body, and her deadly swords.

She'd found the damn dog for Mrs. Bradbury. She'd attended the church's gala in his place. She'd saved him from a suited up lobster, albeit, a demon rather than some guy in a suit. And, she hadn't asked for a damn thing in return.

He'd finally found an honorable woman, focused on the same things he did. She may not want him, may not have him, but he wasn't about to screw anything else up. He needed to give this play a chance.

He called back over his shoulder, knowing that looking at Felicia, naked in the bed they had shared, would tempt him. "I'm going to check on the car and make a call. Stay here, and be certain it's me before you unlock the door."

She called his name, but the closing hotel room door cut her voice silent. Ryan pulled his coat collar up, shielding him slightly against the rain. Spiros's men would be on the hunt. He needed a plan, and he needed time. He had neither. His phone was personal, not department issued, so the encryption on it stood strong against Spiros's hackers. He'd long since disabled the global positioning software. All it had ever brought him was headaches.

He walked down the slick cement stairs, looking both ways as he reached the car. He slipped inside, armed the proximity alarm, tapped the handle of his pistol to be sure it was there, and rested his hands on the steering wheel.

Ryan needed answers about Alexander Spiros, but digging in the police files, the FBI databases, or any corporate assets of Ixion Industries would get him noticed, and most likely killed. He needed a way to snoop without tripping intrusion prevention systems and data breach safeguards. He needed silent, fast, invisible technology if only it existed.

The detective slapped a palm against the steering wheel. Pulling out his phone, he scrolled down until he recognized the number for Shia's artificial butler.

"Jace, this is Ryan. I need a favor."

"You won't possibly paint another masterpiece if you don't stop shaking, Elias."

"I...I can't. You won't let me see what I'm doing."

Alexander Spiros took a sip of his Montrachet 1978. He stared at the naked man trembling on the hotel rug before him.

The man wore only a blindfold.

He held a paintbrush in his left hand. A blank canvas rested before him. A palette of colors sat on the floor.

"Let us review, shall we?" Spiros sipped on his drink. "You are Elias Chevalier. Your art is respected throughout the globe. Critics universally agree that your 2013 piece, titled Fall of the Empire, represented your coming out. You followed it with Solace in Sanctuary, and The Bliss of Pain, each of which fetched over a million dollars at auction."

"I don't know what you want," the artist blubbered.

Spiros continued, "Then, you went off into that dark place where artists and addicts go. You are now famous for benders rather than brushes, celebrity parties over substance, merely a caricature of yourself, and so has your work. Your reputation plummeted, and with it, the price of your art."

"I've cleaned up," Elias answered. "I'm not that man anymore."

"I know," Spiros replied as he stood up. He stepped closer. "That is why you're going to paint your next masterpiece for me...here...now."

"Then take off the blindfold. Let me see what I'm doing."

Spiros smirked. "No. Seeing what you're painting restores the here and now, and we both know that the man you were then doesn't exist here."

Elias lowered his head into his hands. "Why are you doing this?"

"Because," Alexander Spiros said, kneeling closer. "I own The Bliss of Pain. I have seen genius in your work, Elias. Now, you will see it again." He stepped on Elias' right hand, crushing it into the paint as he stood.

Elias Chevalier screamed in pain, clutching his hand to his chest. Spiros adjusted his jacket collar. The artist's suffering was a masterpiece in itself. He hadn't learned his lesson yet.

But he would learn.

"Detective, this is an unusual circumstance. I am accustomed to receiving calls from Lady Ronin only."

"Yeah, and I'm used to dealing with human beings and denying the existence of demons, faeries, vampires, and artificially intelligent technologies. So, I guess we both get to compromise."

"You present an interesting logic path, detective. What is the nature of your call?"

Ryan paused. He was in a battle of wits with a Star Wars droid. "I need you to do some research for me, Jace."

"Sir, I apologize if you have been misled by our previous communications. My services are solely at the command of Lady Ronin. I can only answer her requested call to action."

"She program you that way, or are you afraid she'll yell at you again?"

The AI was silent for a moment. "She threatened to shut me off for the next 85 years."

"If the Mother Demon incapacitates Shia," Ryan replied, unwilling to say kill, even to a computer. "How long are you silent? How long do we all have left?"

"Do you have information regarding the Mother Rissu we are tracking, detective?"

"Jace, I think I may know the human who called her through the portal."

If AI's could snap to attention, Ryan swore he heard Jace do so. "What is it you require of me, detective?"

Ryan was unaware how long it had been since he'd spoken to Jace. He slept, dreaming of demons, gunfire, sex, Heaven and Hell. His head pounded, and he started forward off of the headrest of the seat. A dim light shone from his left, and the hammering resumed. As his head cleared, Ryan realized what he was seeing and hearing. A figure in black slammed the glass of the driver's side window with the butt of a rifle as flashlights encircled the car.

Ryan checked the rear view mirror. A full-sized SUV was parked behind him, effectively cutting off his escape route. He wasn't going to drive his way out of this, unless he wanted to chance driving over a concrete parking divider and into a hotel room. Even the Impala couldn't get all the way through, not without enough room to reach full acceleration.

The butt of the gun hit the glass again. The window

stayed strong. Ryan counted almost a dozen flashlights on the ground floor. He stole a glance up to the second floor. The door to the hotel room was off of its hinges. The front window smashed inward. He cursed under his breath. Felicia was a fighter, but caught, alone, unarmed and naked in a cheap hotel room. He knew they had her.

He clicked a button on the console, and the tint on the driver's side window disappeared, leaving him face to face with the black clad man trying to rifle butt his way through the glass. Ryan drew his own gun pointing it at the man.

The assailant reacted as Ryan hoped. He leveled the rifle and fired. The round ricocheted off of the bulletproof glass, directly backward. The gunman's dead form fell backward as half of his skull disappeared. In an instant, the flashlights followed. Ryan opened the door, rolled across the asphalt, and came up firing.

He landed his first three shots. Cries of pain confirmed each of them. He turned and fired a round into the knee of the operative standing atop the Hummer. The spotlight shifted from the Impala to the sky as the man dropped to grab what was left of his leg. Ryan rushed for the gap between the rows of hotel rooms on the ground floor. The crack of gunfire behind him grew into a cacophony, and he ran harder.

He darted along the perimeter of the courtyard, even as Ixion operatives reached the entryway. They fired, and he ducked and dodged, hoping to reach the exit on the far end of the plaza. Thirty steps, and he could turn and disappear into the night.

Suddenly, the silhouette of a black SUV screeched to a halt, blocking his path. Ryan cursed, but never slowed. His hand reached to his belt as the driver's window lowered. He recognized the form of a H&K automatic rifle. Before the driver could lower the auto-rifle, Ryan raised his hand and fired.

The flare ignited the cabin of the SUV. The driver screamed, firing his ammo upward, ripping through the ceiling. The other members of the team darted away to safety. Ryan reached the burning vehicle, biting his teeth against the smell of frying flesh. He slid across the hood on his hip, landing on his feet in the parking lot. The vehicle now served as a barrier between him and most of the operatives on his tail. He ran two more steps, took a quick glance behind him and fired the flare gun into the vending machine on the second floor.

Red flames mixed with a shower of soda cans, filling the air with small, unpredictable ammunition. The remaining men fired aimlessly, hoping to protect themselves from the chaos around them.

Sirens in the distance joined the gunfire. When Ryan finally stopped running, his lungs burned. His muscles ached, and his skin was torn from every sort of plant he'd run through. He dropped to a knee. He didn't recognize the buildings around him, or the few figures still moving in the hours before dawn. He wiped his mouth with the back of his hand, not surprised to find blood on it. He wanted answers. Felicia was missing. He was only alive through desperate measures and a lot of luck. He didn't even want to think how he was going to explain the mess to his boss.

A dull ache crept into his shoulders; the result of firing so many rounds on the run. Everything hurt. Ryan shook his head to block out the pain. The physical aspect subsided some, but not the desperation. He'd abandoned Felicia. He'd lost touch with Shia. He was alone in a way he had never been before. He slammed his fist into the ground. Breathing hurt. He carried on one more step, finding a reason why.

Everything retreated as Ryan's phone vibrated on his

hip. The detective lifted a rain-soaked head, half-laughing as he answered the call.

"Calder. Jace, is that you?"

CHAPTER TWENTY-FIVE

"Yes, detective, this is Jace. Are you hurt?"

Ryan drew in two more short breaths before responding. "What? Why?"

"Your heart rate is accelerated. Are you injured?"

"No," he replied, amazed at his own condition. "Somehow I'm not. Chalk up another miracle I can't explain."

"I am not certain I follow, detective."

"I avoided three separate teams of contract killers, escaped a tinderbox they mapped out in advance, and managed to escape. Shit, Jace, my former partner has been taken. Can you track her?"

"Do you mean FBI Agent Simone?"

"Yes."

"I'll begin digital identification. This will take a few moments."

Ryan rose to his feet, eying his surroundings. "You didn't call me for my routine physical. You called because you had results."

"Yes, sir."

"And?"

The AI raced into full presentation mode. "You provided me with Abigail Huang's murder record, along with the candid photography attributed to one Carl MacAdams."

Ryan scoffed. "Yeah, he's a parasite."

"His skills are rudimentary at best, but he did manage to capture the image of Alexander Spiros exiting the Huang residence on three separate occasions with no corresponding significance between two of those appointments."

"The third?"

Jace continued, "The third occurred the night of Abigail Huang's murder. The ME's report confirms Abigail died of asphyxiation. She was indeed hurled to her death."

Ryan nodded. "Spiros was there."

"If my records are correct, yes."

The rain pelted the detective's neck and shoulders. He stared at the ground, then glanced in both directions. "Charles Huang didn't kill his wife. Her lover, Alexander Spiros, did."

Jace replied, "The logical conclusion from the evidence."

Ryan shook his head. "Okay, so, who killed Charles?"

"According to his phone records, Charles Huang received a series of calls from untraceable numbers. The first was the night of his wife's death. Charles was summoned to meet an unidentified confidant at the top of the Georgetown stairs. He undoubtedly witnessed her demise and either would confess or flee. Charles chose the latter option, after conveniently leaving his fingerprints along the walls and handrail at the top of the stairs."

"Nice touch," Ryan answered, glancing around.

"The next call occurred later, leading Charles to a spot in Little Falls Park. Nothing happened directly to Charles as a result of the call. Perhaps the predator was testing his ability to respond."

"A few days later, he answered an anonymous call and arrived at the same location. My algorithms surmise the following conclusion: Charles met someone he knew personally. He was stripped to his boxers and socks and driven to a position of humiliation. He was murdered, presumably with a heavy-caliber, American made hand gun."

Ryan paused. All the signs pointed to rich, self-made millionaire Alexander Spiros as the prime suspect in the murders of both Abigail and Charles Huang. He asked the question about Spiros's involvement with the inhuman world beyond, and as the words left his lips, everything seemed to shift into a gateway allowing all realms of imagination to co-exist.

"Jace, listen very carefully. Can you link Spiros to the gateway and the Rissu?"

"I would require his DNA to confirm the connection, but given the information you provided, there is a 98.96% chance he murdered both Charles and Abigail Huang."

"How do we get to 100%?"

"A confession, Detective, or a first-hand eyewitness who survived watching Spiros interacting with the portal."

Ryan tasted the familiar copper taste of blood and spat onto the wet ground. "Alright, leave that to me. I'll find a way to draw the bastard out. Keep me posted if Shia calls, or you find Felicia."

"If you plan on contacting him directly, there might

be an issue."

"What's that supposed to mean?"

The AI sounded hesitant to provide details. "Please wait while I patch in an audio feed from a live interview."

Ryan cursed. He had a feeling he wasn't going to like the next few words. Three seconds later, his instinct was validated.

"…of *The Washington Insider* reporting. As we have confirmed, Ixion Industries CEO Alexander Spiros has been seen on numerous occasions in what can only be described as an insidious love affair with a mysterious mistress. Spiros, who lives with his wife of fourteen years and two sons in his spacious residence in Leesburg, was photographed on multiple occasions with this mystery woman. Who is this Lolita? What is her connection to Spiros? Where is she now? Stay tuned. After the break, we will reveal the identity of this mystery mistress and the incredible details of Alexander Spiros' adulterous actions. This is Chris Weitzel, reporting exclusively."

"Goddamnit!" Ryan shouted into the night sky.

"This will undoubtedly complicate the ability to reach Alexander Spiros."

"You think?" He ran a hand through his hair, pulling away shards of glass. "Concentrate on Shia and Agent Simone. I may still have an idea or two."

"As you wish, detective. Will you need my direct assistance?"

"They shot my car, Jace. Do you have any idea how much that pisses me off?"

"No, sir. I will execute the proper emotions if you would like to indicate which I should power up."

"Never mind. Go. Find Shia and Agent Simone."

"Yes, sir."

The line went dead and Ryan stood silently, letting

the rain course over his skin and soak his clothes. He had lost his former lover and insulted Shia by not believing her. Spiros may be a multimillionaire, but in the end, he was human, he was a man, just a man, and he would be brought to justice for his actions.

Ryan stopped once he reached a main road and recognized the dim lights of a taxi. He hailed the cab, which slowed, but didn't quite stop. Ryan whipped out his badge and gun, and the cabbie slammed on the brakes like he was about to run over a nun. Ryan pulled the passenger side door open.

"Take me to the local District Two Police Station."

The mane looked at him in wide-eyed confusion. When he spoke, he replied in a thick, Kenyan accent. "Is dis some kind of joke, man?"

Ryan shook the pain from his head. "No joke."

The cab driver ducked and pointed out the front window. "You need a ride halfway around de block?"

Ryan followed the man's guidance, recognizing the storefronts that encircled the station's armor pool. He pushed the door back open, staring at the rear of the station. He stopped for a moment and subconsciously reached into his wallet and tossed the cabbie a twenty.

"Thanks for the ride," he said as he closed the door. The cab was already heading southbound before the door shut.

He received plenty of verbal jabs from the skeleton crew working the nightshift. He was bloodied, soaked to the bone, and exhausted. He reached his desk and entered his credentials, scanning his biometrics and entering his passcode. He pulled up the entire Huang Case file and uploaded it to Jace's database, not that Jace couldn't infiltrate the police files. He was, after all, a few decades ahead of them.

Ryan reached into his desk and pulled out the plastic evidence bag. He held it up to the light and studied the simple, long knife. Shia had told the truth about everything else. If this was her knife, she deserved to have it back. He'd figure out how to edit the chain-of-custody forms later. He took the blade from the bag and tucked it into the rear of his belt.

He stopped and rubbed his jaw. He looked to his phone, hoping somehow he had missed Jace's update that Shia and Felicia were both safe and sound. No such luck. He glanced at the monitor on his desk. Alexander Spiros was now his primary suspect. The CEO of the billion dollar defense contractor was challenging to reach. Now that he was the target of a media storm, he would be buffered and defended by layers of marketing and public relations wizards.

Getting to Spiros would be nearly impossible.

Ryan's phone vibrated on his hip, and he grabbed it. "Calder."

The voice on the other end was ice cold and venomous. "Good evening, detective. Let me introduce myself. I'm Alexander Spiros. Perhaps you've heard of me?"

"Is this some kind of prank call? I'm an officer of the law. I will prosecute, even if you are an adventurous kid." Ryan bluffed, tapping in the codes to record the call and to upload it to Jace simultaneously.

"Stop the bullshit, detective. You know my voice. You know my face. You've been on my case far too long, and I think we need to chat about everything you've done to hurt me and the people I love. It's such a shame to hurt the ones we love, isn't it, detective?" As Spiros finished his question, a woman's scream filled the phone's speakers.

Ryan wished he knew the man's voice well enough to swear on it in a court of law. "Alright, so let's assume you're the real deal. Let's talk this out. Tell me what I can do for you."

The voice laughed, accompanied by another female scream. "What you can do for me? You pathetic little maggot. You've already poisoned my legacy with your idealistic actions. You can meet me, in person, and you can die at my hands. If you don't so many others will. Would you like a list, detective? Where should I start?"

Ryan drew in a breath to calm himself. "Let's talk about this, you and me. Hold on, ok? Your issue is with me. What can I do to help?"

"Yes, my issue is with you. That's why I'm going to end Hector Gonzalez, Carl McAdams, and little Mrs. Bradbury, and maybe her damned dog, and then, when your fellow insects are gone, I will kill FBI Agent Simone, and then, when all those humans have given their blood, I will gut Shia Ronin like a pig. Her blood will seal the future, and my rise to power."

The phone line died, and Ryan turned to his laptop screen. It was blank. Two seconds passed, and the phone vibrated in his hand. Ryan nearly dropped it. He took a breath and clicked it to life.

"Detective, I have a location on your incoming call."

"Let me guess, Jace, Little Falls Park."

CHAPTER TWENTY-SIX

Ryan gripped the steering wheel. Spiros was one of the most protected men in DC, and there was no shortage of guarded VIPs in the nation's capital. Instead of having to swim upstream against a tidal wave of security, Spiros called him. Talk about bringing the mountain to Muhammad.

Spiros had done his research. Finding Ryan's connection to Shia and Felicia was easy. That was all in his work files. The others were neighbors and brief acquaintances. Hector Gonzalez and Mrs. Bradbury didn't know anything about Ixion's involvement. And Carl, Ryan thought for a moment. He didn't deserve to die, but if Carl caught a stray bullet in a very painful spot, that would be just fine. Spiros hadn't mentioned Father Munoz, which hopefully meant the priest was all right and somehow off limits. Maybe his faith gave him more strength than some blood pact between a greedy businessman and a bloodthirsty demon. There was always the chance Spiros was accompanied by a small army. Would his men follow his every command if they knew he was dabbling in black magic? Hired guns tended to be skeptical of supernatural urban legend stuff, like Ryan until recently.

This wasn't about him, or any of them. It was about Shia. Spiros said her blood sealed his future. Ryan wasn't going to allow that to happen. He scoffed. It wouldn't happen. Shia was somewhere else. He simply had to find her and stay alive long enough to warn her. If she walked into this trap blindly, Spiros would get his wish. She'd been hit by the smaller Rissu, damaged and bleeding. Ryan couldn't let her face the Mother, not with Spiros loose to blindside her.

He hid the Impala at the southern entrance to the park. The crime scene investigators and the media had all used the northern entrance, which was closer and easier to maneuver. Ryan figured any change might get him an advantage, and he needed every kiss Lady Luck handed out. The man was off his rocker for being in the park. He checked his pistol, secondary weapon, extra ammo, baton and pepper spray, and even his handcuffs, before getting ready for the trek through the woods. He reached the back of his belt, touching the dagger. Confident he had every tool he might need, he sprinted down the path into the park, and his first face-to-face with the head of Ixion Industries.

The moonlight struggled to find its way between the tangled tree branches. Fortunately, most of the leaves had fallen for winter, and Ryan made out a general idea of the trail for most of the way. Thorns tore at his jacket, twice opening gashes on his face. He slipped once on wet leaves and landed hard on a knee. The path crossed over several creeks, and the icy water seeped into the legs of his pants where his boots sank too deep.

He didn't dare use a flashlight. In these conditions, it would have been the equivalent of a bulls-eye on his chest. Instead, he traveled as quietly as possible until he could make out other forms in the distance. Up ahead, he recognized a small, green glow. Taking a breath and looking around for any signs of life, he moved in its direction.

Ryan crouched and crept through the trees, the moldy smell of wet leaves assaulting his skin and his senses, even as frost touched the edges of the foliage. He drew close enough to recognize the artificial glow of the green light. It originated from a set of small LED's set up in a wide circle. Ryan made out two human forms in the light. One paced around the lit area, the other on its knees.

He fought the urge to rush ahead. Only two forms, Spiros had bluffed about all the others, or they were already dead.

As he closed in, he made out the pacing form of Alexander Spiros, who shot glances in every direction. He brandished a G18 pistol with an extended silencer in his right hand. Felicia trembled on her knees near him. Her clothes torn, and her hands bound before her.

Ryan's teeth clenched at the sight of her, wounded and vulnerable. She was a strong woman. She didn't deserve this.

Banking on an ancient trick, Ryan lifted a fist-sized rock and tossed it on the far side of the circle. It landed with a sharp sound as it cracked a branch and launched several leaves into the air. Spiros immediately turned in its direction, raising his pistol and fired. If anything was alive before, it wasn't anymore. The man was a good shot.

Ryan took the opportunity to step into the clearing behind Spiros and take aim at him. He exhaled, feeling the pressure of the trigger against his index finger.

Spiros turned and faced him. "Don't even think about it, Detective."

Spiros' gaze moved away for a half-second, as his gun pushed hard enough against Felicia's temple to make her cry out. Ryan stole a glance at her. Her brown hair was wet and matted, covering half her face. Her face bruised, and her eye swollen. She had been beaten badly. Ryan shifted his gaze to Spiros. Confidence began to swell in his brain. Felicia was hurt, but she had the presence to dress, and hopefully arm herself, before the black suits arrived. She was resourceful. Maybe that would help, after all.

"Throw down the Glock, detective, before you do anything stupid to get your girlfriend here killed."

Ryan stood, trying to get Felicia to recognize him, but she was either too stunned or too subdued to raise her head. He shifted the grip on his pistol so it dangled harmlessly on his finger. "Let her go, Alexander. This isn't about her."

Spiros laughed, and his voice cut through the night. "Of course it isn't, maggot, and it isn't about you either."

"Let's do this man to man." Ryan bluffed again, willing Felicia to look at him.

Spiros shook his head. "This isn't about man, detective. This isn't about mankind. This is about immortality. How do you still not get that?" He shifted his weight to face Ryan. The pistol in his hand followed his gestures, no longer at Felicia's temple. Ryan thanked the invisible maker for a small miracle.

"I get it," he replied. "I'm a human, though, so you can't blame me for thinking about self-preservation."

"Actually, I hoped you would, detective. Now, be a good puppet and give me the blade."

Ryan scowled. Spiros knew he had the dagger. He either had an insider in the precinct or some kind of vision spell. Either way, bluffing might get Felicia killed. He moved his hand slowly behind him and withdrew the dagger.

"Good boy. Toss it here. I need an adequate blade to gut the samurai like a pig."

Ryan pitched the dagger forward. The ancient blade landed softly on the fallen leaves covering the ground. He made a mental count of his remaining weapons as he continued. "How did it come to this, Alexander?"

"You still don't see, do you?"

"This is about Abigail. You loved her." Ryan scanned the area, hoping for an edge.

"She was mine! That parasite Charles used her, and he tarnished her. He ruined her." Spiros spat, his hands shaking with rage.

Ryan moved slowly, trying to increase his leverage. "How are you going to change everything with what you're doing, Alexander?"

"Simpleton. I will draw Shia Ronin to my side, open her veins, and the blood of the Samurai will become mine. I will open the portal and take power over the living and the dead. I will bring back what is mine."

"Abigail."

"Yes, Abigail Renee Chen."

Ryan nodded. "Abigail Huang? There is no Abigail Chen. She hasn't existed in years."

Spiros scowled at the sound of her married name. "I will use the spell to restore her. She will be mine again. You cannot stop me."

"Abigail is dead, Alexander. The person you fantasize about hasn't been real for years. Call her the one that got away. More like the one you killed because you couldn't have her first."

Spiros growled. "Shut up and die."

He raised his pistol, and Ryan dropped to a knee. The bullets fired from Spiros' pistol, but nothing touched him. He lifted his left hand to fire his weapon, when something large and powerful drove him into the dirt. Air left Ryan's lungs and stars filled his vision as he pulled the trigger, firing the flare gun along the ground.

Leaves and branches erupted in flame. A wall of fire rose between him and the thing that struck him. Ryan scrambled back. He found the ability to breathe in, and he worshiped the feel of air in his lungs. He rose back to one knee, catching his breath and looking around. A growl echoed in his skull, and he tried to focus. The form of something that should not be stared back at him from across the wall of flame. He recognized its power, but not its shape.

His vision swam. He couldn't breathe. He couldn't focus. Ryan stopped and put all his energy into a single thought. He opened his mind.

"Shia, I need you here, now."

Around her, dark eyes of monks opened and gazed back at her. She should be startled, angry, but she was too much at peace, even with the Mother Rissu's threats hovering over her.

Stars twinkled overhead.

"What was that creature, Lady?" a soft voice asked. A hiss swept through the other monks.

Shia turned and found a young girl in the saffron robes staring back at her in the darkness. A small fire had been lit between them. A blanket lay long and folded in front of her, something bulky lay between the folds.

They'd been meditating with her, had they?

"Creatures of the other world. Ones such as you should not know."

"But you know them, Lady."

"I do. I do so you do not," she said. She leaned

forward and lifted the edge of the blanket. Her breath caught.

"How do you come to have this?" she whispered. Between the folds of fabric nestled a beautiful, hand carved wooden longbow. The wood freshly oiled, the string newly strung.

"The bow has been in our care for a very long time, Lady Goze--Ronin." Wezu's voice carried through the darkness.

The last time she'd seen the weapon was probably best left unsaid. "It traveled a very long way to rest in our hands. We have passed it down through the generations to keep it in good working order."

Her fingers trailed over the aged wood, flowing over each piece of the carving, every knot, every ridge in loving memory.

A small monk shuffled forward. "The arrows, they brought us two. It took many years, but we think we've crafted those very close to your original ones. The quiver is of our own making as yours was lost."

Shia accepted the small bundle into her arms. The leather was the softest she'd ever felt.

"I don't know what to say." Tears threatened to escape.

Instead, she stood, swinging the quiver onto her body, the bow followed. Everything settled back into place as if they'd never left her. Her swords hummed against her back as if happy to have long time friends returned.

"Thank you all." She didn't know what else to say. To have her weapons restored to her. She'd lost the bow so long ago. Not a weapon easily hidden in modern day, but she'd never missed a shot with it. For them to have taken the time to study her work with a few arrows and then recreate them. "You honor me, even though you don't know me."

"Oh, we know you lady."

Shia opened her mouth, but the world tilted and shifted. What the...She turned, dark eyes gazed back, watchful as her molecules dispersed.

Shia let the world re-form around her, pulling her swords from their sheaths with a slight hiss of metal against leather. She'd shifted often enough to recognize a sister's call and to know to be at the ready. Swords in hand, she eyed her landing space, taking in everything.

A man stood not ten feet from her in a clearing. Little Falls Park and Alexander Spiros, she'd bet. Fire danced along the ground in the background. Two forms danced along the edges of the flames, one on either side.

She expanded her senses.

"He threatened to gut you like a pig," Jace's electronic voice whispered in her ear.

Heavens, he'd been so quiet while she'd been visiting her homeland. Too bad, she didn't have time to answer him.

"I'm sorry. Did you somewhere, someway say, you were going to gut me like a pig?" She stood, battle ready, swords outstretched to her sides, one arched up in front of her and one dropped and ready behind her.

"I will have my vengeance!"

She watched him as a hawk staring down its prey. Yes, she'd heard worse, but she was so going to slice one said human in half. She had the right. Her body hovered in peaceful ease between attack and defend.

"Bigger, badder, and more evil things than you, human, have tried." The sword in her left hand waved around in a laissez faire circle, taunting. "Many things

249

have tried. I have the scars, young man. You want to play in the power realms?" The sword in her other hand whipped around and pointed at his chest, "Then come. Play. Now."

Her swords swished out and settled in a defensive pattern. Again, one behind her back, one in front. She balanced between her feet. Let him try. She'd take his head from his shoulders and everything would be done. He was human, nothing more. He thought he had power. He was mistaken. He'd called the power to him. She'd been made with ancient power, crafted, and finely honed.

"And, by the way, you won't touch the dog or its owner." She ran a glance over him.

She remained watchful as his gaze shifted up and over her shoulder. A warning, it was all she needed. She tensed preparing for the hit as the Mother Rissu's claws sunk into her back.

Ryan stared as the bright light shimmered into form, and knew Shia Ronin appeared across the fire from him. He was paralyzed, dumbfounded by the energy surrounding her. Fortunately, whatever it was surrounding her was enough to send the inhuman beast that had driven him into the mud flailing into the rocks. He shook his head, looking up to make out Spiros' frame in the ring of fire. Spiros had his arm out, aiming his firearm from side to side, unable to draw a bead on his target.

Ryan dashed forward through the flames, and Spiros reacted, lowering the pistol and firing. The detective dove to the ground behind a nearby outcropping of rocks. Gunfire battered against them as he crouched behind. He didn't have long, based on this pattern. Spiros had better guns and a better position. Ryan swore under his breath.

The top layers of the rock shattered, and Ryan rolled

to his left, firing several shots back. For a moment, the sadistic businessman stopped firing. Ryan assumed he was reloading. He took the opportunity to dart behind another rock embankment. When he looked up, his eyes crossed and forced him to glance away. Something in the series of stones warped his vision. He doubled over, grabbing his head as his vision swam. His stomach turned in somersaults. He fought off the myriad of colors stabbing into his skull. He struggled to put one foot in front of the other.

Pain pushed him out of the fog. Fire erupted through his right leg, and Ryan dropped to the bed of burning leaves under him. He grabbed at his leg. Blood trickled between his fingers. Spiros' triumphant laughter brought him back to the moment. He'd been shot. He crawled on his elbows to the nearest cover.

When he finally regained focus, he poked his head out. Spiros's gaze darted from side to side, hoping to catch a glimpse of him. Ryan cursed through the pain. He needed medical help, but he couldn't bring anyone into this carnival of the supernatural. He gritted his teeth, stealing another look at Spiros's desperate behavior and then beyond him. Agent Felicia Simone met his gaze. She nodded and energy snaked along every part of his body.

Ryan clenched his jaw and surged up to his feet, his Glock raised in his right hand.

"Hey, Alex," he called out. "Let's talk about your life in the prison system."

Shia bit back a cry of pain and threatened to send Jace to the nine regions of hell for not warning her.

"Sorry m'lady, she didn't register with the fire," Jace's voice whispered in her ear.

"Shut up unless you can help." She rolled. Her back screamed at her as she came up on her feet, both swords swept out. She kept her arms and swords moving, creating a bladed barrier while she regained her senses.

The Mother Rissu sat a few feet from her, on her haunches, her red eyes staring at her.

"You are an interesting adversary, for a human. I studied you through the portals when my sons ventured here." The demon voice twisted through her mind.

Shia lifted an eyebrow, her swords at the ready. Her bow and quivers rested against her back. She could only hope the Rissu's claws hadn't damaged them. Who knew the females could talk, albeit telepathically? A tidbit of knowledge her sister's would welcome. She'd have Jace updated the demon database--after she rewired him.

"Your sons have all been dispatched. Time for you to go too," she said. Her gaze darted everywhere, taking in the Mother Rissu's stance, her hide, and her positioning. She had nothing to go on as far as dispatching one. None of them had battled a Mother Rissu before. They weren't supposed to be able to transcend the barriers. And yet, here one was. All hers. It figured.

The Mother Rissu went from calm and stationary to moving and attack mode in a matter of nanoseconds. She'd never seen something move so fast. Shia cried out at her claws sank into her shoulders before the demon hit and darted past. She landed on a knee, swords planted tip down, and panted while she took stock. Blood dripped down her arms, down her back.

"Alright, so you're fast," she muttered.

The Mother Rissu sat on her haunches and waited, unblinking. *"You're good, for a human."*

Shia forced her sword tips further into the ground.

"The problem is, I'm not human, not anymore. And,

you're a pain in the everything for a demon," she commented. She'd swear the Mother Rissu smiled at her in the darkness. Maybe it was the firelight. She dropped her hands from her sword hilts. "Albeit, you're faster than your boys."

"*Oh, yes. And I am going to enjoy ripping you to shreds.*" She smiled and lunged.

Shia whipped the bow off her back and notched an arrow as time slowed for her. Her vision narrowed as the bow and arrow settled in her hands.

Thwang.

The Mother Rissu dropped in mid-leap. Her body crumpled to the ground.

Shia laid the bow down on the earth and bowed her head. Thank the Universe that had worked. She let herself breathe and glanced around.

Fire danced in the night. The pain, pinpricks spiked through her shoulder and down her back.

And, so it was done.

Alexander Spiros stole a paranoid glance from side to side. "You have no idea what I'm capable of, detective. Surrender? I hardly think so, not when I have the blood of the Immortals ready at my altar of sacrifice." He leveled his gaze at Ryan. "Whatever you may have wished would happen, it won't. It's over, detective. You lose."

Before the words left his mouth, a figure erupted from behind him.

"Felicia?" Shock raced through Ryan.

She landed squarely behind Spiros. Her hands were visible on his shoulders. The rope from her tied wrists tore at his throat, yanking his head back. Ryan darted forward, adrenaline masking the pain in his wounded leg. He growled, striking Spiros in the gut with the hardest punch he had ever thrown. Spiros pitched forward. A reflection of light blinded Ryan for a split second. The spray of blood struck his face. He turned his head away on instinct, stumbling forward, unable to stop his momentum. It took several seconds to regain his focus. He made out only the outline of Alexander Spiros and Felicia Simone.

And the ancient dagger in her hand.

FBI agent Felicia Simone, who'd been reduced to nothing more than an object of suffering, dragged Spiros' motionless body toward the trees. Her wild gaze flashed on Ryan's for an instant, and that was enough for him to accept it. Felicia pulled her attacker's body into darkness. Try as he might, Ryan could not tune out the sound of the knife digging into Spiros' flesh, again and again.

Ryan rose, caught his breath, and stared into the night until he recognized Shia's triumphant form across the grass and above the haze of the flames. She turned and their eyes met, satisfied, if not glorious heroes. He bowed slightly. She responded in a similar manner.

The sound of physical motion drew his attention, and Ryan turned to his left. He stared for several long moments into the darkness. The blows eventually stopped. He heard muffled sobbing. For all she had suffered, Felicia deserved her vengeance. Ryan gritted his teeth.

He jumped as a hand touched his shoulder. He raised his flashlight, but a trained hand struck his forearm before he could raise it to his shoulder. He gazed down, recognizing the piercing blue-black gaze of Shia Ronin.

"She needs some time. We all do."

Wind blew the ashes into Ryan's eyes, and he brushed at them with the back of his hands. When he looked up again, Shia Ronin was gone. He examined the rocks where the portal had been. Even through stinging eyes, he made out every edge, every crevice and every detail of the stones. The energies that had made him sick and vulnerable were gone. The magic had expired. Only leaves and dirt remained.

He listened for Felicia and turned when he heard her move. She was on her knees, pounding her fist into the ash and leaves around where Spiros' corpse should have been. Ryan put his weight onto his good leg and limped over to her. He slumped down beside her and slowly reached out to put a hand on her shoulder. Felicia fell against him, her arms tight around her body, her head against his chest. Ryan wrapped his arms around her, letting her cry. With care and stealth, he palmed and hid the dagger within the folds of his coat.

He stared into the firelight. His body ached from every pore. His head hurt even more. In the distance, the first in a symphony of emergency sirens sounded. At some point, he would have to explain to his colleagues everything that happened tonight. He scoffed. He would cross that bridge when he got there. Right now, he had a woman who needed him in his arms, and a woman he needed somewhere out there in the world she had revealed to him.

Dr. Shia Ronin had opened his eyes, and his heart, to something he had never imagined. And now, she was gone. Ryan surveyed the area once again. A crime scene obviously, but one none of them could explain. He pulled Felicia a little closer, and a smile broke out across his lips. He loved a good mystery, and Shia Ronin proved to be quite the mystery after all.

EPILOGUE

"Police are still searching for Alexander Spiros, head of Ixion Industries, believed to be on the run for his involvement in a drug trafficking ring with known US Enemies in San Salvador. The FBI has issued no official word at this time. This is Chris Weitzel from *The Washington Insider*, reporting live from the headquarters of Ixion Industries."

"He is pretty much a complete low life, isn't he?" Felicia asked, turning her head away from the TV screen in the corner.

Ryan took a long drink from his coffee. "Yeah, the lowest of the low."

"What was it you called him?" she asked, blowing at the top of her mug. "Pond scum?"

"Something like that." He gazed across the table at her. He noticed the bruising on her cheeks, even behind the Missoni sunglasses. "How are you holdin' up?"

Felicia smirked. "I have separate prescriptions for fluoxetine, setaline and paroxetine. I could spend from now until my 50's in la-la land, if I listened to the doctors."

"Pretty bad, huh?"

"Ryan," she huffed, "I can walk out today and get pension claiming post traumatic stress disorder, and yet, not a single one of those therapists will ever know what I saw or what I did." Her jaw hardened, and she turned her gaze out the window.

He nodded, watching.

She shook her head. "Maybe, I'll get a dog. At least then I won't feel so damn alone at night."

Ryan reached across the table and grabbed her hand. She shot him a surprised look. "Felicia, you hate dogs. You've told me that a thousand times. You need time."

"Perhaps," she answered, eyes hidden behind the dark sunglasses.

"Will there be anything else?" The waitress asked, suddenly appearing between them.

Ryan and Felicia pulled back, releasing their grip on one another. He answered first. "The check, thanks."

"Sure thing," the waitress replied with a grin, setting the slip down on the tabletop.

"I'll..." Felicia started.

"Nope," Ryan countered, snatching the bill. "C'mon." Her gaze skittered away again.

Ryan drew out a few bills, tucking them in the folds of the receipt.

"We played the parts well, didn't we?" Felicia asked.

Ryan slugged down the rest of his coffee. "What parts?"

She smiled. "I was your bride. I was your soul

mate. I was your one true love." She exaggerated, extending her hands above her head. "But, I was never any of that." Her smile remained, despite the change in her tone. She dropped her hands onto the table top. "Ryan, don't be an idiot. Go. Tell her."

Ryan leaned forward and kissed the back of Felicia's hand. "Thank you."

She blinked and smiled back.

He stood and walked toward the door. With one hand on the knob, he stopped and glanced back. "Black Molly."

Felicia shook her head. "Excuse me?"

"You hate dogs. You're allergic to cats. If you get a fish to keep you company, get a Black Molly." He offered a sly smile. "They eat pond scum."

COMING SOON

Stay Tuned for more in the Urban Samurai Series

Coming Soon
From N.S. Kelly

NI
SAN
CHI

....

And don't miss out on the Goddess Chronicles Series
By Stacia D. Kelly
Keep up to date
Visit
www.sybir.com

....

Check on the Catwalk Series
By Nick Kelly

Catwalk: Messiah
www.nickkelly.com

BACK COPYRIGHT

ISBN: 978-0-9852837-8-0
Print Version

ICHI

Copyright© 2013 by N.S. Kelly

For questions or comments, please contact us at: info@catklaw.com.

www.catklaw.com